THROWING STONES

A Glasgow Lads on Ice Novel

AVERY COCKBURN

www.AveryCockburn.com

Glasgow Lads Series

- Play On: Duncan/Brodie novella
- Playing for Keeps: Fergus/John novel
- Playing to Win: Colin/Lord Andrew novel
- Play It Safe: Fergus/John short story
- Playing with Fire: Liam/Robert novel
- Play Dead: Colin/Lord Andrew novella
- Playing in the Dark: Evan/Ben novel
- Play Hard: Liam/Robert novella
- All Through the House: Duncan/Brodie short story
- Playing by Ear: Jamie/Perry novel, coming 2022

Glasgow Lads on Ice (spinoff featuring curling)

- Throwing Stones: Luca/Oliver novel
- Must Love Christmas: Garen/Simon novel

Contents

Dedication

To the members of Potomac Curling Club,
for their cool heads and warm hearts

The Teams

Team Riley

- Luca Riley, skip
- Garen McClaren, vice
- Ross Buchanan, second
- David Moffat, lead

Team Boyd

- Jack Boyd, skip
- Alistair Ritchie, vice
- Bruce Clark, second
- Ian Lindsay, lead

For those new to the sport of curling, a brief summary for easy reference can be found on page 243, as a supplement to the explanations within the book. Enjoy!

Skip

SKIP: *Leader of a four-person curling team. A skip devises the strategy, calls the shots, and usually throws the last two stones in each scoring period or "end." The team bears the skip's name, providing the thrilling yet existentially unsettling feeling of being referred to as a collective noun.*

LUCA RILEY HAD THROWN ROUGHLY a hundred thousand stones in the two decades since his parents had dragged him to his big sister's first curling match. He'd been five at the time, still blithely convinced that despite his short stature and inability to kick a ball without falling down, he would someday grow up to be a famous footballer—or at least famous*ish*, probably playing for a lower-league Scottish team rather than his beloved Partick Thistle FC, much less Glasgow giants Rangers or Celtic, and much *much* less the world-renowned Arsenal or Manchester United.

He'd raged all the way to the curling rink, kicking the back of his mum's seat and moaning about the imminent boredom about to swallow him whole. Miraculously, his parents had not honored his sister's request to leave Luca by the side of the road to find a new home, but rather continued their journey as though their younger child had not combusted in the back seat.

That Saturday afternoon could have changed Luca's life then and there. He could have fallen in love with the idea of sliding hunks of granite down a slab of pebbled ice, could have traded his precious football boots for a pair of shoes with mismatched soles, could have fallen asleep that night dreaming of concentric circles.

But only one of those things happened.

The dream repeated itself in some form for three years, until Luca accepted his tragic footballing deficiencies and joined his sister at Shawlands Ice Rink, where he showed immediate promise and was soon promoted from the "Wee Rockers" kids program up to the juniors league.

After that he mostly dreamed about Pokémon—and, eventually, other lads.

Now, as he stood inside the warm room at that same Southside Glasgow rink, watching through the glass as the ice-maintenance crew scraped the six curling sheets before the Friday night league games, Luca felt utterly at home.

Two of his three teammates stood near him, leaving him out of their banter. They thought Luca needed these pre-game moments to concoct elaborate strategies, but in fact, he just really liked watching the ice prep. It was a time to center himself, to rid his mind of workday irritations and focus on nothing but what was in front of him.

"I should've given myself a head start on not shaving," said Ross, the Team Riley second. "It's been five days and I've barely got stubble."

"The curse of blondness," replied David, their lead. "We gingers are swimming in testosterone. I plan to look like

Tormund from *Game of Thrones* by the time the tournament starts. Psychological intimidation, you know. Of course, it'd be more effective if curling wasn't already a beard-y sport."

"It is that," Ross said. "I wonder why?"

There was a pause. "Do you?" David asked.

"Do I what?"

"Do you wonder why curling is a beard-y sport?"

There was a longer pause, then Ross snapped his fingers. "Because it's cold."

"Clever lad." David lowered his voice. "We'll need all the beard luck we can get, now that Team Boyd's got their fancy Canadian coach."

Luca ripped his gaze from the ice to face his teammates. "What did you say?"

"We'll not be shaving until after next weekend's bonspiel, remember? For luck." David patted his own cheek, where the hair was an even brighter red than that on his head. "Tell me you didn't forget."

"Does it look like I forgot?" Luca scratched his jaw, which already itched like a beast after five days' growth (though he rather fancied the dark, rugged look). The stubble was a constant reminder that the Glasgow Open, the most important tournament of his life, started in less than a week. "I meant, what did you say about a Canadian coach?"

"You've not heard?" asked Ross. "How could you not hear?"

A fair question. Luca's own brother-in-law was the Team Boyd skip. "I guess Jack forgot to mention it at dinner last Sunday." That seemed unlikely. "Or maybe he didn't want to brag."

His teammates laughed, and for good reason. Jack Boyd was the antithesis of the extreme good sportsmanship known as "The Spirit of Curling." Luca often thought his sister's husband had missed his calling as a professional wrestling promoter.

"Jack probably thought the surprise would rattle us." David hugged himself in a mock shudder. "Ooh, I'm pure intimidated."

"Where'd they get the money to hire an imported coach?" Ross asked. "We can't even afford a domestic one."

Luca gave the curling broom tucked under his arm a pensive twist. "What I want to know is, why would someone fly all the way across the pond to coach here when Canada's got the world's best curlers?"

"Maybe he can't get a coaching job there," David said. "Maybe he's a washed-up old has-been."

"Actually," Ross said, "he's—"

"Or a washed-up old never-was." Luca snickered. "He'll spend the bonspiel sitting in the back of the stand drinking a bottle of Buckie in a paper sack. With a pocketful of gum to cover the stench of his own despair."

"Have they got Buckfast in Canada?" David asked.

"No, but we have Brights Pale Dry," came a voice behind them, a voice with a distinct North American accent. "Very popular with all levels of washed-ups."

Luca spun around so fast, he whacked Ross in the gut with his broom. He could only stammer a quick "Sorry, mate" before his tongue was paralyzed by the sight in front of him.

"You want to know why I left Canada?" asked the tall man with wavy nut-brown hair and green-apple eyes, a man who was definitely neither old *nor* washed-up. "You really want to know?"

His question seemed a warning, as though Luca would regret hearing the answer. But it would be twice as awkward to back down.

"Okay." Luca gave a wee cough to clear the squeak from his voice. "Spill."

The man leaned over, so slowly that time itself seemed to pause. Luca held back a shiver, at once wanting to lean into and away from this encroachment.

A warm breath delivered five whispered words:

"None of your fucking business."

Then the man turned and walked away, leaving Luca wearing what felt like the goofiest smile of his life—which was saying a lot.

As he watched the coach join Team Boyd at the warm-room bar, Luca felt his teammates move forward to flank him.

"His name's Oliver Doyle," Ross said, "and he's a former junior world champion. That's what I was trying to tell youse before." He nudged Luca. "Also totally gay and single, according to the internet."

Luca looked at his second. "Ross, you gathered intel on behalf of my love life? Pure sweet of you."

"It'd better work," David said. "I'm sick of our girlfriends moaning about you being 'uncoupled' when we all go out after games."

"Claire says, 'There's no symmetry.'" Ross pitched up his voice to mimic his girlfriend. "'He's so cute, how can he be alone?'"

"I'm not alone, I'm elusive." Luca lifted his chin, feigning indignation. "Like a member of an endangered species."

"A celibate twenty-five-year-old definitely counts as that," David said.

Luca's smile faded. Had he been single so long his mates thought of him as *celibate*? When had he last even kissed a guy? "I can't afford the distraction." He rotated his broom handle against his palm. "Not with the tournament and all."

David snorted. "Och, there's that excuse again."

"Excuse for what?" Garen, the Team Riley vice-skip and Luca's flatmate, was approaching them with his kit bag. "Sorry I'm late, by the way. The bus was…" He trailed off as he followed their eyelines. "What's everyone looking at?"

"Nothing much," David said. "Just the guy who's gonnae make this bonspiel a lot more interesting than we ever dreamed."

"Interesting" indeed. Luca turned back to the rink to ponder this development. His gaze settled on an ice technician showering the surface with water droplets, which would freeze into the all-important pebbles that let the stones glide. But his mind was far from the here-and-now.

Six weeks had passed since Team Riley had shocked Team Boyd by beating them at the Aberdeen Curl Fest in mid-December. That win had left the two rivals tied atop the leaderboard of this season's Scottish Challenger Tour, a series of competitions offering second-tier teams a chance to qualify for the national championship. Whoever finished higher at next weekend's Glasgow Open would likely win the Challenger Tour and thus be bound for Nationals. That would mean TV exposure, invitations to events with bigger cash prizes—and most of all, sponsorships that could transform Luca's obsession from a financial drain into a boon.

Since Aberdeen, Luca had noticed a sudden surge in Team Boyd's level of play. The whole rink had been talking about it. Had this hot young coach been working with them remotely? If Oliver could raise their game by sitting at a computer across the Atlantic, what would they become with him here in person? Had Team Riley's small chance at Nationals just become microscopic?

Enough of that. With a single deep breath, Luca brought his attention back to the present. Next week would see to itself. In the meantime, he'd keep his curlers focused on each shot, always remaining in the moment—and above all, having fun.

His mind calmed, Luca allowed himself another look at Oliver Doyle, just to confirm his initial fleeting impression. He could count on a single hand the number of men he'd wanted at first sight—enough to pursue rather than simply admire.

The coach was holding court at the warm room's far table, his four curlers nodding along with every word and gesture. Though he appeared younger than his thirty-year-old skip, Oliver had an air of authority that even the imperious Jack Boyd seemed to respect.

And yet...Luca sensed another layer beneath that veil of confidence and competence. There was an awkwardness infusing Oliver's robust good looks, and a kernel of uncertainty to his swagger, that made Luca need to know him better.

How would it feel, he wondered, to steady that restive spirit, if only for a moment, and to chase the shadows from those green-apple eyes?

———

OLIVER DOYLE COULD FINALLY BREATHE.

He'd spent the last month holed up in his apartment in New Glasgow, Nova Scotia, studying film of Team Boyd and their rivals, then running that film through video-analysis software and combining the results with a dozen shot-selection spreadsheets. He'd Skyped with the entire team twice a week —and nearly every night with skip Jack Boyd—offering feedback, brainstorming strategy, and assigning drills to improve their performance.

Now here he was, standing beside them in their home rink on the southern edge of the city his hometown had been named after.

Holy jeez, this is really happening.

"Watch Ian's delivery," Jack said as he tapped his broom a few inches in front of the bullseye-shaped house, showing where he wanted the stone to stop. "It's pure straight now." He crouched near the left edge of the house and placed his brush head on the ice for his lead curler to aim at.

Oliver moved behind Jack to get a better look. At the other end of the sheet, Ian placed his right foot into the black-rubber hack, then pointed his toes, hips, and shoulders toward the head of Jack's broom.

It was the essential first step in a good delivery, but even the best curlers sometimes struggled to maintain that perfect line—to "stay on broom"—after launching themselves out of the hack. Maybe a knee would hit the ice and twist the thrower's body, or an anxious hand would push or pull the stone upon release.

Curling is the hardest easy-looking sport in the world, Oliver used to tell his students back home when they shed tears of frustration and threatened to chuck their brooms into the East River of Pictou. Then he'd work with them for hours on practice drills, cultivating one technique after another until their entire delivery was second nature.

Now, he hoped like hell that Team Boyd had been working on *their* drills since hiring him. Otherwise he was in for a short stay.

Ian drew back slightly, then pushed out of the hack with a controlled thrust from his powerful right leg. The sturdy young lead glided forward over the ice, his path straight and smooth, his eyes fixed on Jack's broom. Then he released the rock, its red handle whispering out of his hand with the perfect amount of rotation.

"Nice…" Oliver said. "Real nice."

"Line's good, lads!" Jack called out to Bruce and Alistair,

the Team Boyd second and vice-skip, who accompanied the red rock as it made its way down the sheet. He wanted the stone to land just in front of the house to sit as a guard. If this were an actual game instead of mere practice, that guard would make it harder for their opponent to score.

It just needed a little help getting there.

"Wee bit light," Bruce called out.

"Sweep!" Jack yelled. "Hard!"

Bruce and Alistair leapt into action, furiously brushing the sheet in front of the stone, melting the pebbled-ice surface enough to reduce the friction and let the rock travel farther.

"Up!" Jack called out, and the two sweepers lifted their brooms so the stone could stop exactly where their skip had asked for it. "Brilliant, Ian!" Jack beamed up at Oliver. "Seems daft to be chuffed over such a basic thing, but Christ, I was gonnae have his head if he didn't start placing guards where I wanted them."

"Not daft at all," Oliver said. "When a lead makes his shots, you can spend the end executing your plan instead of putting out fires."

"Jack fancies fires." Alistair glided over to them, pushing his mop of blond curls away from his rimless glasses. "Then he can have me save the day with a double takeout."

"That's why you're here, mate." Jack grinned as he said this, but Oliver saw him glance over at Sheet B, where Team Riley were warming up.

As with so many other rivalries, Luca had been Jack's vice before leaving to start his own team. After a crucial tournament loss to Team Riley last month, the ambitious Jack had sought a coach who could turn Boyd into an elite squad able to compete against the best in Scotland—and crush Luca's band of upstarts in the bargain.

We'll do anything you ask, Jack's email had read. *Please come and change our lives the way you did Team Patterson's.*

After watching one bonspiel webcast of Team Boyd, Oliver had signed on as their coach, unable to resist their mix of raw talent and relentless drive.

Patterson, the women's team Oliver had taken from small-town obscurity to provincial champions in a single season, had just been accepted into Canada's high-performance program. The four ladies were now in the hands of the country's best coaches, fitness experts, and sports psychologists; while Oliver had been left behind, searching for his next challenge.

Jack's P.S. had sealed the deal:

We don't care about your past.

AN HOUR LATER, Oliver sat in the warm room watching Team Boyd's first game of the night, which they were winning handily. But during every break between ends, he kept his eye on Team Riley—especially their skip, who was way hotter in real life than in those grainy tournament webcasts.

On the ice, Luca looked utterly focused, yet he lacked the permanent frown worn by so many skips. Even when he shouted commands at the sweepers, his voice held a strangely sweet serenity.

And when it came to throwing his own stones, Luca was downright mesmerizing. The broom and rock seemed like extensions of his own lithe frame. Though his flexible legs let his body sink low to the ice, he held his head high and shoulders square, arching his back like a swan. As his slender fingers rotated and released the handle, it was like witnessing a fond farewell. If curling were judged on artistic content, Luca would get a perfect score.

Oliver flipped to a blank page in his sketchbook. It was the only paper he carried, now that all his curling stuff was on his omnipresent tablet. For some reason, he did his best thinking while drawing.

Luca was giving him a lot to think about.

It was obvious how Team Riley had earned the nickname "Team Smiley." The four men had an enviable looseness about them, with nearly every interaction ending in laughter. Their front end consisted of an equally brawny ginger and blond who looked like they'd strolled in off the old Glasgow ship-building docks: Lead David Moffat seemed as stolid and stalwart as the guards he placed, while Ross Buchanan was a force of nature throwing second, wielding a takeout stone like the hammer of Thor. Team Riley's vice, Garen McLaren, exuded more energy than the rest of them put together, his mania complementing his teammates' poise rather than clashing with it.

Currently Garen was using his broom as a cane to perform a "Puttin' on the Ritz"-style number as he waited to sweep Ross's next throw, his shaggy mane of sandy hair swaying over his shoulders as he danced.

Behind Oliver, a single sleigh bell jingled, a signal the front door had opened. He turned to see a tall, dark-skinned woman in her early thirties enter the warm room from the foyer. After a pause at the threshold, she spied him and headed over wearing a wide smile.

"If I'm not mistaken, you're Oliver Doyle!" She extended a hand as he stood to greet her. "I'm Heather Wek, from Wek Sight and Sound. I've been hired to do a documentary of sorts on the two Shawlands teams trying to make Nationals."

He froze mid-handshake. "A documentary?" The last thing he needed was someone digging into his past—not that one would need to dig very hard. But if she'd recognized him on sight, she must have already looked him up online.

"Aye, to promote the sport and their club in particular." She reached back and freed her long black ponytail from the hood of her rain-spattered jacket. "Tonight I'm just here to observe and get some background info, as I'm still pretty new to curling."

"Oh, good—I mean, it's always nice to get a fresh perspective on the sport. Helps make it accessible to the public." And the more time Heather spent learning the basics, the less time she'd spend learning his personal history.

He noticed her violet-and-white jacket. "Warriors FC... where have I heard of them?"

"It's an all-LGBT football team." Heather stroked the sword-and-soccer-ball crest on her shoulder. "I'm the starting goalkeeper—and one of the Ts, obviously."

It wasn't obvious, but Oliver didn't say so, as his mind was still chasing the question of why the Warriors were familiar. "I don't follow the sport, so where have I seen you guys?"

"Maybe you watched our 'Football Crazy' video last summer? It went viral."

Oliver remembered now. The Warriors had been every LGBT athlete's heroes of the month. "That must be it. It was fantastic, by the way."

"Thanks." She gave a demure head tilt. "My company made the video, of course."

"I've got my own digital arts business, so I know good stuff when I see it. My work is nowhere near yours." He offered an *I'm-not-worthy* bowing gesture, which made her laugh.

They were joined then by Craig and Anya Sinclair, presidents of the men's and women's competitive curling clubs that had hired Heather. After a bit of small talk, Oliver excused himself to return to work.

Out on the ice, Jack was preparing to attempt a runback double takeout, a shot in which he would hit a guard hard enough to knock two of their opponents' rocks out of the house. It was a big crowd-pleaser when it worked, but when it didn't, they risked giving up a lot of points.

Oliver could see three wiser options available. Had the Boyd skip even considered them?

Ten seconds later, Jack made that question irrelevant. His shooter smashed into his own red guard, which in turn hit one yellow stone, then the other, finally spinning to a stop in the back of the four-foot ring.

"Yaaaas!" Jack pumped his fist, then shared a hearty high-five with his sweepers. Finally he looked at the warm-room window, maybe hoping for applause from his coach.

Oliver gave him a thumbs up, then made a note to work with his skip on shot selection. While he didn't want to discourage Jack's natural intensity, he was hoping to temper it with more...well, *thinking*.

Heather and Anya came to stand behind him, chatting about the basics of the game. To ward off the distraction of their presence, he shifted back and forth between his sketch-book and score sheet.

"A curling game is divided into eight periods called 'ends,'" Anya said. "In each end, all four players on both teams take turns throwing two stones each." She chuckled. "They don't literally throw them, obviously, as they weigh over forty pounds. Anyway, after all eight stones are thrown, whoever's stones are closest to the center of those rings—which we call the 'house'—wins points."

Oliver smiled at Anya's pronunciation, *hoose*. It reminded him of his late grandmother, who'd moved to Nova Scotia from Orkney when she was twelve and never lost the accent.

"So there's a point for each stone in the house?" Heather asked Anya.

"No, only the team with the closest stone can score, and only with the stones which are closer than their opponent's closest stone."

"Ah, I remember now," Heather said. "I was obsessed with curling during last year's Olympics. It's so addictive."

Olympics. Oliver took a deep breath to ease the ache in his chest that always arose when he heard that word.

Soon Anya and Heather headed to the bar to join Craig for a drink, and Oliver returned to his spreadsheet. Within minutes he was fighting off yawns as the jet lag began to wrap around his brain like a wet woolen blanket. He hadn't slept on last night's red-eye flight from Toronto or on the turbulent jump from Halifax before that. As he watched his team take a four-point lead into the eighth and final end, his sandbag-heavy eyelids threatened to turn each blink into a nap.

"Hiya!"

Oliver started at the voice close to his ear. He looked up to see Luca Riley grinning at him around the lollipop in his mouth.

"Hi." Oliver glanced toward the rink. "You finished early," he added, as if Luca hadn't noticed.

"They conceded after six ends. So I'm having a wee recovery snack before we play your lads." Luca sank into the chair beside him, then held up a trio of lollipops: two purple, one green. "Some glucose for your jet lag?"

"Thanks." Oliver snatched the green lollipop, unable to hide his desperate need for a sugar boost.

"I hoped you'd choose that one. It matches your eyes." He smoothed a flop of dark-brown hair off his forehead. "It's apple-flavored, by the way, not lime."

"Good to know." Oliver noticed Luca's own lollipop had turned his lips a rich crimson.

"It's also the closest color to an olive branch."

Oliver hesitated, wondering whether that was a play on his name.

"A peace offering," Luca said, "because I slagged you behind your back earlier. I was still reeling from the fact Team Boyd had hired a coach, but that's no excuse for being a gossipy wee prick."

"Don't worry about it."

"Okay." Luca stuffed the purple lollipops into his shirt pocket and the red one back into his mouth. "As you were." He pulled his feet onto the chair to sit in a lotus position, apparently settling in for a while.

Turning back to the table, Oliver spied his open sketchbook, which still displayed his attempt to capture Luca's graceful delivery. He flipped it over quickly, hoping the sketch was too rough to reveal the subject. Then he moved his tablet's cover to block its screen. "Are you spying on us?"

"Don't need to. Jack and I know each other's curling by heart." Luca's words were slurred by the lollipop. "Until lately, that is. You've changed him this last month—for the better, obviously."

"So...what is it you want?"

"Nothing." Luca folded his hands in his lap, gazing out over the ice with such tranquility, Oliver actually believed him.

He remembered the lollipop in his hand and started to tear off the wrapper. Under the rustle of plastic he heard Luca murmur, "Nova Scotia."

"Sorry?"

Luca pointed to the emblem on the bag beside Oliver's chair. "It means 'New Scotland,' aye?"

"Aye. I mean, yeah." Oliver sucked his lollipop and kicked his tired brain into banter mode. "New and improved."

Luca gasped. "Ooh, sassy. I thought Canadians were meant to be nice."

"And I thought Glaswegians were meant to be obnoxious. Oh, wait."

"Hah! At least one of us is upholding his reputation." Luca held out a hand. "I'm Luca Riley, by the way. Since you asked."

"Oliver Doyle." He shook Luca's hand, which was surprisingly warm considering he'd recently come off the ice. "Jack's told me a lot about you."

"Oh dear. Say, are you doing the no-shaving thing for the tournament? Seems almost every team does it, so what's the point if we're all equally lucky, right?"

"I'm not growing a beard. I—" Oliver stopped, since sometimes people were weirded out by the reason he needed to shave. "Luca: Isn't that Italian?"

"It is, but I'm not, though some say I look it. It's actually short for Lucas. When I was six, I went to the seashore with my family and refused to come out of the water at the end of the day because I wanted to 'swim with the fishes.' My granddad made a Luca Brasi *Godfather* joke—I know, it's actually *'sleep* with the fishes' in the film—and the nickname stuck."

Oliver pulled the lollipop from his mouth, trying not to let it paint his lips green. "Do you like it?"

"I love it. My mission in life is to redeem 'Luca' from its links to a murdered mobster and that poor lad from the Suzanne Vega song. It's now in the top 100 names for Scottish baby boys, so I'll soon have help there. Do you like your name?"

"It's all right," Oliver said, his head spinning from Luca's heavily accented, rapid-fire monologues. "Except for the orphan jokes."

"Orphan?"

"You know. Oliver Twist."

Luca cocked his head. "Who's he?"

"From the Charles Dickens novel."

"Which one?"

"From—" He stopped when he saw the slow grin spread across Luca's face. "Are you always this annoying?"

"Hmmm." Luca pressed a fingertip to his chin. "I don't think so, but I'll ask around."

Holy shit, this guy was cute, in that weird way Oliver really liked. He wished Jack had warned him about his rival's quirky charms.

He saw the rest of Team Riley gathered at the other side of the warm room. "Why aren't you broomstacking with the team you just beat?" he asked Luca. "Is that not a tradition here?"

"It is, and we offered them drinks, but they needed to be up the road. Something about a kidney transplant."

Oliver laughed, hoping Luca was still joking. "And where's your coach?"

"Haven't got one." Luca examined his remaining nub of lollipop, then put the stick back into his mouth. "Are they necessary?"

"It helps, if you want to go far."

"Well, I'm pretty happy where I am just now." He looked down at the space between them, then up into Oliver's eyes.

The bottom dropped out of Oliver's stomach, as if he were descending the first hill of a rollercoaster.

"Desire is a dangerous thing, see." Luca blinked. "In sport, I mean." He broke their gaze and looked out over the ice. "Obviously one should try one's best, but blasting that 'gotta win, gotta win' recording in your head over and over just creates tension. Then you can't perform to your potential."

"For sure," was all Oliver could think to say.

"I teach meditation when I'm not curling or working my inconsequential day job, so I know of what I speak." Luca brightened. "Talking of which, I'm starting a class in meditation for athletes, next Tuesday at the well-being center in Hillhead." He leaned over to give Oliver's arm a fleeting touch. "Beginners welcome."

Oliver tried not to react to this brief brush of Luca's hand. "How do you know I'm a beginner?"

Luca laughed, then pulled the lollipop from his mouth and looked at its naked stick. "Ah, that's my time up. See you at our broomstacking, mate." He clapped Oliver's shoulder as he stood, then crossed the warm room to join his team at their table.

Oliver turned back to the ice sheet in front of him, where Team Boyd were nailing down a victory in the final end of play. Sucking the sweet-tart lollipop, he took a few last notes about their shot choices, but his thoughts kept scurrying back to Luca.

Had he been cozying up to Oliver to distract him from his job, hoping to whittle away Team Boyd's edge? Or maybe Luca was trying to piss off Jack—brothers-in-law were often at odds under the best of circumstances.

Both possibilities seemed contrary to the spirit of curling. And Oliver's gut told him that Luca's flirtation had been genuine.

Unfortunately, Oliver had learned long ago that his gut was a worthless guide to life.

2

Broomstacking

BROOMSTACKING: *Customary post-curling social hour in which the winning team buys the drinks. A chance for alcohol or caffeine to heal any bruised egos or hard feelings so that everyone goes home happy.*

STACKING the brooms with Team Boyd had been a lot more fun when Luca was playing *for* his brother-in-law rather than against him. Now the eight players sat at their communal table, sipping their obligatory drinks in silence. Jack was gulping his coffee so fast, Luca's own throat burned in a sympathetic scald.

The game had gone worse than he'd feared. Usually he could count on Team Boyd to be overly aggressive in the first end, risking difficult shots before evaluating the ice conditions. Riley would then try capitalize on mistakes and take an early lead, thus rattling Boyd and driving them to take more risks in an attempt to catch up.

Not tonight.

Tonight, Boyd had shown a discipline so unlike them,

Garen had wondered aloud if they'd been body-snatched by aliens. But it was clear who'd given them this new attitude.

Luca sipped his bourbon and pondered how to handle the Oliver Doyle Effect. It was a welcome challenge—after all, "waiting for Boyd to screw up" had never been a robust strategy. Clearly Team Riley needed to increase their intensity without losing the stability that made them so formidable in big events.

The awkward silence was broken by the arrival of Craig Sinclair, their curling club's current president. "Great news, lads!" said the burly septuagenarian with bushy white hair. "You're gonnae be stars."

Jack perked up. "Stars of what?"

"The club's hired a local film crew to chronicle your battle to reach Nationals. As part of the journey, we're sending the eight of you—nine, including Oliver—on a wee field trip to Ailsa Craig next Thursday. I hope you can all make it." He handed a stack of papers to Jack. "If you could just pass around these release forms?"

"How are we getting to the island?" Luca asked him.

"Private fishing boat. We've also hired two MPVs for you to drive to the port at Girvan. We've got magnetic Shawlands Ice Rink logos to put on the sides of the vehicles." Craig spread his hands to illustrate. "For promotion and all."

"Brilliant idea." Garen raised his bottle of lager in salute. "The more attention, the better."

Luca held back a laugh. The documentary had been Garen's idea. After six years as Garen's friend, flatmate, teammate—and very briefly his boyfriend—Luca had learned to accept and even welcome his cockamamie schemes.

When Craig had left the table, Jack scratched at his smattering of blond-red stubble. "This field trip seems a big distraction so close to the tournament. Why do we need to all go together?"

"The club's pure proud of us." Garen gestured to the wood-paneled wall's photo gallery of past Shawlands luminaries. "They've not had one team so close to Nationals in decades, much less two."

"But sailing on the Irish Sea in January?" Ian shuddered. "We'll freeze our baws off."

"It'll be fun!" Garen rubbed his hands together. "Glasgow's best curlers visiting the world-famous source of curling-rock granite? That's marketing gold, mate."

"I never agreed to be filmed," Jack said.

"No bother." Garen reached across the table and took Jack's release form. "Just don't sign this. Then you'll not be interviewed, and when you're in the background, your face'll be all pixelated."

Jack tapped his fingers on the table, probably imagining the sponsorships he could pinch with the right exposure. "I never said I wouldn't do it." He snatched the form back from Garen. "I just would've appreciated being informed first."

Luca bit his tongue to stop himself asking Jack, *How ever do you curl with a broomstick up your arse?* It was that very question, among other things, that had led to the demise of Team Boyd 1.0.

He spied Oliver standing alone at the bar with his tablet. "Jack, why don't you invite your coach to join us for a drink?"

"I did, but he's busy making notes for our post-game meeting."

"Maybe he'll change his mind." Luca got up and headed for the bar, his brother-in-law's protests fading behind him. "Fancy joining us?" he asked as he reached Oliver's side. "We'd love to hear any wisdom you'd care to share."

"Hm?" Oliver blinked at him as he covered his tablet

screen. "Oh jeez, thanks, but no. Broomstacking's a time for players to socialize. It's weird when coaches join in. Like having your dad hang out with you at a party."

"'Dad'? You're younger than Jack. Or at least you look it," Luca added, grazing Oliver's arm with his fingertips.

"It's best if I keep some distance between myself and the players." Oliver glanced down at Luca's hand lingering on his arm. "All the players."

"Right." Luca pulled his hand back and used it to smooth his hair. As usual it was sticking up in odd places, judging by his reflection in the door of the fridge behind the bar. "*Oliver Twist* is one of my favorites, by the way. I was just messing you about before."

"I knew that." After a beat, Oliver gave a self-deprecating smile that curled Luca's toes. "Not right away, obviously. The jet lag's left me a bit, um…"

"Glaikit?"

"If that's Scots for foggy-brained, then yes."

"I like 'foggy-brained.' Is it Canadian?"

"No, it's just…" Oliver waved his hand near his own temple. "Apt."

Luca laughed again, relieved a bit of rapport had returned. He pointed to Oliver's cup. "There's a place not far from here with much better coffee. Their espresso's been scientifically proven to make the human mind ten percent more efficient."

Oliver looked amused. "Is that so?"

"They say it's like adding an extra gigabyte of mental RAM. They used to hold coffee-drinking contests on a Saturday, but the health service made them stop on account of all the cardiac arrests. Now Saturdays are icing-sugar paint nights."

Oliver furrowed his brow in the cutest way, which reminded Luca to speak more slowly with foreigners. "Where

I'm from, there's only a handful of fun coffee shops," he said, "but a million Tim Hortons."

"See? Nova Scotia's not a complete improvement on Scotland. Obviously Glasgow's miles better than New Glasgow."

Oliver stiffened. "How'd you know that's my hometown? Did you read my Wikipedia page?"

"One of your curlers told us. I think it was—wait, you've got a Wikipedia page?"

"Forget it." Oliver hunched his shoulders, angling them away from Luca. "It's not worth reading."

"Is winning Junior Worlds enough to get on Wikipedia?" Luca pulled out his phone. "Or are you famous for something else?"

"No! I mean, yeah, I also won a couple Briers."

"'A couple Briers'? As in the Canadian men's national championship? Gaun yersel, mate!" He punched Oliver's upper arm. "That means, 'well done.'"

"It was a long time ago."

"I don't care. I want to hear all about it." Luca climbed onto the barstool beside him. "I'm buying second round, so let's get you a real drink. Unless you'd rather go elsewhere?" He batted his lashes, hoping it looked charming instead of deranged.

"No." Oliver gave him a weary look. "Sorry."

Luca wanted to be sure he wasn't misreading the regret on Oliver's face. "So, 'no' as in 'not tonight,' or 'no' as in 'never'?"

"'No' as in 'never.' See, I'm not actually—"

"Oh my God, I'm chatting up a straight guy." Luca covered his face. "I can't believe this. I finally take the time to—"

"I'm not straight." Oliver lowered his voice. "But I'm also not…interested." He made a wincing noise. "No, that didn't come out right. I'm sorry. You seem like a nice guy, and if the circumstances were different—"

"Right. Of course." Luca lowered his hands, wishing he'd

more experience at flirting so he could gracefully handle a knockback like this. "You said you wanted to keep your distance from the players. I should've listened."

"You were just being friendly. I appreciate that, being new here." Oliver offered a sweetly crooked smile.

"Friendly. Yes. That's it." Oliver's kindness made Luca fancy him even more. "Sorry again, I...okay, bye."

Luca slunk back to his table, which now sat only Team Riley.

"Well?" Ross asked.

"Crashed. And. Burned." Luca sank into his chair. "The glorious beastie is immune to my charms."

"I telt ya." Garen held out a hand across the table to David, waggling his fingers. "That's you owing me a tenner."

David sighed and pulled out his wallet.

"You were betting on my powers of flirtation?" Luca scowled at his empty dram glass. "If I'd known, I would've tried harder."

"You were trying pretty hard." Garen took David's ten-pound note and kissed it. "Practically jumping in his lap, telling him you'd been a good boy this year and please to bring you a new PlayStation and say hi to Rudolph and Mrs. Claus, by the way."

"You're just jealous," Luca said.

"Oh, here we go." David sat back, out of the crossfire.

"Why would I be jealous?" Garen made a show of folding the tenner into a neat triangle. "I've got Steven."

Do you? Luca wondered. Lately Garen's boyfriend was managing to outshine him in the emotional volatility department.

"Doyle's not my type, anyway. Too tall." Garen jerked his head to look at Luca. "Wait—you don't mean I'm jealous of *him*, do you?"

"Why not? I was spectacular when we were together, and I've only improved in the five years since." Luca smoothed his nascent beard. "Now this stubble makes me preternaturally irresistible. Right, Ross?"

Ross assessed him, then shrugged. "If I liked the laddies, I'd have a go."

"You're an absolute sook," Garen told him. "Flattery won't get you promoted to vice."

David snorted. "We all know that's not how *you* originally got that position. Unless 'flattery' is new slang for 'hand job.'"

Garen chucked a sugar packet at David's head, smacking him in the temple. David returned fire with an arsenal of artificial sweetener, and soon it was an all-out condiments melee. Luca looked across the room at Team Boyd, who were hunkered over their own table, solemn as monks. Oliver had joined them, outlining moves using his tablet's curling-strategies app.

If Luca had stayed with Team Boyd, his ticket to Nationals would already be punched. But he wouldn't trade his position, his freedom, and especially his pals for all the sponsorships in the world.

AT LAST, Oliver was home—or at least what would serve as his home for the next two weeks, hopefully much longer.

"Your other work gear came to my house yesterday," Jack said as he carried Oliver's duffel bag up the narrow stairway of the Victorian-era boutique hotel. "I had it brought to your room this morning."

"Thanks. Glad it arrived on time." Oliver grunted as the suitcase in his hand caught the edge of the carved wooden banister. "Without it, Sunday would be pretty dull."

"We'd make it work. And nothing in Glasgow is ever dull." Jack stopped in front of the door at the top of the stairs. "This is you here."

The room was small, but in a cozy rather than cramped way. Its decor was more modern than Oliver had expected based on the hotel's historic-looking lobby. It had a built-in closet rather than a wardrobe, and the double bed's coverings were a muted taupe-and-white stripe. An armless armchair was tucked into the window nook beside a small wooden desk, which was mostly blocked by the crate containing supplies for his other job.

"Ooh, a fireplace." Oliver pointed to the no-smoking sign beneath the alabaster stone mantle. "Gas, I assume?"

"Aye. Would love to have one of these at home." Jack flipped a wall switch. With a tiny whoosh, a pair of flames appeared behind the fireplace glass. "I asked for a room at the back of the building, as Great Western Road can be loud at night with all the Glasgow Uni students." He parted the sheer white curtains and peered out. "There's a wee courtyard back here, and with the leaves off the trees, you can see the Botanic Gardens."

"Great." Oliver eased his backpack off his aching shoulders and let it thump onto the bed. All he wanted was to sleep—or rather, begin his bedtime routine so he could eventually sleep.

"Madeline, the concierge, said occasionally the stray cats fight or mate at night, so if you hear screams, don't assume someone's being murdered."

"Good to know." Oliver rolled the stiffness out of his shoulders. "Thanks again, Jack. Not just for the hotel, but for giving me a chance. You could've chosen a lot of other coaches who had way less baggage." He gestured to the suitcase at his feet. "Literally and figuratively."

"Look, I get it. I mean, not personally, but my wee daughter, Willow—you'll meet her tomorrow—she's got some of the same issues as you. And she's brilliant, like, in every way. So it's us should be thanking you." Jack headed for the door, then stopped. "Talking of family, I'm sorry my brother-in-law was getting on your wick during the broomstacking."

"Oh." Oliver cleared his throat. He knew it was just a colorful British expression, but the image of Luca on his "wick" left him momentarily tongue-tied. "He was fine. Nice guy."

"He is that." Jack rubbed the back of his neck, looking like he wanted to say more.

"But…"

"But nothing. I kinda wish you'd come here two years ago. Maybe you could've kept us together. You've already helped me and Ali get on better."

Oliver nodded. Alistair had skipped his own team before replacing Luca as Jack's vice, and they sometimes butted heads over calling shots. Oliver had held a couple of quasi-counseling sessions over Skype to help the two equally brilliant curlers feel more comfortable in their roles.

"It's not always easy curling with family," Oliver said.

"Me and Luca were more than family. We were friends." Jack shook his head. "But I ruined all that, and now I'm just his sister's dickhead husband."

It pained Oliver to see brothers of any sort on the outs. "What about now? Would you get Luca back on your team if you could?" What he really wanted to ask was, *Should I make it my mission?*

"He's happy where he is, as well he should be." Jack opened the door. "Be sure not to sleep too late. Madeline's breakfast ends at half-ten on a Saturday, and I've heard it's a tragedy to miss."

The moment Jack was gone, Oliver started unpacking. His

body begged him to just kick off his shoes and tumble into bed, but he knew he'd never sleep with his room in chaos.

Halfway through the process, he stopped and pulled out his phone, his already shallow well of willpower emptied by stress and fatigue. His pulse fluttered as he brought up his Wikipedia entry.

The table of contents once again contained an entry marked *Scandal*. He tapped the link to see that the so-called-official rumor had reappeared at the bottom of his entry, making it the last word on his curling career for any Wikipedia reader.

"Damn it." Three times Oliver had had the section removed, and three times it had been resurrected. There was no longer even a note at the top of his entry saying the content was disputed.

The Wiki gods had spoken, as he'd known they would. After all, the story was bullshit only in spirit. The facts of the case were true, and as unassailable as the freezing point of water.

He was an idiot to have mentioned the page to Luca. It never would've slipped out if he hadn't been so tired, if it hadn't been...ugh, a million hours since his last dose of the one thing that could put a filter between his thoughts and his mouth. By now Luca had read all about the "scandal" and probably regarded Oliver with the same contempt as most of the curling world.

He scrolled back up over his Wikipedia page, relieved to see the Personal life section remained brief and boring, containing only his date and place of birth, the name of his business, and the fact he was openly gay.

Oliver set the timer on his phone to five minutes, then managed to finish unpacking three seconds before the alarm sang its merry tune. Then he cleaned his contacts, washed his face, and brushed his teeth—in that order, so he wouldn't forget any of those tasks in his new surroundings, stripped of the familiar visual cues of home.

Finally he switched off the fireplace and crawled beneath the soft sheets. His eyelids drifted shut, then immediately slammed open.

He sat up in bed, heart pounding. He'd almost forgotten the one thing he swore he'd never again neglect.

With trembling fingers, Oliver picked up his phone and set his alarm for the next morning, allowing enough time to lollygag (as his mom would call it) and still arrive downstairs in time to eat. A day without breakfast is hardly worth living, he told himself, as if missing a meal were the worst thing that could happen from a forgotten alarm.

This time when his head hit the pillow, his eyes wouldn't shut, not until he'd run through his mental list of everything he needed to remember for tomorrow, then checked his memory against the list on his phone.

Eat.

Rest.

Visit Jack and his family.

Find the closest pharmacy, in case everything works out.

3

Takeout

TAKEOUT: *A shot in which a rock hits another rock and removes it from play. Incredibly satisfying, if you like that sort of thing, which everyone does.*

WHEN LUCA OPENED his sister's front door Sunday afternoon, he was met with a wave of shrieks. He briefly considered leaving the colorful but sloppily wrapped birthday gift on the foyer floor and sneaking away like some second-rate, off-season Santa.

Then he heard his niece shout from the other room.

"Avaaaaaaaaaaaaaaast!" she cried with a voice far more commanding than the average six-year-old's. The other children hushed, and in the silence, Willow added, "Mummy, what's 'avast' mean?"

Luca swept into the living room and spread his parrot wings. "It means 'stop what you're doing and give your daft wee uncle a hug!'"

Willow hollered his name and dashed over, stomping on the paper-chain pirate ship "ropes" strewn across the floor.

"There's a surprise!" she said as she leapt into his embrace. "And I already know it!"

"There is? Ow." He carefully pushed aside her cardboard cutlass, which dangled from her arm with the help of a blue hair band. "This sword is pure realistic."

"Daddy's coach painted it for me."

"Did he?" He craned his neck to look for Oliver, but didn't see him amidst the fathers gathered by the fireplace with a conspiratorial bottle of whisky.

"Aye, yesterday. He's a artist." Willow scrutinized Luca's parrot-head cap with a hint of pity.

"He's *an* artist, pumpkin, not *a* artist." Gillian looked up at Luca, her kohl-lined eyes a bit bloodshot. "Glad you could make it," she said with sisterly sarcasm.

"I texted you I'd a class until noon." Normally he didn't teach on a weekend due to curling commitments, but the Sunday morning Vipassana teacher had called out ill.

"Uncle Luca, can I tell you the surprise?" Without waiting for his reply, Willow whispered in his ear. "There's gonnae be a real pirate clown!"

The last word stopped him cold. Surely Gillian and Jack wouldn't do that to him. "You mean a real *pirate*?" he said, low enough so the other kids couldn't hear over their rowdy game of Pass the Parcel.

"No, a pirate *clown*." Willow tugged her hat back into place over her strawberry-blond hair. "Real pirates are mean and steal things."

"True." He set Willow down and straightened her eye patch. "But pirate clowns are nice?"

"Yes."

"Always?"

She seemed to consider it further, then nodded once more with emphasis.

"In that case, Uncle Luca needs a drink." He glared at Gillian. "Maybe your mum can help me find one." On his way to the kitchen he waved to Jack, who was at the stereo controlling the music for the game.

Gillian followed, her high-heeled pirate boots clonking on the tile. "There's lager on the fridge door."

"I know." Luca jerked open the refrigerator and pulled out a bottle. "A clown, Gill? How could you do this to me? You know I'm a lifelong coulrophobe."

"Och, away with your fancy words for being a fanny."

"I'm not a fanny for hating clowns, and I'm not alone. No one likes those creepy bams these days."

"Willow and her friends *love* those creepy bams." Smirking, his sister swished her red-and-black-striped pirate skirt. "They also love balloon animals."

"Balloons?!" Luca pointed at her. "I'll not forget this. When I have my own weans, I'll see to it they love spiders. We'll have spider-themed birthday parties every year."

She shuddered. "Spiders kill people. Clowns and balloons don't kill people."

"Okay, but…" Luca sipped his lager, searching for a retort. "Spider-*Man* saves people."

Gillian pursed her lips, then looked him over and started to laugh. "Did you ride the subway wearing that, ya wee numptie?"

"Aye, and I got hunners of crackers from strangers asking, 'Who's a pretty birdie?'" He preened the neon-green feathers glued to the sleeves of his bright-red shirt. "You look pure knackered, by the way. Have you slept this week?"

"As much as ever, so hardly at all." She opened the cupboard and pulled out a box of birthday candles. "But how can I complain? Poor me, suffering from a fantastic job and a fantastic kid to put on parties for."

"And a fantastic husband who does ever so much to help."

"Shut it." She shook the candle box at him. "If you'd helped plan and prepare this party like I asked, there'd be no clown."

"I'm sorry. Between the two jobs and training for the—" He stopped when he saw her scowl. "I'll help tidy up after."

"No, you won't, because curling practice starts at four." She swiped a hand up over her face, nearly knocking the red pirate kerchief from her short dark hair. "It's always the curling with you guys."

And with you, once upon a time, he thought, but didn't say aloud so as not to rub her nose in the fact she'd given up her own love of the ice due to the demands of motherhood and software engineering. "My offer to play mixed doubles stands eternally," he told her.

"As does Jack's. I'm not keen to give your feud more ammunition."

"You know I'd be a better doubles partner than your husband. I can actually make draws, and I'd let you call the shots."

"*Let* me?" she asked, jerking open the cutlery drawer. "How generous."

"I'd be honored if you'd call the shots." He held up his hands in prayer position. "There's a doubles bonspiel next month at Shawlands. Signups start Monday. It'd be a belter!" He flapped his parrot "wings" for emphasis.

The doorbell sounded, followed by a crescendo of kiddie cheers.

"That'll be the clown." Gillian set a cake slicer on the work-top, then slammed the drawer shut. "We'll discuss this later, or better yet, never again."

"What sort of pirate rings the bell instead of invading? Not very authentic." He moved to the sink at the far end of the kitchen. "So I'll just stay here if you don't mind."

"Willow will mind knowing her uncle's a coward." Gillian came over to tug his arm. "C'mon, she'll want you with her."

"What if my nerves are contagious? You want me to sit beside your daughter bracing myself for a balloon pop?"

"They won't pop."

"They. Always. Pop," he said through gritted teeth. "Don't they, Gillian?"

She rolled her eyes. "Then come through after the balloons. I promise this clown's not scary. He's actually—"

"Just gross and annoying? Fantastic." He waved her out. "Fine, I'll be there soon."

"Thank you." Gillian stalked out of the kitchen, but Luca heard her footsteps stop just outside the door. A moment later, the edge of a red balloon appeared at the side of the doorway.

"Stop it, ya cow!"

Gillian chucked the balloon into the kitchen like a grenade, then ran away, cackling.

Luca took the balloon's dangling ribbon and pulled the floating fiend over to the sink, where he tethered it to a cupboard handle so he could keep an eye on it.

Then he started on the pile of dishes, partly to be useful but also to take his mind off the noise from the other room. The clown was spouting the usual pirate clichés but delivering them with a not-terrible Cornish accent, a clever nod to *Pirates of Penzance.*

By the time Luca had set all the clean dishes in the drainer to dry, his curiosity was urging him to have a wee peek at this so-called pirate. He took a step toward the kitchen door.

From the living room came the distinctive squeak of a twisted balloon.

None of that. Luca retreated to the sink, grabbing a tea towel on the way. As he dried the dishes, he hummed to himself, but every creak of latex broke through his manufactured white noise, until it felt like the clown was literally unnerving him, crumpling and fraying his neurons one by one.

Finally he stopped and closed his eyes. With a pair of long, deep breaths, he let his mind settle on the feeling of the tea towel in one hand and the stainless steel mixing bowl in the other.

The towel was soft and slightly damp. The smooth bowl held a lingering warmth from the dishwater. His thumb brushed the bowl's beveled edge, where a bit of dried cake batter remained. *This. Here. Now.*

Luca's pulse slowed and steadied. *Everything's fine*, his body and mind seemed to agree.

POP!!

Luca yelped, losing his grip on the bowl, which ricocheted off the worktop edge, then tumbled to the floor and bounced across the stone tile with a series of metallic bangs.

The living room fell silent for a moment before a wee lad shrieked, "You killed my balloon parrot!"

"Did not!" said another boy.

"You did, I saw you poke it!"

"It's all right," the clown said, his accent never faltering. "I can make more. See?"

Another balloon popped with a rifle-like retort.

"Ha! Revenge!" yelled the first boy.

A third pop resounded, and the other children began to scream and laugh.

Luca had to get out. He yanked the bag from the kitchen rubbish bin and hurried toward the door to the back garden.

Of course the latch stuck, and he was left rattling the knob in frustration just as the clamor in the living room began to die down.

"Uncle Luca, where are you going?"

Luca looked through the dining room to see everyone at the party staring at him—including the clown.

He held up the bin bag. "Just...taking this out?"

"I'll get that later," Gillian said. "Right now I think Captain Arrrgh needs a first mate to help him with the balloons."

Luca's jaw tightened as he tried to think of the word for murdering one's sister. Was it *sorocide* or simply *fratricide*?

"Ahoy, matey!" the clown cried out. "There'll be great booty for you as a reward."

"I...I don't...okay." Luca set down the bag, then forced his feet to cross the floor until he stood as close as he could bear to the looming pirate—who, to his credit, didn't have a big red nose or a ghastly fake grin like a regular clown. His stage makeup consisted of a jagged cheek scar and gray lines to make his face look rugged and gaunt. The near eye was covered by a black patch, so Luca couldn't properly estimate the pirate's age.

Captain Arrrgh picked up a long, bright-green balloon. "Now, wee Willow, where was I in my grand tale of derring-do?"

Willow stood to answer, her face pure earnest. "Your zoo boat was being attacked by Bad Billy's Bogus Buccaneers."

"That's right! Clever lass." The clown shook his long, black curls as he twisted one end of the balloon—the far tip of which, Luca noticed, was left uninflated. "So my mateys and I, we had to fight off Bad Billy, or those scallywags would scuttle our ship and turn us into shark bait. Now someone tell me— what do pirates fight with?"

"Swords!" half the kids shouted, and lo and behold, Captain Arrrgh had transformed the balloon into a cutlass, complete with a three-part hand guard.

"My first mate, see, is also my armorer. He'll be keeping the weapons until there's enough for everyone." The pirate held the sword out to Luca—handle first, as though the blade could actually be sharp.

Luca snatched it from him. That was the weird thing about his globophobia: A balloon wasn't scary in his own hands. He knew *he* wouldn't pop it, but others, like his sister, weren't so trustworthy.

Captain Arrrgh continued the story as he twisted a red balloon into a saber, with a curved blade and a half-circle hand guard. When Luca saw the saber was finished, he quickly gathered it into his arms with the green sword.

As the pirate kept up the patter, his hands' rapid contortions became strangely mesmerizing. Luca realized he was witnessing a form of art. Despite their inherent evil, the balloons were becoming something beautiful.

Eventually his elbows started to lock up from cradling nearly a dozen swords, so he straightened his arms, lowering the weapons in front of himself. Immediately he heard a chorus of non-childlike giggles break out in the corner of the room. A group of mothers stood there, drinking wine and peering at Luca's midsection with great amusement.

He looked down to discover he was now displaying the swords in front of his crotch like a giant bouquet of cocks.

Don't laugh. Don't laugh. Don't laugh. But he had no free hand to wipe the grin off his rapidly warming face.

One of Gillian's friends leaned over and whispered in her ear. She looked at Luca and snorted so hard she started to cough on her wine.

The dads were noticing now too, some snickering outright and others covering their eyes. Even Jack was cracking a pained smile that looked almost sympathetic.

Gillian raised her hand. "Captain Arrrgh, shall we pass

around some of the balloons now? I think the armory is getting full."

The pirate clown turned and froze at the sight of Luca's magnificent display. Then his gaze flashed up, showing his unpatched eye. It was the same color as half the balloons in Luca's arms, the same color as the lollipop he'd given away Friday night.

The same color as a ripe green apple.

WHEN OLIVER SAW the shock of recognition sweep over Luca's face like a rogue wave, he felt a glow of pride in his powers of disguise, and also relief that Luca's hiding in the kitchen hadn't been an attempt to avoid him.

"A brilliant idea," he said to Gillian. "First Mate, give these swashbucklers their weapons!"

Luca stepped back as the children rushed forward, clamoring for their balloon swords. With each creak of latex, his shoulders tensed and his forehead crinkled. Oliver's heart went out to him—if Luca was sensitive to loud noises, he would hate what was about to happen.

"Can we sword fight now, Captain Arrrgh?" Willow hopped up and down, brandishing her curved green cutlass.

Oliver looked at Luca's paling face. "In just a moment, me heartie. Right now I need to send our First Mate on a secret mission. Let's give him a big 'Yo ho ho' for being such a brave helper."

The kids thrust their balloon swords in Luca's direction and shouted, "Yo ho ho!"

"Thanks," Luca croaked out. "Erm, same to you?"

Oliver leaned over to whisper in his ear. "There's a treasure-hunt game upstairs under your sister's bed. If you could get the clues organized, it'd be a huge help to me, and by the time you're done, the sword fight'll be over."

"Thank you." Luca clutched Oliver's gloved hand. "You're only a wee bit terrifying." He dashed up the stairs, stumbling halfway to the top.

When he heard the distant bedroom door shut, Oliver raised his arms to the children. "All hands hoay, now...heave ho!"

It was no surprise the young Scots were even more ferocious at swordplay than Canadian kids. Oliver was glad the Boyds had signed a waiver saying they wouldn't sue him in the event of injury or property destruction.

When the war was over and most of the swords had been popped into saggy rubber plowshares, the backyard treasure hunt began. Luca assisted, looking perilously adorable in his parrot costume.

Oliver was surprised to see no judgment in those lively brown eyes when they turned upon him. Maybe Luca hadn't yet investigated the story behind Oliver's early retirement. Or maybe he was sympathetic, perhaps with Jack's help.

Either way, Oliver found himself rapidly losing the will to avoid the Riley skip. So when his contracted two hours were up, he waited until Luca was fully occupied—in this case, cleaning cake off the wall—before waving goodbye to the kids and slipping out the front door.

Hurrying down the brick stairs outside, Oliver spied the taxi he'd reserved. As requested, it was parked halfway down the quiet, tree-lined street, so as not to destroy the pirate illusion in case any children were watching from the windows.

"Was this why you needed to shave?"

Oliver turned to see Luca standing on the front porch, the brisk wind fluttering his green wing feathers. He tugged his fake beard. "Yeah, this stuff sticks better to bare skin." His real accent sounded strange in his ears after all that pirate talk.

"It's impressive." Luca started to descend the steps toward him. "Your whole act, I mean. Not just the beard." He paused halfway. "I don't like clowns."

"I can tell."

"Do you like them?" Luca asked with a puzzled look. "Do you like being one?"

Oliver held up a finger toward his taxi to signal the driver to wait. "For sure," he told Luca. "I wouldn't do this otherwise."

"Plenty of people do stuff they hate for money. Then again, clowning seems like something you can't fake loving."

"Still, I wouldn't do it for free. Jack's team pays me to coach them, but it's not enough to live on. Since I'm on a six-month visitor visa, the UK government won't let me get a real job while I'm here."

"So you're stealing gigs from hardworking British clowns? I like you even more now." A gust of wind came up, ripping off one of Luca's feathers. He reached out to catch it but missed. "Are you always a pirate, or do you also do the monstrous sort of clown with the big red nose and stretchy grin?"

"There's not much demand for straight clowns these days—and by 'straight,' I mean straightforward, classic." Oliver snatched the wafting green feather as it passed him. "Though there is a healthy niche market for gay clowns."

"You're joking, right?"

"I am, but that doesn't mean it's not true."

Luca laughed, looking suddenly more relaxed. He peeked back at the house before continuing down the steps, like a dog checking to see if its owner had spied its escape. "Thanks for being so nice today about my, erm, difficulties with clowns and balloons."

"I'm used to it. Most parties have at least one kid who's afraid, especially if they've got sensory processing issues." When Luca raised an eyebrow, Oliver hurried to add, "Not that you do, or that you're a kid. Sorry."

That could have been more reassuring, he thought, wishing just once he could say the right thing to this man.

"It's more of an aversion than a fear," Luca said. "I'm not truly afraid of balloons and clowns, I just really don't like them, the same way some people don't like coriander leaves because they taste like soap. Of course, that's genetic, so—"

"If one of your meditation students had this problem, what would you tell them?"

"Good question." Luca tucked his fingers into the front pockets of his jeans while he thought. "I'd say, 'Next time you're faced with the object of your fears, take a deep breath— in through the nose, out through the mouth.'" He demonstrated, his tight red shirt expanding across his front.

"Sounds like good advice."

"Aye, well, the more relaxed you are, the faster you can run away." When Oliver laughed, Luca came closer. "Hey, I've always wanted to kick a clown. May I?"

"What, kick me?"

"Uh-huh."

"Sorry, no."

"All right." Luca rotated his parrot-head cap to the side, drawing a wayward lock of dark hair across his forehead. "Can I chuck you off a cliff?"

"Sorry, no."

"Hm." Luca sidled closer, almost near enough to touch "Just one more question, then."

Oliver's pulse raced with anticipation. "Yeah?"

"When Canadians say, 'sorry,' do they always mean it? Or is it just a word?"

The laugh caught in Oliver's throat, trying to force its way past the sudden constriction there. After a moment it gave up and became a gurgle.

"I..." Oliver felt his lips move but heard no more sounds come out. He gestured to his taxi. "I should..."

"Right." Luca backed up, looking confused and a bit alarmed. "On you go. I guess I'll see you...somewhere."

Oliver nodded and turned away, feeling like a complete tool.

Inside the taxi, he pulled out his phone and hit a well-rehearsed series of numbers.

"You have one saved message. To hear your—"

-Beep!-

"First saved message, received on—"

-Beep!-

Oliver rolled the shaft of the green feather between his fingertips as he rested his head on the taxicab window and listened to the lost voice:

"Agent O, this is Agent N." A nervous laugh. "Jeez, that sounds so dorky. Anyway, um, things are bad here. Really, really bad. So if you could come get me, that'd be cool." A heavy sigh. "Sorry to make you do this again. I know you said, 'You can't be brave if you're not scared,' but I just can't today. Too much scared, not enough brave. So...I guess I'll just wait at the usual place? Thanks...see ya."

"To save this message, press—"

-Beep!-

"Message saved."

Oliver hung up. "I'm so sorry, Noah," he whispered. "Again."

4

Draw

DRAW: *A shot that lands in play without hitting another stone. Teams who prefer to draw tend to be more offensive-minded, since having many stones in play can lead to big gains but also big losses. Curlers who prefer to draw tend to be more secure and mature, not requiring all that smashy-smashy to feel good about themselves.*

LUCA SAT ALONE in the well-being center's meditation studio. With his eyes closed, he could smell the fresh polish on the hardwood floors and hear the tick of the radiator on the wall to his right, two things he'd not noticed upon entering the room.

Oliver's painted, eye-patched, pirate-bearded face kept invading his thoughts, but that was fine. Each time Luca found himself distracted from the rhythm of his own breath, he would picture the thought as a thistle seed stuck to the sleeve of his jumper. At the first puff of imaginary wind, the thought would simply let go and blow away.

At least, that was the idea. Trouble was, each appearance of that face in Luca's memory was accompanied by a pang of sorrow. When Luca had joked about the Canadian penchant for apologies, the look in Oliver's one visible eye...

A soft chime from his phone signaled it was okay to let his mind do whatever it wanted—which was fortunate, as it very much wanted to work out what the hell he'd said to upset Oliver.

The man didn't seem particularly sensitive to Canadian stereotypes, and anyway, he did say *sorry* a lot, though probably not more than anyone here, including Luca. Had the word itself triggered Oliver's alarming response, or had it been the question? What had Oliver once apologized for that had left such a scar?

The answer probably lay online. But Luca knew the internet was full of lies, and besides, it was much more fun to get to know someone without Googling them first. Soon, he hoped, he'd learn the secret from a more reliable source: Oliver himself.

A rustle in the corridor outside the studio coaxed Luca out of his conjecture. He opened his eyes and returned to the here-and-now, ready to greet the students of his inaugural Mindfulness for Athletic Performance class.

The first to enter was a welcome sight.

"Drew." Luca stood to greet the young lord, who'd stopped attending advanced meditation lessons two months ago. "It's good to see you again."

"It's good to be back." Lord Andrew Sunderland's smile was strained but determined. He looked as though he'd lost weight, and not in a good way.

Luca tried to figure out how to offer his support without mentioning Andrew's public panic attack the previous week. The media had made it sound quite the spectacle, so he was no doubt sensitive about it.

Andrew beckoned to someone out in the hallway. "Come on, I promise you won't perish."

"I'm not feart, I was just having a drink of water from the fountain." A tall, well-built lad Andrew's age with black spiky hair walked in, wiping his mouth with the back of his hand. "All right?" he said in greeting to Luca.

"Welcome." Luca came forward as Andrew introduced them in his usual by-the-etiquette-book fashion. "It's a thrill to meet the famous Colin MacDuff."

"*In*famous, more like." Colin shook Luca's hand, then passed a wary gaze over the pale teal walls. "Andrew's been nipping my head to try meditation. He says soon every foot-baller'll be doing it, so I should get an edge now while I can."

Luca smiled. Andrew clearly knew how to motivate his boyfriend. "It is catching on big time amongst athletes. I'm happy you're here." He turned to Andrew. "And happy you've come back. How are you?"

"Better," Andrew said with doubt in his voice. Then he cleared his throat and spoke more forcefully. "*Working* on better, which I hear is half the battle."

"It's all of the battle, actually, so well done." Luca resisted the urge to offer a reassuring arm squeeze, wanting to give Andrew the space he needed to relax.

Other students filed in, and Luca was glad to see a variety of genders, ages, and body types. While he wouldn't have been disappointed to spend an hour with a dozen fit young footballers like Colin, the diversity in students told him he'd done well in widely advertising the class.

"Come through, make yourselves comfortable," he told them. "As you can see, there's all sorts of ways to sit." He had set up two rows of chairs behind three rows of floor cushions and another row of yoga mats. "Plenty of extra seats, so feel free to switch mid-session if your bum falls asleep or you fancy a change in scenery."

After everyone had found a place, Luca introduced himself and asked the class about their experiences with meditation. Out of the fifteen students, only two besides Andrew had any previous training, which explained the mood of uncertainty in the room.

Luca took a seat on his own cushion at the front of the class. "Now, you may think meditation's all about relaxation. And it can be relaxing, but not as much as, say, a warm bath or a stiff dram. The point of mindfulness is simply to notice yourself."

In the front row, Colin told Andrew, "Now I see why you're so good at this."

Andrew squeezed his boyfriend's knee and mouthed, "Sorry" at Luca.

Luca chuckled. "No bother. We keep things loose and informal here. So, before we talk about what we're *trying* to do, let me tell you about some cool sport-science-type side effects that happen without us even trying. Question: Who here's got stress in their lives?"

Everyone's hand went up, including Luca's. Some people raised both hands.

"It's part of being human," Luca said. "And it's not just in our heads. When we're under stress, our bodies release a hormone called cortisol. In olden times it helped us run away from saber-toothed tigers and such, and it still helps us react quickly in an urgent situation, including sport. But too much cortisol day in, day out can lead to fatigue, inflammation, reduced immune function, and even muscle breakdown."

Several of the students blanched, no doubt imagining the continuous corrosion within them.

"The good news is," he continued, "mindfulness meditation has been proven to significantly reduce cortisol levels, even in people who say they don't feel less stressed after meditating. Our blood doesn't lie."

Luca listed a few other health benefits, then leaned forward and lowered his voice as if sharing a secret. "So these are some pure lovely side effects, but let's face it—we're here because we want to win."

Colin grinned. "Fuckin' right," he said, provoking laughter from the other students. "But how can this meditation stuff make us perform better?"

"It doesn't *make* us perform better. It *lets* us perform better. After years of training, our bodies know what to do. But sometimes our minds get in the way." Luca tapped his temple, nodding at his students' murmurs of assent. "Overthinking in sport leads to tension, and tension leads to mistakes. But mindfulness helps us stay in our bodies—and stay in the moment—instead of drifting off into thoughts of the past or future."

Stop talking, he told himself. *You've got them, now just start.* Luca was always nervous at the beginning of a new class, worried he'd come off a bit bonkers in his passion for meditation and living a mindful life. But ideally his opening lecture would give them good reason not to quit in the middle of class.

He began with a simple breathing exercise, having them inhale from the abdomen instead of the chest—already a familiar practice to most athletes. When he asked his students to close their eyes, he kept his own open but unfocused, not examining anyone in particular, just getting a general sense of their postures. Over the next minute, he saw shoulders drop into peaceful resting positions, and all fidgeting came to a halt. Even Colin ceased his restless foot waggling.

Just as Luca was about to end the exercise, the studio door

eased open a few inches. A familiar face appeared, contorted with regret.

Luca smiled, because he couldn't help it, then beckoned Oliver inside. As the contrite-looking Canadian entered, the door gave a loud creak. He froze as half of the students turned to him.

"Now," Luca said softly, "if we've not already done, we'll just gently open our eyes."

His students sighed as they blinked and stretched. Oliver quietly slipped into the chair nearest the door, draping his blue quilted coat over the back.

"In case you're wondering," Luca said, "I asked Oliver to come a few minutes late to test your levels of relaxation. As we release stress, see, we become less vigilant and less prone to distraction."

Andrew arched a skeptical brow at Luca. Oliver just looked at the floor, his face still flushed but with a hint of a smile teasing the corner of his mouth.

"For our next bit of fun," Luca said, "we'll do what's probably the most rewarding and important exercise for an athlete: the body scan."

He began the session by having them focus on their breath, then led them to mentally scan themselves from head to toe, taking an inventory of how each body part felt. This time he kept his eyes closed, sweeping his awareness down over his own body. He noticed that his pulse had sped up since Oliver's arrival.

"It's tempting to start thinking about these sensations, especially if they surprise you." Luca was coaching himself as much as his students. "But there's no need to analyze or judge them, and least of all to change them. Simply acknowledge each feeling and move on."

When he finished his own scan—his feet were a bit cold, he

noticed—Luca opened his eyes, which naturally landed on Oliver.

Don't stare at him. It's creepy. Besides, a passing glance was enough to see Oliver was struggling, his eyes squeezed shut and his face scrunched up with the effort to focus.

"If it's too much," Luca said, "just pause your scan and come back to the breath for a wee while. The breath is always there, waiting for your attention, like a faithful puppy dog."

Most of the students smiled, but Oliver just squinted harder. Luca had the worst urge to give him a scalp and face massage, to smooth the deep crevices in that forehead and bring peace to those spectacular cheekbones.

He closed his eyes, semi-regretting inviting Oliver to join this class. How dare Luca teach the body-scan exercise while his own mind was scanning one of those bodies?

After another minute, he told his students to let their minds wander if they wanted. Then he brought them briefly back to their breath before saying, "And now, each in our own time as we're ready, let's open our—"

Luca nearly gasped when he saw Oliver's empty chair.

"Erm…open our eyes," he managed to finish.

Luca scanned the room, hoping Oliver had moved to a cushion or a mat. But there was no sign of him or his coat. He had gone, silently, as if he'd never been there at all.

5

Hammer

HAMMER: *An entirely virtual item of power. The team with the hammer—aka, the "hammer team"—gets to throw last in the end and therefore has an advantage. If the hammer team scores, the hammer passes to their opponents; if the hammer team fails to score, they keep the hammer. It's a fairness thing.*

THURSDAY MORNING, the sky was again the color of granite when Oliver arrived at the Shawlands Ice Rink parking lot for the journey to Ayrshire. Jack had warned him the weather in Scotland was "pure shite," but at least it was warmer than home. It was a joy not to wade through shin-deep snow every time he stepped out the front door.

The Boyd skip was chatting with Heather, who'd brought a cameraman with her today. Spying Oliver, Jack beckoned him over.

Oliver held back a sigh of irritation as he approached them. He didn't mind talking to Heather, but he was beginning to have his fill of Jack. The skip had taken the week off work to prepare for the bonspiel, which meant hours-long one-on-one meetings and practices. Oliver admired Jack's dedication, but there was such a thing as overpreparing for a competition.

"Here's the big man himself." Jack clapped Oliver's shoulder and beamed at the camera. "Our savior, come all the way across the Atlantic."

"Aww, thanks," Oliver said, "but you don't need saving, just some fine-tuning." *And a Valium.*

They made small talk for a few minutes with the camera off. Then Heather said, "I've been doing a bit of research. Apparently your compatriots like to claim that whilst Scotland may have invented curling, Canada has perfected it."

"Sorry," Oliver said, "that's not very diplomatic."

"But is it true?" she asked, then nodded to her partner to turn on his camera for the answer. "Can you comment on the relative quality of play here compared to Canada?

Do I have a choice? "For sure." Oliver checked the front of his jacket to confirm he hadn't dropped bits of Madeline's croissants upon himself in the taxi. "The competitive spirit here is just as fierce. And while it's true that Canada wins most of the international gold medals, Scotland is right up there with us. On any given day, your best can beat our best."

He wondered if he should have used *your* and *our* that way. Oliver was a loyal Canadian, but he had a duty to his team. If Boyd ever had the honor of representing Scotland or Great Britain against a Team Canada, which side would Oliver choose?

He derailed that train of thought immediately. To play in the world championship, Boyd had to win Nationals, and to get to Nationals, they had to win the Glasgow Open, or at least finish better than Team Riley.

As Jack answered Heather's next question, Oliver saw Luca standing alone near the club entrance, his back to the brisk wind that ruffled his dark hair. He seemed to be frowning down at his phone.

"Coach?" Jack nudged his arm.

Oliver blinked. "Sorry, what?"

Heather laughed. "Forgive me," she said. "It's too early for such deep questions. Have a think on it, and I'll find you later."

"Great!" he said, hoping to find out what the question was before she asked it again.

As Jack took Heather and her cameraman to interview the rest of Team Boyd, Oliver went over to Luca, who looked up with a distracted smile.

"Sorry, am I interrupting?"

"Nah." Luca stuffed his phone into the pocket of his steel-gray tweed coat. "Just a text from my mum saying she can't come to the bonspiel. She lives in Jersey now—the island, not the shore. Five hundred miles is a long trip, and her job is... och, it's some boring finance thing, but very demanding."

Mentally converting miles to kilometers, Oliver realized it was roughly the same distance between Halifax and Montreal, a ninety-minute flight his parents would happily take for a major tournament (when they could afford it, which wasn't often). It was a stark reminder of how massive his own country was compared to this one.

"That's too bad. And I guess your dad's not coming." Gillian had told Oliver that their father lived in Boston with his new wife.

"No, but he'll be watching the webcast," Luca said. "So how are you?"

"I'm sorry, that's how. For leaving your class early the other night, especially after showing up late. By the way, it was nice of you to cover for me by saying I was an intentional distraction."

"I was just returning the favor." Luca leaned in and lowered his voice. "I don't think my students bought it, any more than the kids at Willow's party believed you were sending me on a special mission away from the balloons. But people enjoy playing along with acts of kindness. It makes them feel warm in their tummies."

Oliver took a sip of coffee to hide his smile.

"Obviously it's better not to be tardy to a meditation class," Luca said, "but newcomers to Glasgow have an excuse. I imagine where you're from, the buses run on time."

"Not really. But I like when buses are late, because then I get to feel early."

"So what made you scarper?" Luca shook his head. "Not to imply you were running away. I meant, what made you decide the class wasn't for you?"

"I really want to learn meditation. I *need* to." Oliver fidgeted with his jacket zipper. "But in that class, there were just so many people. I couldn't focus, and the harder I tried, the worse it got." He remembered how his thoughts had buzzed around his brain like hornets trapped in a jar.

"Focus isn't about 'trying,'" Luca said. "You can't force it. If a group class doesn't work for you, I can recommend some good apps for meditating on your own."

"I've tried a few, but then it's the opposite problem. When I'm by myself, there's nothing to keep me on track. After the first ten seconds, I'm lost in a spiral of thoughts without realizing it. I don't even hear the voice in my ear until it says we're done."

He noticed Luca was gazing up at him with what seemed like a mixture of amusement and...could it be awe? Oliver wasn't always the best at reading faces.

"Why are you looking at me like that?" Oliver touched the corner of his mouth. "Do I have crumbs?"

"No, you're fine. I just love your arse."

Oliver's jaw dropped. "Uh…" He glanced down and back, feeling his cheeks flush. It seemed rude not to reply in kind. "Yours isn't bad either…I guess?"

Luca squinted at him. "My what?" His eyes widened suddenly. "No, I said your *R*s. The way you pronounce the letter *R*."

"Oh jeez. Right. Sorry." Oliver rubbed his face, which was heating more each second. "I don't really think about it. It's just how I talk."

"It's nice."

"To me it sounds ugly compared to how you say *R* here in Scotland. You know…" He sipped his coffee and looked away. "With your tongues." *Shit, we're flirting. This can't happen.*

"Pfft. I hear those *R*s all the time." Pulling a set of keys from his pocket, Luca started to turn toward the Team Riley minivan, then stopped. "Did you think I was complimenting your arse?"

Oliver took a step back. "Um, well, I wasn't sure—"

"Because that would be highly inappropriate." Luca smirked. "After all, you did say, 'No as in never.'"

Then he spun on his heel and walked away, twirling the key ring around his finger.

Oliver forced his eyes away from Luca's retreating figure, which moved as gracefully across a parking lot as it did on the ice. Despite their chemistry, the two of them were a terrible idea—and not just because of the obvious conflict of interest.

According to his contract, Oliver's coaching gig would last only as long as Team Boyd's hopes of reaching Nationals. A tournament loss this weekend would put him on the first plane back to Canada, branded with yet another epic failure. Which meant getting involved with Luca could make Oliver blow his big chance at redemption *and* leave a perfectly nice guy in the lurch.

In the not-too-distant past, Oliver wouldn't have hesitated. He would have careened down the path of chaos, fueled by instinct and hormones, following the scent of his latest whim. Consequences, schmonsequences.

But he wasn't that person anymore, not here in Scotland. Oliver had come to the Old World to make a new start, and he'd let no one—especially himself—take that away.

As Luca walked toward the MPV without looking back, he reviewed the last minute of conversation with chagrin. Oliver had been trying to open up about his difficulties, and instead of helping, Luca had simply mooned over his accent. He wasn't used to wanting someone enough to make a fool of himself over them, but that was no excuse for being an insensitive wee shit.

Those *R*s, though…like the letter was being bitten off and chewed. It made him think of Oliver's perfect teeth and how they might feel on the back of his neck. Based on what Oliver had said about Luca's tongue, maybe the *R*-induced fascination was mutual.

"Stop it," he told himself as he climbed into the driver's seat of the multi-purpose vehicle. A fleeting bit of flirtatious banter didn't mean Oliver had changed his mind about the two of them. After all, he was *Team Boyd's coach*. They'd be like the Romeo and Juliet of curling.

The thought amused Luca, as he imagined this weekend's bonspiel culminating in a broom fight to the death between Jack and David. On second thought, maybe Ian and Ross would better fit the Tybalt and Mercutio roles. Garen would definitely be Benvolio.

The passenger door opened, and David jumped in beside him. "Fuck's sake, put on the heating."

"Good morning to you, too." Luca turned on the engine, then fumbled with the climate controls. "Thought you were bringing coffee."

"I delegated to Ross. Seniority and all."

"You're the lead and he's the second. Technically he's got seniority."

"Aye, but I know how much you hate hierarchies." David pointed to his wing mirror. "That's him now."

The rear door slid open to Ross and Garen, the former carrying a quartet of large cups in a cardboard tray and the latter singing the theme to *Convoy*—one of many habits that made Luca dread road trips with his flatmate.

"Garen, gonnae stop that song or I'll choke you," David said. "I don't care if the team's got no alternates. We can play with three men."

Garen just sang louder.

Ross leaned forward between the seats to hand Luca his coffee. "One Americano for the skipper—my shout, of course. Dave, your massive triple mocha macchiato is five quid."

"Put it on my tab."

"I'll put it all over your lap if you don't gie's a fiver."

"Lads, lads." Luca took a sip of coffee. "Christ, that's good." He remembered the writing on the sleeve of Oliver's cup. "Team Boyd's coach drinks decaf in the morning, like some sort of depraved supervillain."

"Maybe that's why he was chucked out of Canada." David snickered as he counted out five pounds in small change for Ross. "He broke the Tim Hortons Act of 1938, which famously forbade antemeridian consumption of non-caffeinated beverages."

"It's *ante meridiem*," Luca muttered into his coffee.

"Actually…" Ross took his money and sat back. "What David said, it's not far from the truth."

Luca froze mid-sip. "Hmm?"

"You know." Ross hesitated. "Oliver's doping scandal?"

Garen stopped singing, then started again, much more softly.

"Doping scandal?" David spun in his seat. "What sort of doping?"

"Amphetamines," Ross said. "That's what it says on the internet. In more than one place, too. I checked."

Luca struggled to swallow his mouthful of coffee. "I don't believe it. He doesn't at all seem like-like…"

"A speed freak?" David offered.

Garen stopped singing. "His teeth are too nice." He started a new tune, the theme to *Orange is the New Black*, slapping his knees to accompany himself on drums.

"Amphetamines aren't the same as meth," Ross said. "They're PEDs—performance-enhancing drugs. Like steroids."

Luca shook his head. "There must be some explanation."

"Besides the obvious?" David asked. "Curling in Canada's not wee like it is here. There it's massive, on TV all the time. Stands to reason a guy would do what he can to get an edge."

"It's *curling*," Luca said. "We're not meant to get an edge. It's better to lose than to win unfairly. And why would a curler take speed? If anything, you'd want something to calm you down." He'd heard of golfers using beta blockers to lower their heart rates for better putting.

"Extra energy for grueling bonspiels, maybe?" David gasped. "What if he smuggled in some Canadian uppers for his curlers to use? We should demand Team Boyd all piss in a cup."

"Separate cups, though," Garen said, mid-verse.

Luca was ready to skelp his flatmate in the head. "That's ridiculous."

"Is it?" Ross asked. "Maybe we could phone in an anonymous tip to the tournament. If nothing else, it'll put Boyd out of sorts."

"You've all lost the plot." Luca jammed his coffee into the cup holder and put the MPV into reverse. "We'll go to this tournament and curl the best we can, and we'll forget about Team Boyd until it's time to meet them on the ice."

"Okay," Ross said. "Except we're on a boat with them to Ailsa Craig in an hour."

6

No Handle

NO HANDLE OR NO HAND: *When a curler forgets to rotate the stone as it's released, resulting in an unpredictable and often entertaining trajectory.*

"FOG'S GONNAE LIFT," the captain said as he checked the boat's moorings. "Guaranteed."

Oliver nodded at the grizzled sailor, then gave a contented sigh as he surveyed his surroundings—what he could see of them, anyway. The small fishing vessel rocked gently in the center of an upside-down bowl of white. On the other side of the dock, another fisherman had just brought in a literal boatload of jam-packed lobster traps.

During his handful of curling-related visits to Scotland, Oliver hadn't seen much to remind him of Nova Scotia or give him a clue why his province had been named after this nation. But now, sitting on a patch of gray water amid a fog so thick he could almost spoon it into his mouth like ice cream, he felt at home.

Chattering voices came out of the mist in the direction of

the parking lot. Team Riley appeared on the dock, Luca leading the way. At the sight of Oliver, they all grew quiet— even Garen, who'd been humming some repetitive tune. Luca mumbled a greeting to Oliver as he passed, not meeting his eyes.

There was only one explanation for this sudden change in demeanor: Somewhere along the A77 between Glasgow and Girvan, Luca had learned the truth—or at least what passed for it on the internet.

Oliver's face burned with shame. The Atlantic Ocean wasn't big enough. Planet Earth wasn't big enough. His mistakes were a part of him now, and he couldn't shed them any more than he could shed his own bones.

In the past he would have slunk into a corner, kept his head down, and focused on the people who already accepted him. But Oliver couldn't stand to slink away from Luca and let him believe an incomplete truth. He had to explain.

The boat's seats were arranged in two back-to-back rows of six, half facing the port side and half facing starboard. When he saw Luca take the last one next to the stern, Oliver slipped into the one behind him. The seat backs were short, so when he sat up straight, his shoulder blades pressed against Luca's. The Riley skip tensed for a moment, then relaxed against him with a welcome warmth.

Luca wasn't fleeing. That was a hopeful sign.

Revving its engine, the fishing boat left the dock and headed out into the fog-draped harbor. The seaside town of Girvan rapidly receded behind a curtain of white.

Soon they were in open sea, though Oliver knew this only by the way the wind whipped through his hair. He could see nothing beyond the boat's creaking walls apart from a few frothy waves fading into gray oblivion.

Sitting to Oliver's left, Jack said, "Next stop: the Isle of

Avalon." This was met by nervous laughter as everyone scanned their surroundings for anything solid with which to orient themselves. Even Heather and her cameraman had fallen as still and silent as the mist.

When Oliver's ears began to ache from the chill, he pulled his gray-and-green tuque from his pocket and slipped it on his head. As he did, he looked back to see Luca doing the same, only his hat was black and made to appear like a rabbit's head, with white eyes and whiskers across his forehead and floppy white bunny ears serving as the dangling flaps.

Does he have to be so goddamn cute?

At full speed now, the boat's motor was loud enough to shroud conversation, so Oliver shifted his legs into the narrow walkway between his seat and the wall of the stern. Then he nudged Luca's shoulder. "I take it you heard."

Luca jumped. "Heard what?"

Oliver raised his eyebrows, and Luca seemed to deflate like a leaky balloon, his chin sagging and his shoulders folding in.

"Aye," Luca said. "But I don't believe it. Just now I was sitting here trying to think of a way to ask you what happened." He turned to face the stern, legs parallel to Oliver's. "So what happened?"

An extra-large wave came up, and Oliver braced himself both physically and mentally. "Nothing I'm about to tell you counts as an excuse. I've done more stupid things in twenty-nine years than most people do in a lifetime."

"I doubt that," Luca said, twisting one of his rabbit ears. "But go on."

"I wasn't taking amphetamines to perform better on the ice." He scratched his forehead, which was warming despite the clammy sea air. "I take them to perform better *off* the ice."

"'Take'? As in present tense?"

"I have ADHD. Attention Deficit Hyperactivity Disorder."

He hated spelling out the acronym, and even eight years after his diagnosis, it still felt like a confession. "Prescription stimulants help me focus. They help me remember things. Most of all, they regulate my moods."

"So they're like anti-depressants?"

"Not exactly, though they do stop my thoughts from spiraling into a pit of doom. By 'moods,' I mean they manage my irritability. I call them my 'anti-dickhead pills.'"

Luca laughed, then covered his mouth. "I'm so sorry. It's not funny."

"It is funny. I have to joke about it, or I'd hate myself all the time." *Instead of just most of the time,* Oliver would have added had he not had a good night's sleep, a high-protein breakfast, and a timely dose of Vyvanse.

"If you've got this condition and a prescription," Luca said, "then how'd you get suspended? Haven't they got waivers for athletes who need drugs for medical reasons?"

Oliver nodded. "They're called TUEs—Therapeutic Use Exemptions. But they expire and you have to reapply. After I was diagnosed, I got my four-year waiver, no problem."

As the boat rode another big wave, Luca grabbed the side of his seat. "And then?"

"When I tried to renew the TUE, my application was rejected. This was about five years ago, when the anti-doping agencies had started cracking down across the board on every substance. I think they wanted to see how many applicants they could weed out by making us jump through more hoops."

"What utter pish. You couldn't appeal it?"

"I could." Oliver's throat constricted. "But I didn't."

Luca's face held the neurotypical person's usual benign bewilderment. "Why not?"

"Because." Oliver stared at the boat's churning wake. "I just...didn't."

After a short pause, Luca said, "I don't get it."

"Of course you don't get it. You literally *can't* get it. Your brain developed like most people's. You can't possibly fathom how anyone could put off something so important day after day after day after day."

"I can fathom it. Everyone procrastinates. Usually it means there's some sort of block or fear about that task." Luca gave Oliver's shoulder a soft tap. "Maybe deep down you didn't want to curl anymore. Maybe it was taking over your life. Maybe this was your way of getting out without having to quit."

Oliver knew his meds were all that kept him from kicking the boat wall in frustration. He'd hoped Luca would magically understand. But like everyone else, he needed Oliver's help.

"Maybe that's why most people procrastinate. But for us, it's not so complex." Oliver took a deep breath, preparing to feel ridiculous. "The appeals process had so many steps. Every one of them was tedious or frustrating or both. I'd get up every day and tell myself, 'Just start the process. Just start.' But I couldn't see the start. All I could see was the entire journey." Oliver shifted his feet apart, bracing them on the rolling deck. "I know this sounds insane, but the thought of filling out that paperwork and making those phone calls felt like a spike through my skull. Just imagining it made me want to take a nap, or have a drink, or play a video game. Anything to dull the dread." Oliver gave a bitter laugh. "People asked me, 'Didn't you think about your future?' as if the future was something I could clearly picture. As if the future was something that mattered."

He stopped when he heard Luca sniffle.

"Sorry, I'm not crying, my nose is just runny from the chilly air." Luca rummaged through his coat pockets and took out a ragged tissue. "Curlers should be immune to the cold, but for some reason I can only handle it indoors." He dabbed at his nose. "So here's my silly question. If you were already taking these meds which fix your ADHD, why didn't they help you fill in that paperwork?"

"That's actually the opposite of a silly question."

Luca beamed. "Is it? Well done, me."

Oliver felt himself start to relax. Luca's curiosity might mean he was open to understanding. At least he hadn't called Oliver *lazy* or *stupid*.

Before answering, Oliver checked to see whether anyone was listening. The wind was blowing their voices away from the other passengers, who were either having their own conversations or looking too seasick to care.

He turned back to Luca. "The thing is, stimulants don't fix ADHD any more than insulin fixes diabetes. They just manage it so we can live better lives. I can't remember the last time I flew into a rage or wasted an entire day surfing the internet. But meds haven't cured my inability to see the distant future as a real thing."

"Hm." Luca rubbed his dark stubble, which was becoming a pretty decent beard, Oliver had noticed. "So what you're saying is, the way your brain is built keeps you from seeing the consequences of your actions?"

"Sometimes, yeah. People call it time-blindness, but it's more time-nearsightedness."

"That makes sense, though here we say 'shortsighted' to mean myopic." Luca winced. "Sorry. I edit medical textbooks for a living, so I can be both pedantic and sesquipedalian."

Oliver wondered whether that last word was real. Maybe Luca's accent had obscured it. "Anyway," he said, "that's why I tend to be late, and why I put off doing things."

"So if your appeal had been due, say, the day after you got the rejection, you would've done it?"

"Absolutely." Oliver's hope began to grow. Maybe Luca would really get it. "I can move mountains on a tight deadline or in a crisis—all that adrenaline helps me focus. But the agency gave me ninety days, which was like an eternity. It might as well have been stamped 'Due Never.'"

"That makes sense, because tight deadlines are close to you, so you can still see them. Like some people are so short-sighted, they can only read the giant *E* on the eye chart, but nothing below it." Luca's eyes popped wide. "So your meds are like contact lenses for your brain?"

"Yes! Exactly!" Oliver wanted to hug him. "I still can't see *all* of the chart. The teeny letters at the bottom will always be fuzzy. But now I can read most of it, and that feeling is…" He rubbed the back of his neck as he searched for the word. "Miraculous."

"Wow." Luca regarded him for a long moment. "I'm happy for you."

"Thanks." Oliver couldn't tear his eyes away from this man. He knew that by now the others were probably all watching, wondering why his and Luca's heads were bent so close together and what they could be discussing to make their faces so earnest. It seemed that this connection they'd formed, the one that felt like it could turn the very wind around, must have been obvious to even a casual onlooker.

"There it is!" someone cried out behind them.

Oliver turned to see a great dark mass appear out of the fog. A gust of wind swirled the mist upward around the giant rock, unveiling first gray stone, then green grass, and finally white snow, as if the island were being conjured by elemental forces. "Is that…"

"Aye." Luca's voice filled with awe. "It's Ailsa Craig."

———

"BE BACK IN AN HOUR, or I'll leave you here!" the captain called out as Luca stepped onto the island's rickety dock. "Low tide'll come in and strand the boat at the jetty, and you're not paying me enough to stay here all day."

"Right, then." Jack held up his wrist. "Watches synchronized, everyone. It's half-twelve now. The trail to the quarry is that way." He pointed north toward the rocky cliffs, then south along the beach. "And the lighthouse is over there. There's probably not time to see both, so go where you like, but let's meet back here no later than twenty past one, for the sake of this good man's sanity." He gestured to the boat captain, who saluted him with his cigarette.

As Heather and her cameraman followed Jack toward the trail, Oliver asked, "What are all those stones there?" He pointed down the shoreline to a large pile of jagged rocks. "Is that the curling granite the quarry's left for pickup?"

Jack shaded his eyes as he peered that way. "Maybe. Why?"

"If it is, then we don't have to choose between seeing the rocks and seeing the lighthouse."

Jack frowned. "It could just be pieces of concrete or something."

"I'll take my chances." Oliver put his hands in his pockets and started trudging down the shore without looking back.

Luca shrugged at his teammates, then trotted after him. He was chockablock with questions for Oliver—who was being pure patient with his ignorance and curiosity—but didn't know where to start.

Oliver offered a vague smile when he caught up, but said nothing. It occurred to Luca a minute too late that Oliver might have come this way for some solitude. Or maybe like

Luca, he wanted to experience Ailsa Craig without a film crew hovering over his shoulder.

Apart from the wind and waves, the island was dead silent. When Luca had visited in summertime, the place had been roiling with thousands of nesting seabirds. Now the steep, pale-green, snow-dusted hill above them seemed devoid of life, though he knew the island was home to wee rabbits and snakes, which obviously couldn't fly south for the winter.

"This is a plug," he blurted.

Oliver squinted at him. "A what?"

"A volcanic plug. The island. It's when magma clogs up a volcano's vent. Sometimes it can cause a massive explosion, like *pshhooo!*" He soared his hands upward together, then apart, knowing he sounded an absolute dunderhead. "But other times the volcano dies and then the glaciers come and smash away everything but the vent."

"Neat."

Luca looked back to see his teammates about a hundred feet behind them, where they'd stopped to throw stones into the sea. He felt a bit bad that apart from Oliver, the two teams had split up entirely. This trip was meant to bring the eight of them together before the weekend's big curling clash.

The beach grew rockier, so he turned forward again to keep his footing, scouring his mind for more fun facts. "Did you know 'Ailsa Craig' is Gaelic for 'fairy rock'?"

"Interesting."

"Yes. Very." Luca chewed his lower lip as they kept walking in silence. By now he was pretty sure Oliver wanted to be alone.

Oh well, too late for that. "This island is owned by a duke," Luca said. "It's for sale, actually, a bargain at three million pounds."

Finally Oliver chuckled. "I'll keep that in mind. It'd be cool to put a curling rink here."

"Ailsa Craig is a bird sanctuary, so you'd have to leave it be." Luca kicked a small rock ahead of them.

"Sanctuary sounds perfect." Oliver kicked the same rock, angling it back into Luca's path.

"Doesn't it just?" Luca sped up toward the rock, planning a perfectly bent free kick. But his instep scuffed the stone, which bounced against the toes of his planted foot. "Ow!"

"You okay?"

"Aye." He sat on the cold white sand to rub his toes. "This is why I started curling. I'm crap at football."

"Don't take this the wrong way," Oliver said as he crouched down beside him, "but I'm glad football failed you."

Luca felt it again, that buzzing up and down his spine, the one that had smoothed into an addictive hum whilst they'd spoken on the boat. He wanted to know this man, inside and out.

Then Oliver cleared his throat and stood up. "You're a gift to our sport, I mean." He looked down the beach. "Not much farther."

Luca got to his feet and brushed the sand off his arse. Then he finally thought of easy small talk. "So what do you do when you're not clowning or coaching? Did you leave a day job back in Canada?"

"Temporarily. I'm a freelance artist. Mostly sports-related." He pulled out his wallet and handed Luca a business card:

OD Graphic Arts: High-Octane Digital Design

"'OD'?" Luca asked. "Ah, your initials. I thought maybe it stood for 'overdose,'" he added with a nervous laugh.

"That, too." Oliver smirked. "Figured I might as well have some fun with my reputation as a drug fiend."

"Heh." Luca relaxed a little. If Oliver could joke about it, maybe it was okay to ask more questions. "Talking of which, I'm not clear on what happened after you missed the deadline for your appeal. Did that mean you weren't allowed to take your meds anymore?"

"I could take them on most days, but I was supposed to avoid them during competition. Which I tried doing, but the withdrawal made me edgy and gave me screaming headaches. Imagine being told you couldn't drink coffee during a tournament."

"Ooft." The very thought made Luca's head pound. "I'd be in absolute shambles. My hands would be shaking too hard to throw."

"Exactly. And for me that was just the *physical* part of it. Going back to that feeling of walking blindfolded through quicksand—the way I'd felt my whole life before the meds—was torture. Eventually I decided it was bullshit to have to choose between my mental health and the sport I loved. I couldn't choose, so I didn't."

"And you got caught."

"I got caught." Oliver hunched his shoulders as he walked. "I was suspended for two years from the entire sport. I couldn't compete or coach at any level. I couldn't do bonspiels, even for non-cash prizes. I couldn't even play in my rink's Sunday pizza league."

"What a farce!" Luca kicked another rock, sending it bouncing into the frothy waves to his left. "Those eejits robbed you and the world of curling, all because of some stupid paperwork."

"Rules are there to make things fair," Oliver said. "No one should get special treatment. If anything, being at the top of your game makes it worse. When a scandal happens, everyone wants to drag you off your pedestal, then burn the pedestal and piss on the ashes so you can never climb back on."

"True." Luca had seen it happen in every sport. He'd aimed his own harsh judgment at celebrity athletes who'd turned out to be as human as the rest of society. Those people had seemed as far away and untouchable as the stars in the sky.

"I can't blame the curling folks for feeling betrayed," Oliver said. "In any other sport, my mistake would've been forgiven —or at least conveniently forgotten in the name of winning. But curling's all about honor and sportsmanship. By breaking the rules, I tainted my character forever. I shamed the entire game."

"That's a bit dramatic," Luca said.

"Is it? Then why did they rescind my medals and points from that season—and my teammates', too? Why did they make me pay back all my prize money? If I did nothing wrong, why was I punished?"

Luca flinched. It wasn't enough they'd stolen Oliver's future, they'd had to erase his past as well? "It sounds like they wanted to make an example of you."

"It worked. You know, I can't believe you didn't hear about this. It felt like the whole curling world was talking about it forever."

"If it was five years ago, I would've been at university. I barely had time to curl, much less follow the gossip." Luca lifted a broken conch shell from the sand with his toe, which he used to toss it into the waves. "What about after the two years? Did they let you play again?"

"After my suspension, I got another Therapeutic Use Exemption. I could curl and take my meds at the same time, just like before."

"Fantastic."

"But I couldn't get back onto an elite team."

"Why ever not?"

"It wasn't really the curlers' choice. Their sponsors

wouldn't go for it." Oliver joined Luca's effort to kick every last shell into the Irish Sea. "Besides, everyone had already formed teams to qualify for the Sochi Olympic trials. There was no room for me." He snorted. "At least I could stop worrying about being a gay athlete in Putin's Russia."

Luca could hear the raw heartbreak in Oliver's voice. No doubt he, like Luca, had spent his life watching the Winter Games and picturing himself atop that podium. After winning two Canadian championships, Oliver would have had reason to believe that dream within reach.

"I tried to stay active in the game, though." Oliver's posture straightened a bit. "I finished my coaching and instructor certifications. I got serious about studying curling stats. I even joined the board of our local rink, which had totally stuck by me during the whole scandal. It's almost a cliché that curlers are the kindest, most supportive people in the world, but it's true."

"Good," Luca said, noting Oliver hadn't mentioned doing any actual curling himself. Surely he could've formed a new team and worked his way back toward the top level. Why would he let his dream die without an ounce of resistance?

They reached the stone pile, which did indeed consist of granite chunks slightly larger than their heads. Luca could still make out the tracks in the sand from the vehicle that had carried the rocks from the smaller southern quarry.

It was hard to savor the sight in front of him, though, as his mind was still pondering Oliver's situation. "Mate, this isn't just about the sport. It's a disability-rights issue. Someone should've fought for you to get accommodation or—"

"That couldn't happen."

"Why not?"

"Because I never went public with why I was taking the drugs. The only people who knew were my doctor, my family, a few friends at the club, and of course the anti-doping agency. I never gave a single interview." He tapped his toe against a hunk of granite. "I didn't fight for myself, so why should anyone fight for me?"

Now Luca understood why the internet thought Oliver a speed freak. "Were you—are you ashamed of your condition?"

"If I was, I wouldn't be rambling on about it to you. I didn't want to use my disability as an excuse."

"It's not an excuse, it's an explanation," Luca said. "People understand the difference."

"They don't, not with this. Lots of people still think ADHD isn't even a real thing. It was bad enough I'd disgraced my sport, my country, my province, and the LGBT athletic community. I couldn't do that to my fellow ADHDers. The stigma's bad enough without people like me proving the screwup stereotype."

This mystifying martyrdom made Luca want to hurl the rocks at his feet into the sea. "So is this your penance?" He flapped his hand at their barren surroundings. "Exiling yourself to a lesser curling nation?"

"It's not like that. I'm here because—" Oliver stopped and looked past him. "Here come your friends."

"Och, this is amazing!"

Luca turned at the sound of David's voice. Team Riley seemed to be having a race to cover the last hundred yards.

David reached the pile of granite first and began to circle it in such a reverential way, Luca half-expected him to start genuflecting. "Did you know these things break off from the cliffs in perfect-size pieces for curling stones?"

"You're talking pish," Ross declared as he arrived to stand beside Luca.

"It's true! I saw it on TV last year before the Olympics. BBC sent a crew out here to talk to the guy who owns the factory."

David tapped a light-colored fragment. "Blue hone. That's the stuff they use for the rocks' running surface."

Garen stood at one end of the heap, unusually quiet. "All right, mate?" Luca asked.

"It's just massive, being here." Garen crouched down to caress one of the chunks. "Those rocks we obsess over, we're seeing them in the raw in the place they were born. It's like going to Bethlehem or something."

"It does feel sacred," Oliver said.

Garen looked up at him. "Will you give us a prayer?"

"Oh jeez, no." Oliver took a step back. "I'm not really a praying person."

"But you're Canadian," Garen said. "That makes you like a high priest of curling."

"Come on, mate." David patted the coach's back. "Just try. We'll not judge you."

Oliver adjusted his knit cap, tucking a stray clump of brown hair under the front edge. "Okay, here goes." He leaned forward and placed his right hand on a rock. They all followed suit.

"So...hey God," Oliver began. "We stand here, um, humbly before you...I guess. We give thanks for the volcanos that made this granite, and for the glaciers that made this island. Sorry, I mean, the glaciers," he repeated, this time pronouncing the c like an s instead of a sh. "And for everything in the fifty million years since then. It's all pretty good. Um...also we ask that you grant us a safe trip back to Glasgow and keep us all healthy and reasonably sane this weekend." He paused, blinking rapidly. "In your name...good curling."

"Good curling," they all echoed

As they stood in silent reverence, Ross pulled a flask from inside his coat and passed it around. Then he and Garen and

David turned without a word and filed uphill toward the nearby lighthouse.

Oliver stood staring at the pile of stones, his face full of longing.

"Do you miss it?" Luca asked softly.

Oliver's lips flashed into a frown, then he made a noncommittal noise in the back of his throat.

"When was the last time you curled? Like, really curled, not just demonstrating techniques for your students or whatever."

"It's been a while." Oliver shoved his hands deeper into his coat pockets. "Enough about me, eh? You owe me a dark secret."

7

Vice

VICE OR VICE-SKIP: *The second in "command" after the skip. Usually throws third and is often the best all-round shooter. A vice does several important jobs which the skip can't be arsed to do, such as writing definitions to introduce book chapters once His Excellency has finished the glamorous bits.*

"Hmm." Luca leaned back and scanned the gunmetal-gray clouds, as though they held the answer. "Can't think of anything dark. If my secrets were beer, there'd be no stout on offer. I could maybe dredge up an IPA, or even a maibock if you catch me in the right mood."

Oliver wasn't about to let Luca change the subject. "Why'd you leave Team Boyd?"

"Because it stopped being fun. Och, that sounds such a shallow reason when I say it out loud." He turned and headed up the hill toward the lighthouse.

"It's the best reason." Oliver followed, ready to be the interrogator for once. "Why did it stop being fun?"

"I used to curl with David, Ross, and Garen at Glasgow

Uni, did you know that?" Luca's foot twisted a bit on the wet grass. "It was mostly for laughs, as I was still skipping my competitive junior league team as well. As soon as I turned twenty-two, Jack invited me to join his team as lead."

Oliver remembered his own leap from juniors to men's curling. "That's always a tough transition, being a skip in juniors, then suddenly being low man on the totem pole. You gotta learn to take orders again."

"I don't give orders," Luca said, "I build consensus. I see to it that the lads know what I've got planned and why. If they disagree, I listen."

This was the ideal approach for a curling team, but Oliver knew many skips—Jack included—who preferred not to be questioned. "Do they disagree much?"

"Nah." Luca smirked. "Mind, I am brilliant."

"And yet so humble."

"Truly. Anyway, I improved a lot on Team Boyd, got made vice-skip, and won far more games than I'd ever done before. That made it harder to leave, and with Jack being my brother-in-law...och, I still feel a bit shit about it."

"Where I'm from, it's pretty common for curlers to switch teams." Oliver leaned forward into the steep, rocky slope, spreading his arms for balance. "Breakups are hard, but sometimes it's the only way to make it big if you're podium material."

"Podium material," Luca said. "That's so far from my reality. The thought of going to Worlds or the Olympics, heh— might as well imagine a trip to Mars. But Jack totally believes he can get there. Maybe he can do, with your help."

"I hope so."

They reached the stone wall surrounding the abandoned lighthouse, only to discover there was no opening on the seaward side.

"There's a gate to get in, but I'm not sure where." Luca reached up to place his hands atop the wall. "The lads must have climbed over."

"Need a boost?" Oliver knelt down and formed a stirrup with his hands.

"Aww, such the gentleman." Luca stepped onto the makeshift support, then let out a whoop as Oliver lifted him up to straddle the wall. "Oh good, it's not as far down as it is up." He slung his other leg over and landed with a slight grunt.

Hoping he wasn't about to look like an idiot, Oliver took a running leap at the wall and pulled himself up. The top edge was made of vertically placed stones, the ends of which had been weathered down to points that were merely bruising rather than gut-piercing.

He landed on his feet on the other side, stumbling only a little. Luca was surveying the looming lighthouse tower and its attached building, which were surrounded by a gray brick wall even higher than the one they'd just climbed. Then he pointed to an opening about a hundred meters away.

As they weaved between the rocks scattered over the patchy grass, Oliver's curiosity nagged him to ask the big question:

"Do you ever regret leaving Team Boyd? Would you come back if you had the chance?"

Luca sighed. "I regret the wee rift I caused in the family. But I wouldn't trade my lads for anything, even a gold medal. Besides, Team Boyd wasn't right for me. Jack and I are... dissimilar." He shook his head hard, making his rabbit ears swing back and forth. "I won't run him down. He's a good guy and a great skip."

"He is."

"But Jack wanted us all to be as intense as he is. I *am*

intense, but in here." He poked his own chest. "He wanted me to show my passion for the game by cursing and sulking when things go wrong and leaping about when things go right. So that last season I was emoting all over the place, jumping up and down, punching the air like a total fucking loon, just to make my skipper happy. That's when I started missing shots."

Oliver began to step from one rock fragment to the next, seeing if he could avoid touching the grass. "Probably because you weren't yourself on the ice anymore. It's draining to pretend to be someone you're not."

"Exactly. I play better when I'm loose, like, having a laugh with the other curlers and keeping them happy." Luca joined Oliver's don't-touch-the-ground game. "Also, when I'm pure focused, my face goes blank, so Jack thought I was bored. But I can't help I've got Resting Eejit Face."

"You don't look bored or idiotic. You look peaceful."

Luca stopped, balancing on one foot atop a wobbly stone. "You watch me? When I'm just standing about doing nothing?"

Busted. Oliver looked away, out over the sea. "Wow, it's really clearing up. You can see the mainland coast now."

Luca made no comment, but looked pleased to know Oliver had been checking him out.

They entered the lighthouse's courtyard to find the rest of Team Riley seated in a semicircle on the sandy floor.

"Fancy a cuppa?" Garen raised a white ceramic teacup and saucer, one of five settings arranged in front of them. "We found these in a cupboard inside." He gestured to one of the abandoned lighthouse's open doors. "Totally clean apart from some dust, and anyway, the whisky'll sterilize them."

Oliver sat beside Luca and picked up his cup, which held what looked like two drams. "I feel like Alice at the Mad Tea Party."

"Luca's definitely the Hatter," Garen said, "cos of that fucking mental cap."

Luca just smiled and preened the white bunny whiskers on his forehead.

"But it's a rabbit hat," David said, "so he should be the March Hare."

"Don't be so literal." Garen gestured with his chipped teacup. "You're the March Hare, cos you're the hare-iest. Ross is definitely the Dormouse."

Ross pouted. "Why am I the Dormouse?"

"Then who are you, Garen?" David asked. "We've no more tea party characters."

Garen bowed his head in mock humility. "I am Time, of course—the all-powerful off-page deity who dictates that it always be six o'clock so the tea party never ends."

Satisfied with the casting, they commenced drinking, and when Ross's whisky was gone, David pulled out his flask of bourbon, which they also made short work of.

Sheltered from the wind here in the courtyard, surrounded by his new friends, Oliver felt more content than he had in years. He wished Garen really were a time god who could make this "tea" party last forever.

Oliver wondered whether he was being unfaithful to his own curlers by hanging out with their rivals. After spending nearly every moment with Team Boyd this week, when he'd found the chance to strike out on his own, he'd taken it without thinking twice. Story of his life.

On the other hand, Jack and his teammates hadn't followed him down the shoreline. Luca had.

Luca, whose knee now brushed his from time to time as they leaned forward and back in conversation with the others. The slight touch sent a warm shiver up Oliver's thigh, settling in the base of his spine. The feeling made him simultaneously want to spread his naked body atop Luca's but also long to just...sit with him, listen to his lilting voice, and watch the never-ending animation of his face.

Far too soon, the timer app on Oliver's phone chirped its invasive melody. He silenced it in his pocket. "We need to head back to the dock."

Luca looked at his watch. "Oh my God, you're right." He nudged Oliver. "Thought you were always late."

"I would be, without electronic help."

They took their cups and saucers back to the cupboard inside the lighthouse kitchen, which was centered around a crumbling wood stove topped by a rusty iron skillet. Garen left a bit of bourbon in a saucer—"for the faeries"—outside the main door.

Oliver walked beside Luca down the long tram track toward the dock, taking care not to trip over any rails in his semi-inebriated state. "You're wrong, by the way."

"I'm wrong about a lot of things," Luca said, "but what specifically this time?"

"There's nothing lesser about Scotland—as a curling nation or anything else. This weird sport we play, it all started in your country five hundred years ago." He pointed to the peak of Ailsa Craig, which was once again shrouded in mist. "And it will always start here, with that granite."

"Does this mean that coming to Glasgow isn't your penance?" Luca punctuated the question with a sly wink, as if he already knew the answer—which would have been ironic, given that Oliver didn't know it himself. "Regardless..."

Oliver tensed, wondering what dramatic statement would follow this pause. "Yeah?"

"You were pretty clear about the two of us not, you know, having anything or doing anything. And I'm totally cool with that."

"Okay." Oliver was no longer sure *he* was cool with it, but didn't trust his judgment at the moment.

"Still, I'd a nice time palling about with you today, and I'd like to do it again. As mates, of course. Or whatever's appropriate."

"Me too." Oliver coughed. "'Mates' sounds good."

"Specifically, I was thinking about what you said this morning, how meditating in a big class didn't work for you but meditating alone was also a bit crap. So maybe I could give you a private lesson?" He rolled his eyes. "Och, that sounds such a chat-up line. I mean, I could book a small room at the well-being center. Quiet, but practically public."

Oliver could think of nothing in the world he'd rather do—well, almost nothing. "Tomorrow morning? Maybe ten o'clock or so?"

Luca smiled. "Ideal, mate."

Jack met them at the dock, checking his watch in an obvious way.

"We're bang on time," Luca said before Jack could speak, "thanks to your exceptionally responsible coach."

As Team Riley moved on to board the boat, Oliver stopped next to his skip. "How was the quarry?"

"Very cool, though there were spots of ice on the trail." Jack grimaced. "We almost lost Kevin, the camera guy."

"'Lost' like you couldn't find him?"

"No, 'lost' like—" Using both hands, Jack mimed a body falling off a ledge.

"Holy shit. Would've been interesting footage, though."

Jack laughed. "Less than a week in Glasgow and already making death jokes." He glanced past Oliver toward the lighthouse. "Did you gather any useful intelligence?"

"About the island?"

"About Team Riley. Like their strategy for the weekend and all."

"We didn't really talk curling."

Jack gave him a flat look. "Seriously? What did you talk about?"

Oliver dredged his memory, feeling suddenly naive. Perhaps curling was more predatory here than it was back home. "Let's see, we talked about...uh, hats...and which Avenger gets more screen time than they deserve...and whether eating cows is worse than eating fish. Morally, that is. See, Luca's got this friend Andrew, who—"

"Right. Forget it." Jack started to turn away, then changed his mind. "If you've ever another chance to get inside their heads—especially their skip's—please take advantage of it."

"You want me to spy on them?"

"Not—no. No, that would be wrong. Just try and get some insights if you can. Any small clue could make the difference. You want to win, right?"

"Of course. We win this tournament, we win the Challenger Tour. We win the tour, we go to Nationals."

"And you get to keep your job." Jack took half a step back, frowning. "Sorry, that sounded harsh. I just—I'd really like you to stay on, but we need that prize money to keep paying you."

"I know." Oliver had hoped the progress they'd made so far would convince Jack to give him a long-term contract regardless of this weekend's results. But financial realities didn't bend under the weight of mere hope.

Did Luca know about the temporary nature of Oliver's tenure? Probably not, given the way he'd just talked about the two of them hanging out, like it could be a regular thing going forward. Oliver could ask Jack whether Luca knew, but the question might spark suspicion. And since there wasn't technically anything between him and Luca, it shouldn't matter, right?

The whole situation was starting to feel like a fraying tightrope. Were he a wiser man, Oliver knew, he wouldn't think of walking it at all.

———

"BAGSIES ON FIRST SHOWER," Luca said as he pushed past Garen into their flat. They'd less than an hour before the Glasgow Open's big welcome dinner, and the trip to Ailsa Craig had left him feeling pure bedraggled.

"Don't forget to not shave," Garen said.

Luca hurried into the bathroom, where he swept Garen's scattered hair products off the sink into the plastic storage container he'd bought for the purpose. Garen never used the bin himself, but it lowered Luca's blood pressure to have a handy repository for his flatmate's crap.

Tomorrow and Saturday nights, Garen would stay with his boyfriend, Steven, who lived close to the rink and who would theoretically be cheering on Team Riley (though he'd missed last month's bonspiel in Aberdeen, citing budgetary constraints). Since Ross and David both had plans with their girlfriends, Luca might be able to recover from the first day's games with some blissful privacy.

Unless...

No, he couldn't let himself hope Oliver might keep him company. Even thinking about his rival's coach that way was a clear violation of the spirit of curling.

But maybe next week, after the Challenger Tour was over?

Luca found the towel rail empty, as was the shelf above the toilet. "Garen, please tell me you brought the washing up from the launderette. Mrs. Watson from 103 said the underwear bandit struck again this week." When Garen didn't answer, Luca stalked into the living room. "Did you hear—" He stopped when he found his flatmate staring at his phone, face twisted in what looked like disbelief. "All right, mate?"

"No, I—" Garen punched his fingertip against the screen and turned away, raising the phone to his ear. "Straight to voice mail," he muttered a moment later. "Fucking coward."

Luca stood frozen, wondering whether he should retreat to the bathroom and pretend not to witness the approaching cyclone.

"Are you fucking kidding me, Steven?" Garen shouted into the phone. "A fucking breakup text? You couldn't say it to my face? What are you afraid of?"

Luca edged backward, trying to be quiet, but then tripped on the kit bag Garen had left in the middle of the floor. He yelped, catching the bathroom doorpost just in time to stop himself falling on his arse and potentially ending Team Riley's tournament before it began.

Garen gaped at Luca's near-tumble. "You know what, Steven, ya worthless wankstain? I nearly just accidentally killed Luca, so I'm not wasting any more breath or-or-or thoughts on you. So fuck off forever!" He lowered the phone. "Sorry, you okay?" he asked Luca.

"I'm fine. Are *you* okay?"

"No! Steven left me, less than twenty-four hours before a tournament." He held up a hand. "Don't you dare say it should be *fewer* than twenty-four hours.'"

"It shouldn't be. Time, money, distance, and weight are— never mind. Steven's an eejit."

"Is he? Cos it sure feels like I'm the eejit this time. Or maybe we both are. Maybe that's why it lasted so long." He slouched to the sofa and flung himself down on his back. The spring made a spine-grating creak. "I miss him already."

Luca sat on the arm of the adjacent comfy chair. "You've not been happy since before Christmas. You told me on Hogmanay you might break up before the midnight fireworks."

"I knew Steven didn't love me anymore, but I thought we were still in the let's-pretend-for-one-or-two-more-weekends phase. I figured he'd leave me right before Valentine's Day so he wouldn't have to buy me anything."

Luca sort of admired Garen's awareness of his relationships' transactional nature. Rather than rationalize his waning interest in a particular lover, he'd be frank about no longer enjoying someone enough to waste time and energy on him.

Now Garen seemed to be on the other end of that calculation. If Luca didn't care so much about his friend, he'd find the turnabout sadistically satisfying.

"What did I do wrong?" Garen asked in a forlorn voice.

"Maybe nothing. Maybe it just wasn't meant to be."

"Och, that's useless. C'mon, think about it: If *you'd* dumped *me* all those years ago instead of the other way around, what would've been the reason?"

"Other than your tendency to scratch your balls when you're not alone?"

"Would that have been enough?" Garen asked.

"After another month, probably."

Garen looked as though he believed this.

"I'm kidding," Luca said. "More likely it would've been your inability to take seriously a single honest human emotion. But that was a long time ago."

"It was. I've changed. I loved Steven. I took us seriously." His mouth twisted, as if the word tasted rotten. "Maybe that was the problem."

"If you're suggesting that being shallow worked better for you—"

"I'm suggesting I was trying too hard. I wasn't the guy he fell for. I was someone 'better.'" His fingers curled into inverted commas. "Maybe I can win him back by being Summer Garen again."

"It's January."

"I still look good in a Speedo."

"I mean, it's curling season." Luca went over and sat beside Garen's head. "It's not easy being the boyfriend of a world-class athlete."

"Is that what you think I am?"

"It's what we all are." He stroked Garen's hair, tucking a pale-brown strand behind his ear. "And if Steven's ego can't handle it, fuck him."

"Yeah." Garen shifted up to lay his cheek on Luca's thigh. "Fuck him."

"Not literally, though."

"But what if he comes crawling back tomorrow? Makeup sex is the best." He turned his head to look up at Luca. "Remember?"

"Be serious."

"When are we ever serious?" Garen sat up and examined him. "You're dead nervous about this bonspiel, aren't you?"

"I'm not nervous, and we were talking about you." Luca assumed, with good reason, that Garen would be happy to turn the conversation back to himself. "If this thing with Steven was doomed anyway, then he did us all a favor by ending it now instead of stringing you along another weekend and distracting you from the curling."

"I know, I know." Garen slumped against the couch and tapped the back of his head against the wall. "This breakup's been hanging over my head for weeks. Now it's done and dusted, and there's nothing I can do, so I may as well curl my arse off."

"Exactly." Luca squeezed his shoulder. "Seeing as it won't be getting much use otherwise."

"Oh, fuck off!" He slapped Luca in the head with the wee sofa cushion, but was laughing too hard to put much force behind the blow. "Nice one from a guy who's not seen a naked man this entire calendar year."

"It's only January, ya slag."

"It'll be February on Sunday, and you'll still be mooning over the forbidden fruit of Yukon Cornelius."

Luca ripped the cushion from him. "If you're referring to Oliver, we're officially just friends, and I feel fantastic about that."

"Do you, aye?"

Luca hugged the cushion to his chest and gave Garen a bug-eyed grimace. They started laughing even harder.

"Poor Luca. Now who's distracted all weekend?"

"I'll get my head together, don't worry. Much meditation planned for tomorrow morning."

He wasn't about to tell Garen about the private session he'd planned with Oliver. Right now it was their own wee secret, a rendezvous of passionate minds, if not bodies.

Luca only hoped he could keep his own body from responding to the nearness of Oliver Doyle. No mantra in the world was strong enough to tame the attraction he felt for that man. But he'd take each moment as it came.

Apart from the next few minutes in the shower, when he'd let his imagination run free. There were limits to serenity, after all.

8

Guard

GUARD: *A rock placed in front of the rings to protect either a rock that's already there or a rock one plans to put behind it. Makes shots more difficult for the other team—and often for one's own team as well, because life is like that, innit?*

OLIVER SAT BACK in his dining room chair with a satisfied groan. His arteries wouldn't miss these full Scottish breakfasts, but his mouth certainly would. Coming from a Scot-centric province like Nova Scotia, he'd always rolled his eyes at the kilts and bagpipes put on display for tourists in Halifax. But now that he was living in the real Scotland—and it didn't get much realer than Glasgow—he couldn't get enough.

Stifling a yawn, he checked the grandfather clock at the side of his hotel's dining room. Soon he'd feel more awake. His meds always took longer to kick in when he was sleep-deprived.

Today's drowsiness had nothing to do with jet lag and everything to do with Jack's reminder that Oliver might fly home a failure next week. A familiar nightmare had woken him at three a.m., and he couldn't get back to sleep until he'd reviewed the Team Boyd stats to reassure himself how much they'd improved.

He had every reason to be confident. Boyd's destiny was in their own hands. If they won the Glasgow Open, they'd win the overall Scottish Challenger Tour—with its fifteen-thousand-pound prize—and thus qualify for next month's national championship in Edinburgh. Simple as that.

Moreover, they had a bit of a safety net. According to Oliver's calculations, Boyd could finish as low as third place this weekend and still win the season-long Challenger Tour, as long as they did better than their two closest rivals, Teams Riley and MacDougall.

"More decaf, Mr. Doyle?"

Madeline, the hotel's concierge, stood beside his chair holding a silver carafe with a red lid.

"I'm not sure where I'll put it," he said, patting his stomach, "but yes, please. And call me Oliver."

"Of course," Madeline said, as she'd done the other five times he'd asked her to use his first name.

"Mr. Doyle is my dad," he said, "so I feel ancient when people call me that."

"Ohhh, I see." She set down his coffee cup, leaving room for milk. "Father issues," she muttered as she walked off.

Oliver's phone buzzed in his pocket. He pulled it out to see a text from Luca.

Still want a go at meditation at 10?

A flame of anticipation whooshed through him.

Yes! About to leave. Early this time, promise.

He set down the phone to pour milk into his coffee. In a minute, another text appeared from Luca.

Great! Slight change in plans. No rooms open at wellbeing ctr. Can you come to mine? Garen's at the wheelchair curling, so we'll have privacy.

Then Luca listed his address.

Oliver's face and hands turned hot. Alone with Luca in his apartment for over an hour? What would start as meditation could quickly become something much less cerebral. Oliver knew himself well: He'd never have the strength to resist such an impulse.

But did he really have to resist? What would be the harm in a brief hookup? Luca didn't seem to want more than friendship, so maybe they could keep things casual. That way, if Team Boyd failed this weekend, it wouldn't hurt so bad to say goodbye.

"Ha!" Oliver said out loud, startling the businessman at the next table. "Sorry, I just…thought of something funny."

His thought hadn't been funny at all. Because again, Oliver knew himself. If he so much as kissed Luca, he'd be hooked, and flying away next week would be like leaving part of himself behind.

His phone buzzed again.

Luca: You there?

Oliver grabbed the phone and replied before he could reconsider.

Sorry, something's come up and I need to get to the rink early. Some other time? Sorry again. Really sorry.

Then Oliver waited, taking half-hearted sips of coffee and feeling like the worst person in the world.

Luca's reply arrived several minutes later, and its two tiny letters made Oliver's heart fold in half.

ok

As Luca and his fellow curlers followed the bagpiper into Shawlands Ice Rink for the tournament's opening ceremony, he was reminded with bitter certainty why he didn't bother himself with men during the curling season.

His mind wasn't on their first of five round-robin games, beginning in less than half an hour. He wasn't contemplating how he wanted David to lay down the guards or whether the ice might be too keen for Ross's finesse come-arounds, or even whether Garen's breakup rage might make him throw too hard, sending his takeout hits *through* the house instead of clearing it. He definitely wasn't savoring the moment—the biting smell of fresh ice, the echo of each musical note against the ceiling, the soothing caress of cold air against his skin.

No, he was playing that stupid text conversation over and over in his mind. Had he scared Oliver off by inviting him to his place? Why would Oliver lie to avoid being alone with him? Why not just show up as a pal, like they'd agreed? Was Oliver actually attracted to Luca and couldn't risk the temptation, or was he profoundly *un*attracted to Luca and couldn't risk leading him on?

Luca couldn't claim total innocence, at least not to himself. He'd felt no disappointment upon discovering the well-being center was entirely booked. He'd hoped that if the two of them were truly alone together, something would happen.

The final piped notes of "Flower of Scotland" faded, replaced by cheers of the crowd in the small open spectator stand above the warm room. Luca spied a few rainbow flags, which he assumed were for him and Garen, unless another curler had come out in the six weeks since the last major event.

Half of the front row was taken up by eight giant foam-board versions of the curlers' faces, one for each member of Teams Riley and Boyd. Luca had seen the big heads on TV, wielded by fans at curling competitions in North America. Maybe Oliver had carried the tradition across the Atlantic. Luca appreciated the support but felt a bit unnerved at the sight of his own ten-times-normal-size visage staring down at him. (Was his smile really that wide? He could fit his real-life head into that mouth.)

Ah well, he would just toss it onto the pile of things to banish from his mind, along with the knowledge that Oliver himself was sitting in the stand—at the end of the front row, of course, so he could quickly come down to the ice during a timeout to advise his team.

Garen nudged him. "Give Ben a wave."

Luca held up his hand to their fan-turned-friend Ben Reid, who stood in the middle of the crowd bobbing a *Riley Rocks* sign above his head. The winsome lad had supported Team Riley when they'd played at Glasgow University. In fact, it was Ben who'd convinced Luca to leave Team Boyd before last season and reunite with his uni mates. He also provided an endless supply of romantic advice—some solicited, but most not so much.

"That's the same sign he brought to Aberdeen when we won," Garen whispered to Luca as Craig stepped to the microphone to make the host club's opening remarks. "He wanted to bring a bigger sign today, but I said, 'Don't you dare—that one's good luck.'"

"Cool." Luca used to worry about Garen's superstitions until he noticed his mate only seemed to believe in good luck, not bad.

"I bet Ben'd be interested in my newfound freedom," Garen said. "It's been a wee while since he and I—"

"Why don't we both calm our jets and focus on the curling, okay?"

"I'll do if you do."

"Deal." They exchanged a surreptitious fist bump, then turned their attention to Craig as he welcomed everyone to Shawlands Ice Rink.

When the ceremony ended, Luca followed his team to Sheet E for their pre-game practice session. The sight of his mates in their black-and-midnight-blue Team Riley kits, striding with calm determination toward their first battle-ground, brought a sudden sharpness to Luca's mind. At last he felt fully *here*.

As he took his first practice slide out of the hack—with no stone or supportive broom, just his arms outstretched like wings, demonstrating his impeccable balance to any opponent who might be watching—Luca realized he needn't have worried about his focus. This was all he needed to get his head in the game: the arch of his back, the fix of his gaze on the far end of the sheet, the feel of pebbled ice gliding under his left shoe's Teflon sole. These things connected him to himself and the universe better than any yoga pose.

At the end of their ten-minute practice, Team Riley prepared for the Last Stone Draw (or LSD, as people loved to call it). Winning this duel would give them the hammer—the advantage of throwing last—in the game's first end. All Luca had to do was throw two rocks closer to the button than his rival skip, Cameron MacDougall.

Luca got into the hack and crouched down to clean his

stone. As he tilted it on its side to wipe off its running surface, he gave but a brief thought to the importance of this game. Team MacDougall currently sat third on the Scottish Challenger Tour leaderboard and were therefore the main threat to the dual dominance of Riley and Boyd. Beating MacDougall right now would make the rest of the weekend a lot less stressful.

Stop thinking, he told himself. *You're in an empty rink, with no crowds, no media, and no cute Canadian coaches. It's just you, this stone, and this ice.*

Luca stood and took a deep breath to calm his pulse. He focused on Garen standing in the house at the far end of the sheet. His vice set his mustard-yellow broom head on the tee line bisecting the circles, adjusting the line for today's ice, which would have less curl thanks to the rainy weather and the damp coats of three dozen spectators.

Ross and David stood near Luca at either side of the sheet, ready to defend their reputation as the competition's strongest sweepers. He could err on the side of throwing light, knowing their brooms could add several feet to the stone's journey.

Luca settled into the hack, aligning his body and the stone with Garen's broom. Then he rotated the rock's yellow handle to the ten o'clock position so that when he released it at the twelve o'clock, the stone would spin clockwise and thus curl from left to right. Like some of his fellow right-handed curlers, he preferred this "in-turn" position for a draw and the opposite "out-turn" for hits.

He shifted back, then thrust forward out of the hack, perfectly straight. Gliding forward, he waited until he was nearly at the hog line to release the stone.

"Line's good!" Garen said.

Ross and David accompanied the rock down the sheet, their brooms at the ready.

"Wee bit heavy," Ross said.

"Back eight, maybe?" David added.

What? Luca stood up and examined the stone's speed. He'd thrown too hard without realizing it. If anything, he'd tried to ease off to compensate for adrenaline.

The rock slid to a stop at the back of the eight-foot ring, just as David had predicted. Not good enough.

Luca tried to dial it back on the second try—his less-favored out-turn draw—but this one went even farther, ending up in the back of the twelve-foot ring, almost leaving the house entirely.

"Sorry, lads," he told his teammates when he joined them on the carpeted catwalk at the end of the ice sheet.

"Better to bottle a draw *before* the game than during it," David said. "This way we avoid overconfidence."

"Exactly." Garen patted Luca's back. "In the theater world, a poor dress rehearsal is meant to be good luck for opening night."

"Oi, you guys," Ross said, "Luca's throws weren't *that* crap." He gestured with his broom to their opponents, who were now taking the ice for their own practice. "They're probably just as nervous. So we might still win the LSD and first hammer."

Luca gave his mates an appreciative smile as he slipped the black-rubber gripper over the sole of his sliding shoe. Most people credited him for Team Riley's *joie de vivre*, but he knew that without these three lads, he'd be as moody as Jack Boyd.

They retreated to the warm room, but went directly to the window to observe their opponents' practice. Team MacDougall was a formidable foursome of Highlanders who always wore kilts on the ice, a feat Luca had attempted but once. Once.

Ross never failed to bring it up. "Remember that time in Inverness," he said, "when we all tried curling in—"

"Yes," the other three said in unison, then gave a collective shiver at the memory. It had taken hours for Luca's bits to fully thaw.

They watched as MacDougall's lead curler stepped into the hack, his foot dwarfing the black rubber contraption. He was the biggest man in the rink in both height and brawn—a fact he demonstrated by picking up the forty-plus-pound stone and rubbing its underside against the front of his green short-sleeved shirt.

Garen gave a low whistle. "That's way more intimidating than David's beard."

Ten minutes later, Cameron MacDougall had narrowly beaten Luca's LSD, which meant Team Riley would start the game by throwing first. It was a disadvantage, statistically speaking, but one they could overcome with the right strategy and execution.

"Ideally we'd like to steal a point," Luca reminded his team as they headed back out to the ice. "But if we can't, we want to force them to score just one so we get the hammer in the next end." He clapped like a circus seal. "And don't forget to have fun!"

After the teams exchanged handshakes and wishes of "good curling," the two skips went to the other end of the sheet. Luca tapped his broom head a few inches in front of the blue twelve-foot circle to show he wanted a tight center guard.

"Top of the house is second best!" he called to David and the sweepers. Team Riley always had a Plan B and a "pro-side error"—i.e., which sort of miss would be the least unfortunate. In a sport where Murphy's Law ruled supreme, there was no place for blind faith and blithe hope.

Luca watched as David launched into his impeccable delivery, displaying not an ounce of nerves. The Riley lead gave the stone a gentle release.

"Weight's good!" Ross called.

"Line's good!" Luca replied. "Just clean," he added, telling the sweepers to gently brush ahead of the stone to clear any debris. The tiniest piece of fuzz could disrupt a rock's trajectory and send it drifting out of control, like a car with a flat tire.

Luca could have kissed David for this ideal first throw. The stone would end up exactly where he wanted it—assuming Luca called the sweep correctly.

The key was in the timing. If he asked Ross and Garen to brush too soon, the stone would travel too far before curling and probably land inside the house, which wouldn't be the end of the world. If he waited too long, the stone could come up short, perhaps even sitting as a corner guard, offering MacDougall the cover they needed to score multiple points.

It was always best to play it safe.

"Yes!" Luca called out. "Hard, lads! Haarrd! Haaaaaaard!" He moved forward as the stone approached the house. "Yep! Go, go, go. Wee bit more. And, off!"

Garen and Ross pulled back their brooms as the rock made one final half-spin to rest bang on the center line a few inches in front of the house.

"Good throw," Cameron said. "Good sweep, too."

Luca's face warmed in the obligatory curling humble-blush. "Iceman did a fantastic job, especially for the weather." Then he turned to David, kissing his own fingertips and popping open his hand like an Italian chef. "Ya beauty!"

As he moved behind the house to await Team MacDougall's first throw, Luca pulled in a long breath, then let it out slowly as he mentally recited his mantra.

This. Here. Now.

David's guard had given Team Riley an auspicious start, but it was only the first stone of hundreds they would throw this weekend. Luca would take them one at a time, like always. He wasn't the most talented or clever skip in the rink, but if he stayed true to himself, he could be by far the most chill. And no tall, handsome, *R*-chewing coach could stop him.

Probably.

9

Shot Rock

SHOT ROCK: *The stone closest to the center of the house. The second-closest stone is called "second shot." A team with two stones closer to the center than their opponents' nearest stone is said to be "sitting two"—or "lying two," because heaven forfend there should be but one term for anything in curling.*

OLIVER WAS grateful that Boyd's first opponents were Team Laing, the lowest-rated side in the tournament. Jack had been so wound up before the opening ceremonies, he'd been unable to eat for fear he'd "boak all over the ice and pure melt the sheet." Stealing three points in this game's first end had done wonders for the skip's nerves.

To their credit, Laing hadn't self-destructed, but instead put up a good fight, placing lots of stones in the house in an attempt to get a big score in the second end.

"What are Laing's chances of clawing their way back into this game?" asked Heather, who'd sent her cameraman down to the ice with strict orders not to get in the way. "In football a three-nil lead is insurmountable—well, usually." She gave a wistful smirk, perhaps remembering such a comeback by her own team.

"Statistically, they still have about a fifteen percent chance of winning," Oliver said. "In the olden days before the free guard zone, it would've been less than one percent."

"Free guard zone? Wait, don't tell me." Heather looked up at the ceiling as she thought. "That's the rule saying you can't take out the rocks sitting outside the front of the house until after the...fourth stone is thrown?"

"Exactly. Before the nineties, teams would get an early lead and just start knocking out their opponents' stones left and right. It was super boring for spectators. But now, having all those guards forces curlers to play with more strategy and finesse."

As he watched his team—who were wearing new red-and-white uniforms in honor of their coach's home country—Oliver marveled at how hard they'd worked on the goals he'd set for them. Bruce had grown more assertive in calling weight as he swept, shouting out to his skip how far he thought the rock would travel. Alistair was mastering the hit-and-roll shot, in which the shooting stone, after knocking out its target, would move to a spot in the house where it would be hard to hit.

And Jack...well, Jack was learning to make life easier for his team.

"What do you tell yourself before deciding each call?" Oliver had asked his skip today as they'd wrapped up their pre-game practice, arranging the stones in the proper order beside the hack.

Jack had hesitated a moment before his face lit up. "The best shot is the one you can make."

"And?"

"The shot you make matters less than the shot you leave your opponents."

Oliver hoped Jack would take these curling adages to heart. The skip loved attempting glamorous, YouTube-worthy take-outs, even when there was an easier shot staring him in the face.

Just as he had this thought, Oliver saw Jack preparing to throw, cleaning his yellow stone and wearing a predatory grin. Based on Alistair's broom placement, it looked like they were attempting a double takeout of the two red stones Laing had placed in the back of the four-foot.

Wait…were they going for a *triple* takeout, including the red stone in the front of the four-foot? "Around the horn, no less," Oliver said. "Jesus."

"What's 'around the horn'?" Heather asked.

Oliver kept his eyes on Jack. "That's when the shooting stone ricochets off one rock, then another, in such a way that it ends up traveling in the opposite direction it started."

"So it'll come back toward the thrower? How is that physi-cally—hold on." Heather spoke into her comm. "Kevin, be sure and get Boyd's next shot on Sheet C. Could be a belter."

Oliver's pulse quickened. If Jack succeeded, Boyd would be sitting three again, forcing Laing to make a tough draw just to score one. If Jack missed, Laing could score two, three, or even four points.

It would be futile to try to change his team's aggressive approach. Moreover, Oliver didn't want to. He'd crossed the Atlantic to help Team Boyd because he believed in them. He had to keep believing, every step of the way.

Jack surged out of the hack, then waited until nearly the last moment to let go of the stone, delaying his release to coun-terbalance the power of his legs, hopefully achieving a perfectly calibrated weight.

Then his job was done. The shooting stone had to hit that first Laing rock at just the right angle, which meant Alistair and the front end had to fine-tune its journey with precise brushing.

Oliver leaned forward, his gaze snapping between the rock and the house as Ali shouted to the sweepers. The line looked perfect so far, but were the red stones in the house too far apart for this shot to work?

Jack's shooter smacked into the first Laing stone, then the second, sending them both out the rear of the house as it spun back the way it had come, toward the third red stone. The crowd around Oliver began to cheer.

The cheer faded into an "Awwww" when Jack's yellow shooter merely grazed the third stone, then glided slowly out of the house like a rogue asteroid leaving a star system after destroying a pair of planets.

"Whoa." Heather sat with her hands on her cheeks and her mouth open wide. Then she joined the applause for Jack's effort. "That was definitely not boring!"

On the ice, Jack gave a shrug to his teammates, who saluted him with their brooms. He had, at least, cut their opponents' potential score from four to two.

The Laing skip made a draw to earn the deuce, and the second end was over. During the one-minute break, Oliver checked the Sheet E scoreboard to see that Team Riley were down by a point at the start of the third end. Their scarlet-kilted opponents, led by Cameron MacDougall, were Team Boyd's second closest rivals, so Oliver knew he should keep an eye on that game rather than simply review its stats afterward. Not everything in curling could be reduced to numbers.

If only he could look at Luca without feeling sick. Canceling their meditation session had been a dick move. If Oliver had had time to think about the change in venue, he probably would've done the right thing and gone to Luca's apartment, if only to be polite. But in the moment, he'd panicked and obeyed his instincts—his stupid, unreliable instincts.

He'd find a way to make it up to Luca, to let him know... what, exactly? That he wasn't afraid to be alone with him? That he trusted himself not to act on his impulses? Those would be lies.

"Question about that last stone there," Heather said. "Laing wanted it to curl more at the end so it would be shot rock, but they kept sweeping it. I thought sweeping made it go straight."

"Actually, it just makes the stone continue to travel the way it's already traveling. If it's going straight, sweeping keeps it straighter. But once it starts to curl, a brusher can make it curl even more." Oliver went on to explain how each sweeper could affect the stone differently depending which side they were on at which point in its journey.

"Fascinating." Heather scanned the notes she'd jotted down. "Every time I think I've got this sport figured out, there's a whole other layer of physics underneath."

"It makes a lot more sense once you get out on the ice and try it yourself." He nudged her with his elbow. "Like maybe tonight after the last game?"

She shook her head. "I've got a football match tomorrow. My manager would have my head if I got hurt in a freak curling accident." Heather laced her fingers and pushed her palms forward to stretch her shoulders. "So this 'spirit of curling' thing I keep hearing of. What's that all about?"

Oliver shrugged. "It's just a fancy term for sportsmanship."

"Extreme sportsmanship, more like. In football, we claim we're good sports cos we shake hands after a match, but between the whistles it's murder. When I'm in goal during a penalty, I'll do anything to mess with a player's head. And when somebody scores, my God, they celebrate like they've cured cancer. But if a curler gives a wee fist pump after a great shot, people say he's showboating."

"That's a bit of an exaggeration," he said, "but yeah, we try not to make our opponents feel bad."

"Even if their feeling bad would help you win?"

Oliver's expression must have been comically horrified, because she burst out laughing.

"Seriously," she said, "why are curlers nicer and humbler than other athletes?"

"We're not."

"And by saying that, you just proved you are."

Okay, he'd walked into that one. "I guess it's just tradition. Some sports are all about intimidation. With curling it's all about etiquette, which falls into two categories: Don't mess up the ice and don't be a jerk."

"Seems a sound philosophy," Heather said. "Maybe the world would be a better place if it had more curlers?"

"I think so." Oliver watched Team Laing's lead attempt a center guard to open the third end. "But it's not for everyone. The sport attracts a certain type of person."

Her brows popped up. "What type?"

Oliver tried to think beyond the clichés. "People who can go with the flow, who don't need to control everything. A sense of humor comes in handy, because everyone loves to mock curling. And yeah, it helps if you're nice."

"But how did it get that way to begin with? Curling was invented in Scotland, but we Scots are known for being pugnacious, not polite." Heather gasped. "It was Canada, wasn't it? You made curling nice!"

"I don't think it's quite—"

"That must be it." She rapped her fists against her thighs

like a little kid awaiting a birthday cake. "And *that's* the real story here. For the film, I mean." She flipped a page in her notebook and started to scribble. "This piece needs a big theme. It needs to say something about our culture."

"Whose culture, yours or mine?"

"Both." Heather suddenly looked up from her notebook, her dark eyes gleaming. "And you're the one at the crossroads. Could we do a more in-depth interview about your own journey?"

Oliver looked away, then pretended something on the ice had caught his attention. "Just a second." He hunched over his tablet, running a new regression in his spreadsheet while his mind worked the problem Heather had just dumped in his lap.

An interview could open up old wounds, the ones Oliver had sustained long before the doping scandal. But Heather's film would promote Team Boyd, maybe even earn them sponsorships that could pay a coach's wages. Besides, she was really nice, and Oliver had always found it hard to say no to nice people.

"I might be able to do an interview tomorrow morning," he told her. That would give him time to figure out what he should and shouldn't say—or even time to decline if he thought better of it.

"Tomorrow's no good," Heather said. "I've got my own match, remember?"

He'd forgotten already. No surprise there. "Right," he said, trying to hide his relief. "Good luck with that."

"Thanks. How about tonight after the last game?"

Oliver hesitated. After saying yes, he couldn't just wimp out—he'd already done that once today, with Luca's meditation offer.

And maybe this interview could be an opportunity. Maybe he'd finally found a place where it was safe to be real and tell his story. Since the day he'd set foot in Scotland, he'd felt the shackles of shame begin to loosen.

"Yeah," he said, "tonight would be great."

———

LUCA HAD several theories as to why whisky tasted best after a stellar day of curling. Perhaps the victory-induced endorphins activated the brain's pleasure centers. More simply, it could be that standing about on a sheet of ice for several hours made one long for the inner warmth granted by a good single malt or even a decent blend.

Team Riley had won both of today's round-robin games by a single point. Luca didn't mind a close score—in fact, he rather enjoyed the challenge of keeping his wits under pressure. He couldn't help but notice the other skips' frustration as Riley erased deficit after deficit, never giving up or losing their heads.

"They call you the 'Comeback King,'" Heather had told Luca tonight during the post-game interview. *"What's your secret to winning?"*

It was an easy question with a simple answer: *"We're not afraid to lose."*

Now, he sat watching David and Ross at the other end of their pub table as they reenacted the day's best throws for their girlfriends, even though Lisa and Claire had already seen everything firsthand. The lads were using chips from one of the table's three baskets as substitute stones—the burnt ones were their opponents' rocks—to illustrate each shot. Garen sat between them and Luca, correcting David and Ross when they misremembered.

Luca was just happy to be away from the rink for a few waking hours. The warm room had cheap drinks, but the hot food had all been eaten, so after the broomstackings, several of the curling teams had retreated to the pub across the street for a late-night "calorie restoration project."

He turned to Ben sitting across from him. "Tell me something that's got nothing to do with curling. What's new with you? Made any more history?" In addition to his studies at Glasgow Uni, Ben was a wedding planner specializing in same-sex weddings, which had recently been legalized in Scotland.

"Got a big one next Saturday." Ben peered through his black-rimmed glasses at his phone screen, then nodded. "Just confirmed I'm meeting with the couple tomorrow at noon, so I'll be missing your first two draws. But of course I'll be here for the marquee shootout with Team Boyd."

"Och, I said no curling talk." Luca made like he was plugging his ears. "Met any new lads?"

"I'm always meeting new lads." Ben gave a sheepish smile at the reference to his active social life.

"But anyone special?" Luca felt old-fashioned asking in such a way.

"Maybe. There's one guy I chatted up at the wedding I did on Hogmanay. The ex-boyfriend of one of the grooms."

"How awkward." Luca tried to remember what Ben had told him about the wedding. "Was this the groom who captains that LGBT football team?"

"The Warriors, yeah. The whole team was invited to the wedding, but Fergus—that's the captain—he didn't think Evan would actually show up."

"Wait, this guy you fancy is a footballer? I thought you hated the sport."

"I do." Ben wrinkled his nose. "It's so uncivilized compared to curling."

"Tea with the queen is uncivilized compared to curling. Now back to Evan…"

"He asked for my number, so I gave him my business card. But it's been a month and I've not heard from him." Ben sighed and took another sip of ginger ale. "I'm punching above my weight with that one. He's, like, an eleven on the hotness scale. Absolutely stratospheric."

"But you chatted him up anyway. Well done, mate."

"Eh, nothing ventured, nothing gained." Ben fake-preened the swoop of black hair ascending from his forehead. "Audacity goes a long way, I've found."

"Sometimes." Luca peered over at Oliver, who was deep in conversation with Heather at a small table near the back of the pub. "But not always."

Ben followed his gaze. "Your brother-in-law's coach? Doesn't get more audacious than that."

"He's not interested, at least not enough to overcome the wrongness of it all." Luca briefed Ben on the events with Oliver thus far.

"Seems a waste to avoid someone you get on with so well." Chin in hand, Ben examined Oliver again. "Hmmm." He tapped his fingers against his cheek. "Hmmm," he repeated in a lower tone.

"You're scheming. What are you scheming?"

"Oliver's been talking to Heather for over half an hour," Ben said, "and it seems to be getting intense, maybe even uncomfortable. He's shifting about in his chair more, breaking eye contact, angling his shoulders away."

Luca looked over to see Ben was right. "How'd you get so observant, Mr. Holmes?"

Ben kept his eyes on Oliver as he spoke. "I've watched my mum make couples happy since I was big enough to hold a cake server. Spend enough time around brides and grooms, you learn to spot unspoken tension." He pulled a pen and a cream-colored business card from his pocket. "Right. Fist pressed against his mouth. That means he's done talking and ready for a savior." He scribbled something on the card, then stood up. "Back in a mo'."

"What are you—"

But Ben was already heading toward Oliver and Heather's table. When he got there, he bent over and said something to them. Oliver seemed confused at first, but when Ben handed him the card, his eyes widened. He looked at his watch, then gave Heather an apologetic shrug before shaking her hand and picking up his bag.

Ben made a *yay!* face at Luca as he led Oliver through the crowd straight toward Team Riley. Oliver slowed down when he saw who was waiting for him, but he didn't stop.

Ben set Oliver's glass of whisky on the table across from Luca. "Another round?" he asked everyone.

After his teammates had ordered, Luca said, "Nothing for me. I'm away soon."

"Me too," Oliver said.

"Oh, I do hope so." Ben winked at Luca, then headed toward the bar.

"I didn't ask him to do that," Luca said as Oliver draped his red-and-white Team Boyd jacket over the back of the chair across from him. "What did he do, by the way?"

"He 'reminded' me that he was supposed to interview me at ten for the LGBT magazine at Glasgow University. Then he gave me this." Oliver sat down and flipped over Ben's business card, which read *Come with me if you want to escape.*

"Must've been a pretty dire interview."

"Heather was just doing her job," Oliver said, "which means exploring my past."

"So she asked about the doping scandal?"

"No. Well, yes, but that wasn't the part I wanted to escape. This was more personal stuff."

"Personal like boyfriends?"

"Personal like family." Oliver drained his whisky. "You guys played great today."

Luca took the cue to change the subject. "Why, thank you. All down to them, of course." He nodded toward his team-mates, who were now eating the demonstration chips. "They left me some criminally simple draws for deuces and threes."

"But you orchestrated their shots perfectly."

Luca felt his face warm under Oliver's praise. "I won't complain about being 2-0 at the end of the first day. Though your team is ahead of us on shots difference. I imagine you'll be up all night running the numbers, working out how you can squeeze an extra five percent more magnificence from them tomorrow."

"Maybe, but when a team's playing the way they are, sometimes the best thing a coach can do is just not interfere." As he spoke, Oliver rocked his glass along its bottom edge. "Like you said in your class, overthinking creates tension, and tension—"

"Creates mistakes. So you *were* paying attention." Luca paused. He was pretty sure he'd made that statement before Oliver's arrival. Had he stood outside Luca's classroom to listen before entering? The image of a nervous Oliver working up the courage to step through that door made Luca's heart feel all sorts of squishy.

"Speaking of meditation…" Oliver kept his eyes on his rotating tumbler. "I'm sorry about this morning. And before you ask, yes, I really mean it when I say I'm sorry. It was a shitty thing to do."

"What was, exactly?" Luca asked, not yet ready to let him off the hook.

Oliver frowned. "To lie about why I couldn't come to your place. I should've just said I wasn't comfortable being alone with you there."

Luca regretted fishing for this truth. "I make you uncomfortable?"

"No." Oliver met his eyes for a split second. "I mean, yeah, in a way."

"What sort of way?"

"In a...not completely bad way." Oliver tapped his glass against the table. "If you gave me a third chance, I'd jump at it."

Luca had to stop himself from dragging Oliver out of the pub that moment. "Well, the studio is open now, and I've already booked the room for myself at eleven-fifteen, so—"

"I don't want to interfere with your mental preparation for tomorrow."

"Och, this'll be decompression from today. I'll worry about tomorrow when tomorrow comes." Luca stood and put on his jacket. "We shouldn't leave together, so wait at least five minutes before you follow." He decided not to point, in case anyone was watching. "Turn right when you leave the pub. I'll be at the next junction." He said goodbye to his teammates, then gave a quick thumbs up to Ben, who was still at the bar ordering the next round.

Outside, the torrential rain had eased to a steady drizzle. Luca stopped beneath the awning of a newsagent to phone a taxi. Cabs could be a bit scarce on the outskirts of the city, and he didn't want to waste time waiting for one to happen by— not when that time could be spent alone with Oliver in a nice warm meditation room.

Luca still wasn't sure what might happen when they got there. He half-expected Oliver to invent another excuse to avoid him.

So he was pleasantly surprised when he saw his "date" leave the pub five minutes later and amble up the pavement toward him. It was a long, steep street, which gave Luca time to shamelessly catalog his physical attributes.

Oliver had clearly stayed in shape since leaving the sport. His chest and shoulders were still broad and powerful, like many front-end curlers who do a lot of sweeping. His long legs ate up the hill between them, swinging easily even though his hands were stuffed in his pockets. His head was bent against the rain, taking the brunt of the water with his gray-and-green knit cap. Luca imagined pulling off that cap, then running his fingers through the mussed brown hair it left behind.

A beep to his right aborted this wee fantasy. He waved to the taxi driver who'd just pulled up, then turned to see Oliver quickening his pace to a jog.

Once they were in the cab together, Luca felt an unbidden attack of shyness. He couldn't think of a single thing to say. But Oliver seemed content to peer out the window as his new home passed by, so Luca relaxed again. Silence was nothing to be frightened of, he was always telling his students.

"I love this bridge," Oliver said as they passed over the Clyde Arc into Glasgow's City Centre.

Luca tried to think of an interesting fact about it. "They call it 'The Squinty' because the arch looks twisted from this angle. 'Squinty' is slang for crooked."

"I know."

"Oh." Luca glanced at the gaping space between their bodies. Before tonight, he'd never noticed how wide these cabs were.

The drizzle strengthened into a downpour again, sweeping against the windows in a low roar.

"Sorry about the rain," Luca said. *Oh my God, we're talking about the weather. Could I be any less sexy?*

"It's snowing at home, so no complaints here." Oliver turned to face him. "I have a confession to make."

Luca sat up straight, relieved there was interesting conversation to be had but also dreading what it might be. "Go on."

"One of my so-called stretch goals as Team Boyd's coach was to convince you to play for Jack again."

Luca had definitely not been expecting that sort of confession. It made him a bit queasy.

"But now that's changed," Oliver said. "After getting to know both teams this week, I realized you're all exactly where you belong." He met Luca's eyes. "Especially you."

"Well...thanks." Luca appreciated his honesty, though he felt naive for not considering that Oliver might have had an ulterior motive for spending time with him. "I feel the same way. About being exactly where I belong, that is."

As they looked at each other across the back seat, Luca wondered whether the taxi driver had suddenly turned up the car's heating.

"Here we are, lads," the man was now saying as they reached the well-being center on Byres Road.

Oliver pulled out his wallet. "I've got this."

"Nope. My invitation, my shout." Luca stuck his credit card through the sliding window to the front of the taxi.

"Technically I invited myself," Oliver said as he opened the door. "But thanks." He paused. "For everything."

Luca gave him a smile, which Oliver returned tenfold, making Luca's entire spine glow.

Still looking back, Oliver stepped out of the cab. There was a loud plop. "Oh jeez."

"What happened?" Luca leaned over to see Oliver had just stepped into an ankle-deep puddle. "Oops."

"'Oops' is right. 'Oops' should be engraved on my headstone." Oliver scooted sideways out of the car, taking a wide step to avoid a second puddle.

Luca retrieved his receipt and credit card, then followed. "On behalf of all Glasgow, I profusely apologize for the state of our pavement." He looked at Oliver's soaking wet foot. "You can't walk about like that. But I'm not sure where we can get you dry socks at this hour."

"Actually." Oliver looked uphill toward Great Western Road. "My hotel's not far."

10

Hard

HARD: *The command to sweep, usually shouted at the top of one's voice and thus providing an excellent outlet for the day's frustrations. Often combined with* Hurry, Yes/yep/yup, All the way, Gotta go, *and other suggestive urgings. Curling is pure hot, lads and lasses.*

"I'LL JUST WAIT HERE," Luca said as he took a seat at the bottom of the hotel's interior staircase. "You'll be only a minute, aye?"

Oliver hesitated, his hand on the banister. It would definitely be best if Luca stayed behind, but the mere fact that he'd offered to do so made it hard to say yes.

Besides, after that gut-piercing interview with Heather, Oliver was all out of willpower. He needed to feel good again, and nobody made him feel as good as Luca did. "Come on up."

"You sure?"

"I'm sure I don't want you sitting here like a dog tied up outside a restaurant."

Oliver didn't look back as he ascended. Though the stairs

were carpeted, their footsteps seemed to echo against the walls. Was this the first time they'd been truly alone together? They'd felt alone so many times before, even within the sight of others.

"Ooh, nice," Luca said when they entered Oliver's room. "Jack pays for this?"

"It's not terribly expensive, with it being January and the hotel giving us a weekly rate." He headed for his closet, hoping he hadn't left it a complete mess this morning.

"Why the *weekly* rate? I thought your visa was for six months."

Oliver stopped with the closet door half open. It was certain now: Luca didn't know Oliver's future depended on this weekend's results. So it wasn't common knowledge, which could mean Jack didn't want anyone else to know. "Maybe there's no monthly rate?"

"Ah." Luca didn't question further, just wandered over to the window above the desk.

Oliver stepped out of his shoes and pulled off his socks, then took the wet one to the bathroom to hang. Sticking to the mirror above the sink was his neon-yellow note reading *What time is it?*—one of half a dozen various reminders adorning his room. Luca hadn't commented on them yet, but he must have been wondering whether Oliver had lost his mind.

As he retrieved a fresh towel to dry his feet, he saw Luca move toward the crate tucked into the corner of the room.

The clown crate.

Luca tapped the lid. "This looks intriguing."

"You don't want to open it."

"What's inside, the Ark of the Covenant?"

"You don't want to open it," Oliver repeated.

"Are you saying I can't?"

"You can, but again, you don't want to."

Luca flipped the latch. "Now I simply must, after you—
och!" He dropped the lid and sat down hard on the bed. "You
sadist! How could you let me look at clown stuff?"

"I told you not to open it."

"You should have told me harder!" Luca started laughing.
"How can you even sleep in the same room as that?"

I guess this means he's not staying, Oliver thought, disappointed at his own disappointment. "I've learned to embrace
the darkness that is clowning," he said as he moved to join
Luca. "Then it's not so scary." He put his hand on the edge of
the crate. "You want to try?"

"God, no. Could you nail it shut or something while we're
here?" He laughed as he made this request, but Oliver couldn't
tell if he was completely joking.

"How about this?" Oliver sat on the crate and crossed his
legs. "Now it can't get out."

Luca laughed again, and this time it sounded real. Then he
looked down at Oliver's bare feet. "Is that a birthmark?"

"This tattoo?" He pulled up the hem of his jeans to display
the thumbprint-sized maple leaf etched upon his left ankle.
"All Canadians are required to get them at age eighteen. Same
goes for new immigrants."

"Naw, you're at it," Luca said with a laugh.

"It's true. We're a fiercely patriotic bunch."

Luca smile faltered. "Does it have to be on the ankle?"

"Most people choose a less bony part so it doesn't hurt so
much." Oliver spread his thighs and gestured down. "The
bravest men get one maple leaf on each ball."

Luca's jaw dropped, then jutted out as he picked up on the
joke. "Och, away, you!"

Oliver laughed. "I'm a terrible liar, so you must be really
gullible."

"I am. When I was a wean, I noticed our dad was two years

older than our mum *and* our granddad was two years older
than our gran. When I told Gillian, she said it was the law, that
couples couldn't marry in Scotland unless the man was exactly
two years older than the woman."

"And you believed her?"

"Yes, for ages! Older sisters are the worst." Luca eyed the
crate, as though making sure its contents weren't about to
escape. "Have you got siblings?"

"No." The word came out smoothly, because strictly speaking, it was the truth. Before they could come closer to *that*
subject, Oliver held out his left foot. "I did get this when I was
eighteen, so that part's for real. It was the week before I went
to the Junior World Championship. It was also the week I
came out, so I almost got a rainbow-colored maple leaf. But
now I'm glad I went with the standard, except for the fact that
red tattoos do look like birthmarks."

"Wait—if you're twenty-nine now, and you were at Junior
Worlds when you were eighteen, then I would've been…"
Luca scanned the ceiling, then gasped. "Was your hair longer
then?"

Oliver nodded. "And I wore glasses. It wasn't a good
look."

Luca smacked his hands together. "I remember you! I'd
heard there was a gay curler from Canada, so I looked for
pictures online. I thought you were so cute." He grinned. "You
may have inspired a wank or two."

"Oh. Thanks, I guess?" Oliver knew it was meant as a
compliment, but picturing a fourteen-year-old Luca in *that*
way felt a bit creepy.

"It's weird, isn't it?" Luca leaned back on his hands. "You
don't feel much older than me now, but if we'd met then, the
age difference would've raised a few eyebrows." He tilted

down his chin, then looked up at Oliver through his long, dark lashes. "Not that you would've looked twice at me."

"Okay, I can't win here. Saying I would've checked you out sounds kinda pervy, but saying I wouldn't sounds like an insult."

"Yes, let's erase this whole discussion." Luca waved his hands like he was wiping a chalkboard. "We're here and it's now."

"It is," Oliver said softly. Only the whisky humming through his veins gave him the courage to keep his gaze on Luca.

Looking suddenly shy, Luca folded his hands together and stuffed them between his own knees. "So, are you going to put new socks on or…" The question hung in the air, loaded with implication.

"I don't know." Oliver gave Luca's leg a playful tap with his bare foot. "Should I?" Another tap. "Hmm?"

On the third tap, Luca jumped up and moved away. "What the hell are you doing?"

"I THOUGHT I WAS FLIRTING." Oliver looked hurt. "Guess I'm not very good at it."

Yes you are, you bewildering bastard! "I thought—" Luca pressed his fingertips to his temples. "Last weekend you said—"

"'No as in never.' I'm sorry." Oliver drew in a deep breath, then let it out. "You know how sometimes a skip sees a throw that seems way too heavy, so he yells, 'Never!'?"

"Yeah…"

"But the sweepers have to stay with the rock, because the

skip might suddenly change his mind and shout, 'Hurry hard!'"

"What's your point?" Luca didn't dare to hope Oliver meant what he thought he meant.

"Well, if you still want…" Oliver's gaze dropped to the floor.

"I do want." Luca took a few steps forward, then stopped. "But you need to say it."

"Say what?"

Luca lifted his chin. "The opposite of 'never.'"

"Oh." Oliver's eyes crinkled, then softened into sincerity. "Hurry hard."

Though his legs weakened at the sound of those words, Luca turned his head and touched his earlobe. "Sorry? Can't quite hear you."

Oliver stood, stepped close to Luca, then leaned over, just as he'd done the night they'd met. "Hurry hard," he said, his warm breath caressing Luca's ear.

Oh God yes. Exhaling, Luca reached up and took Oliver's face in his hands. "I can kiss you now, aye?"

"You'd better."

So he did. Oliver's warm, soft lips soon parted, and as their tongues met, he emitted a moan that Luca felt to the tips of his fingers and toes.

When Luca's knees buckled, Oliver guided him back to sit on the bed. They shed their jackets, and before Luca knew it, they were lying face to face, hands wandering over shirts, exploring the planes of chests and backs. The intoxicating scent of Oliver's hair and skin made Luca want to taste him everywhere, everywhere, but for now this mouth was his entire world, and it was a good world.

Oliver slid a leg over Luca's, pulling their hips together and offering a very clear mental picture of what he wanted.

Luca shuddered just imagining it. If *that* could make him feel as delirious as these kisses, then it could be a glorious night.

Problem was, *that* rarely lived up to the hype, Luca had found. Sex often reminded him of those anticlimactic main courses that followed amazing starters—by the time he got to the big event, his appetite tended to wane, and he mostly just looked forward to the dessert of an orgasm-induced slumber.

He pulled back to put a few significant inches of space between them.

"You okay?" Oliver asked.

"Aye." Luca fidgeted with the edge of Oliver's shirt collar. "I don't really do this very often...at all."

"Do what?"

"This."

"What's 'this'?" Oliver asked with a slight smile.

"Sex stuff. I probably gave you the wrong idea, the way I've been flirting. You might think I'm a player or something, but I just don't...think about it much. Being an athlete and working two jobs, it's just not a priority." He winced inwardly at the excuse. This wasn't about his demanding schedule. But it was so hard to be fully honest. "Rather a shame, really. Glasgow's got one of the best gay scenes in the UK, and I pretty much ignore it."

"Why would you think I care?" Oliver blinked. "Sorry, that didn't come out right. I mean, why would that bother me?"

"It bothers some lads." Luca averted his gaze. "It bothers some lads a lot."

"Not this lad. Unless you're trying to discourage me."

"Never." Luca tugged on Oliver's collar. "I just don't want you to expect much."

"I don't expect anything. Just you." Oliver brushed his lips over the tip of Luca's nose. "How about we just kiss for a while, and then you can finally teach me to meditate?"

Luca hadn't realized how tense he'd been until he felt his body relax at this suggestion. "Sounds perfect," he said, though he actually wanted to do far more than just kiss.

That fact in itself perplexed him. Usually Luca needed to know a man a lot longer than a week before naked things happened. But Oliver was different, and if he knew he was different—that Luca literally fancied the pants off him—he might be scared away by so much seriousness.

So Luca would play it safe, for as long as he could bear.

———

"A LOT of people think meditation's about clearing the mind and getting rid of thoughts. But it's actually the opposite."

"Good." Oliver looked at Luca sitting cross-legged on the bed beside him. "Because I'm having a lot of thoughts right now."

"Me too." An impish smile lit up Luca's eyes. "The more the better, because it gives our brains practice. It builds the mindfulness muscle, so to speak. Anyway, the objective is to be comfortable with our thoughts and feelings—to just sit with them, not follow them down a rabbit hole or try and stamp them out."

"Okay." Oliver felt his spine relax against the wooden headboard behind him. His mind definitely needed an off-ramp from the endless roundabouts it was always trapping itself in.

Luca led him through a series of deep breaths, then had him close his eyes. Immediately Oliver's brain went into over-drive, weaving memories of the last half hour's make-out session with fantasies of other things they could do together wearing way less clothes.

"The next thing we'll do," Luca said, making Oliver

wonder what they were supposed to be doing currently, "is a body scan, like we did in class."

Oliver resisted the obvious joke about wanting to scan Luca's body with his bare hands and instead focused on sliding his awareness down from his own head to his toes.

Luca's voice took on a soothing cadence. "Mind, we're not judging these sensations or trying to change them. We're merely noticing, not just the places where our bodies feel bad, but also where they feel good."

Oliver noticed his body felt particularly good on the left side, the one nearest Luca. His skin tingled there, like every cell and hair follicle were reaching out, drawn by the waves of reassurance his tutor emitted.

"Now for the simplest part," Luca said. "We just follow the breath in and out. Notice what it feels like, but again, don't try and make it deep or steady or anything. Just let it be, almost like you're watching the most riveting film you've ever seen."

Oliver did as he was told, and found it was easier than he'd expected. He hadn't truly focused on his breath since his last time on the ice. When he'd left curling, biofeedback was starting to become popular, and many of the top players would take a moment before delivery to lower their pulse and respiration rates to avoid adrenaline-fueled overthrows.

"If your mind starts to wander," Luca said, "just gently bring it back to the breath."

Of course Oliver's mind *had* wandered, thinking about the biofeedback and how long it had been since he'd curled. Maybe this wasn't so easy after all.

Luca continued. "If it helps, you can count the breaths."

It did help, so much so that the next time Luca gave an encouraging reminder, Oliver barely heard him.

What might have been thirty seconds or several minutes

later, Luca said, "All right, for a few moments, just let the mind do whatever it wants."

Strangely, Oliver's mind didn't burst into a rampage like an uncaged tiger. It didn't want to wander or think or worry. It wanted more of this staying-with-the-breath thing.

"Now you can bring your awareness back to the room around you—the sounds, the smells, the weight of your body pressing down on the bed." Air whistled through Luca's nose as he pulled in a deep sigh. "And whenever you're ready...just open your eyes."

Oliver did so, and was relieved to see Luca wasn't staring at him expectantly but rather gazing ahead, his face smooth and serene.

"Wow," Oliver whispered.

"How did that feel?"

"Good." He stretched his neck from side to side, returning himself to the real world. "I feel calm. Much better than I did in that studio."

Luca gave his leg a playful poke. "That's because you were late for class and missed my intro."

"Sorry. Again." He looked at the bedside clock. "That took ten minutes? It felt like a lot less."

"Did you fall asleep?"

"No. It was more like...falling awake."

"Perfect! Next time we'll do it for an hour." He laughed at Oliver's shocked expression. "Kidding. It'll always be ten minutes, unless you want more or less. For my own practice, I try to sprinkle in a few three-minute sessions throughout the day to keep myself centered." He rolled his eyes. "Och, 'centered' sounds so pretentious. I mean, to stop myself spiraling."

"Spiraling. You do that too?"

"Everyone does. It's natural. We feel a feeling or think a thought we don't like, and instead of letting it go, we double down on it. We meet our anger with more anger, or fear with more fear. It's only when we train the mind to notice the cycle that we can break it. Sometimes." Luca squeezed Oliver's knee. "Questions? Comments? Adulation?"

"Just this." He leaned forward and kissed Luca. "That's where most of my thoughts were."

"Mine, too. I'm a poor role model." He pulled away with a groan of regret. "I should be away home. I need my sleep." When Oliver glanced at the pillows behind them, Luca said, "I need *good* sleep. Big day tomorrow, in case you've forgotten. So unless bedding me is part of your plan to undermine Team Riley—"

"Don't even joke about that." To dispel the sudden tension Luca's jest had brought him, Oliver added, "It's the clown crate, isn't it? If it'd make you feel better, I could find a welding torch and seal it shut."

"Haha." Luca poked Oliver's chest, then froze, his brows scrunched together. "Wait a minute..." He slid off the bed and stood beside the crate. "May I open this?"

"If you dare. But why?"

"When I was meditating just now, I remembered seeing something in here before, something that wasn't horrible." As Luca lifted the lid, he leaned back as though expecting an actual clown to pop out. "There it is!" He reached in and pulled out the bright-green feather that had once adorned his parrot costume. "You kept this."

"I did."

"Why?"

"Why do you think?"

"You fancied me then?"

"Way before that," Oliver said. "It might have been the lollipop. I'm a sucker for sweets."

Luca dropped his gaze, spinning the feather's shaft between his thumb and forefinger to create a green blur.

Then his eyebrows suddenly rose. "Your trainers." He bent down and picked up one of Oliver's black-and-red runners, then one of his own blue ones. "They look the same size as mine." Luca peered inside Oliver's shoe. "Yours says ten, and mine's nine-and-a-half, but North America uses a different scale, right?"

"I think so. Why?"

"Just a thought." Luca set down the shoes, then sat on the bed, still holding the feather. "I could lend you my curling shoes, if you want to throw a few stones during practice tomorrow."

Oliver could barely speak, overwhelmed at the thought. "That's...that's nice of you, but I'm okay."

"Are you?" Luca asked, his tone gentle but clearly tolerating no bullshit.

"Not really," Oliver said. "But I'm getting there, lately." He looked down at the ivory duvet beneath them, tracing the curved seam with his first two fingers. "I wish I'd had the courage to come to your place this morning. My whole day would've been better if I'd meditated, and I wouldn't have hurt your feelings."

"You didn't—" Luca stopped himself. "You did hurt my feelings. I was raging. Not just at you, but at myself for being presumptuous. But it all worked out in the end, aye?"

"This isn't the end," Oliver said. "This is just the beginning."

"Good to know I'm not a one-night snogging stand. 'Snogging' means kissing, by the way."

"I know. What I meant was, this is the beginning of difficulties. I'm your rival's coach. If anyone finds out we're together, it would be a scandal."

Luca frowned. "I get it. You've had enough of those."

"I'm thinking about our two teams. We don't want them distracted by the Loliver Affair."

"'Loliver,' I like that. 'Luliver' or 'Olica' would be a bit more balanced, but yours sounds happier." Luca gave a definitive nod. "Fine. We keep us a secret until the end of the tour. For forty-eight hours, I can pretend you don't exist."

"But then there's Nationals."

"Wheesht!" Luca put a finger against Oliver's mouth. "Don't jinx it. It's only Friday. If one of our teams goes to Nationals, we'll work out what to do about us. Until then, one moment at a time, aye?"

Oliver took his hand, working up the courage to reveal the terms of his contract. Luca would be upset, but it wasn't fair to keep him in the dark. "If Team Boyd don't win Sunday—"

"Oliver, listen. It's one thing for you to drive your own self round the bend with what-if scenarios. You're sitting in the stand." Luca held up a palm. "Not saying your job isn't important. But I'm the one out there on the ice. I need my head clear every second."

Oliver's stomach felt suddenly heavy. Luca was right. It was already too late to tell him the truth. They were already too entangled. If Luca knew he could lose Oliver by winning this tournament, his head would be anything but clear. He might not consciously choose Oliver over that trophy, but the athletic brain was a funny thing. And with a sport like curling, where a steady hand and mind were key, such a conflict could destroy Luca's performance.

"Okay. We'll ignore the future and focus on now." Oliver shifted closer. "I'm kind of an expert at that."

"Good, because I like now." Luca lifted Oliver's hand and kissed it on the knuckles. "I like now a lot."

11

Line

LINE: *The path of a moving stone. A rock with a good line is traveling the way it was intended. A rock with a bad line can be aided by strong sweepers, but is often well and truly gubbed. There's a metaphor in here somewhere.*

SATURDAY MORNING, Luca and Garen went to the rink early to meet with David and Ross and prepare for the day's three tough draws.

When they arrived, they found Team Boyd huddled near the back of the warm room, looking serious as ever. Luca gave them a vague wave without looking directly at their coach. He and Oliver had made plans to "hang out" tonight after the curling, but Luca knew he needed to avoid the dreamy Canadian in the presence of others. One look would give him away, as the mere thought of last night made Luca's face feel like a giant heart-eyes emoji.

"Wonder what magical new strategy their coach has cooked up?" Garen said as he and Luca entered the changing room.

"Something involving spreadsheets, databases, and chicken entrails, no doubt." Luca set his kit bag on the bench in front of his locker, hoping his voice sounded innocently neutral. He focused on the combination lock to hide his face from his flatmate.

"Doyle's probably got a plan to beat us," Garen said. "I heard Jack sent him film last month."

"What sort of film?" Luca asked, imagining secret spy cameras.

"Like webcasts from tournaments." Garen sat on the bench and started untying his street shoes. "Does it bother you?"

"That we're filmed? Of course not. It's the internet age. Nothing is private." Luca spun his lock's dial to reset it, having lost track of the numbers.

"So you don't care that Oliver's had his eye on your cute wee arse for weeks?"

Luca's fingers slipped on the lock. "Why would I care?"

Garen didn't reply, but Luca could feel his scrutiny. It was like standing too close to a heat lamp.

"Aww, ya wee bam," Garen said finally.

"Sorry?"

"Where were you last night after the pub?"

"I told you, I was away to the studio to meditate." Technically this was true.

"Aye, with Oliver Doyle hot on your trail. And I saw what happened when we walked in just now."

"Nothing happened just now." Luca reset his lock a second time. "We didn't even say hi."

"Exactly. After the way you two were palling about on Ailsa Craig, you should at least give a nod. But you're very loudly ignoring each other. You might as well wear matching 'I winched him' T-shirts—the ones with the wee arrows?"

"Shut it!" Luca lowered his voice to a whisper-shout. "You can't tell anyone."

"I'll never do. On one condition: You tell me everything."

"Och, fine, but only the basics, no details. Just give my head peace for a second?" He finally managed to open his locker and retrieve his curling shoes. Then he went with Garen to the back section of the dressing room, which held a pair of long blue mats for warm-ups and stretches.

The skip of Team Laing was already there, so the three of them made small talk as they jogged in place.

When Laing left, Luca asked Garen, "So how are you today? With the whole Steven situation and all."

"Steven who?"

"Mate…"

"Seriously, I'm way too focused on this competition to think about that prick. Or any other part of Steven." He stepped forward into a lunge. "So thanks for asking, but back to you and Oliver…"

Luca sighed as he pulled his right foot behind him into the dance pose, a yoga position Andrew had taught him for loosening the quads and lower back. "We hooked up at his place."

"But you were home before two." Garen took another lunging step. "Was it bad sex? Is that why you're avoiding each other?"

"No!" Luca's vehemence made him wobble on his left foot. "We're avoiding each other to hide our relationship. Jack would probably sack Oliver if he knew there was something between us."

"So it was *good* sex, then?"

Losing his balance, Luca let go of his foot. "Not that it's any of your business, but we only snogged."

"Clothes on or off?"

"On." Luca started a high-stepping march, touching his

elbows to his opposite knees. "Apart from shoes. And in his case, socks. Funny story about the socks. That's actually how we ended up—"

"So you don't know if he's cut."

"If he's cut what?"

"If he's circumcised, ya loon."

"Oh!" Luca stopped marching. "It never occurred to me. You think he could be?"

"Most Americans are, but I don't know about—hang on." Garen pulled his phone from the pocket of his tracksuit bottoms. "Siri, what's the percentage of Canadian men circumcised?"

After a long pause, Siri replied in her BBC-robot voice. "Skies are fifty percent cloudy in Ottawa tonight, decreasing to thirty percent tomorrow."

"She'll never understand our accent," Luca said.

"One day she will. Until then, I'll Google with my thumbs, like they did in Victorian times." Garen tapped on his screen for several moments. "This chart says thirty-one percent of Canadian men—but wait, which province was he born in?"

"Nova Scotia, I think. That's where he lives now." Luca had avoided Oliver's Wikipedia page, since he'd seemed so spooked at the mere mention of it.

"Ooh, the rate there's only seven percent. Two percent in Newfoundland. Those fishermen must fancy their foreskins."

"Or maybe they're just more European, being on the east coast." Luca started marching again. "What if he *is* circumcised? I've never seen one like that in person. I wouldn't know what to do with it."

"It's a penis, Luca, not an alien," Garen said, just as David and Ross entered the warm-up area.

"What's a penis?" Ross asked.

"Nothing is," Luca replied.

David gestured to Luca's crotch with his water bottle. "You needing medical attention down there?"

"It's fine," Luca said. "Everything is fine." But he knew the tightness in his voice belied his words.

As the rest of his team discussed what it would be like to curl with an injured cock and how one's delivery could be altered to accommodate such a disaster, Luca mostly tuned them out, focusing on a series of slow kicks to warm up his hamstrings.

During yesterday's games, it had been easy—or at least possible—to banish Oliver from his thoughts. But today, Luca's mind swirled with the sensations of last night, replaying memories so vivid, he could still feel those arms and taste those lips. What would it be like to curl with Oliver watching him?

Knowing Oliver had *already* been watching him for weeks, and now they were...whatever they were...it felt intrusive, like Luca had been stalked.

But this was reality now, he reminded himself as he wind-milled the last few kinks out of his shoulders. If Team Riley qualified for Nationals, they'd be observed every day by people they'd never met—maybe even people who'd ask for their autographs or want to go home with them at the end of the night. For years Luca had prepared physically and espe-cially mentally for the day he made the leap to the next level.

Now that day had arrived. He was ready.

Well, almost ready. He just needed to turn the energy between him and Oliver into a fuel instead of a distraction. Because if ignoring Oliver on the outside wasn't fooling Garen, then surely ignoring him on the inside would never fool himself.

"MISTER OLLIE, SAY 'GUARD' again."

Oliver gave the side-eye to Willow, who was sitting beside him in the stand as her father battled Team MacDougall on the ice below. "Why?"

"Just do it." She covered her mouth to suppress the giggles. "Say 'guard.'"

"How much will you pay me to say"—he paused to watch her eyes widen with anticipation—"that?"

She looked up at Gillian. "Mummy, how much have we got?"

"Willow, love, leave him be. He's trying to work."

"But he's not doing anything." Willow swung her legs, banging her heels against the bottom of her seat. "Daddy's doing everything."

"Gee, thanks," Oliver said. "I'll just go home, then, and you'll never, ever hear me say that word."

She laughed and repeated the word *word* with an exaggerated *R*. "You sound like a pirate." Willow grasped his arm and leaned her head against it. "But a nice pirate. So don't go home, okay? Ever?"

Oliver looked at her mother, who winced. "Sorry," Gillian said. "She gets attached to people very fast."

"So do I, so it's cool. She reminds me of…" Oliver cleared his throat. "She reminds me of myself at her age."

"Well, you've certainly calmed down a lot," Gillian said. "Gives me hope." She ruffled Willow's mass of cinnamon-blond hair. "I think this one needs a slice of pizza."

"Yaaaaaaaaas!" Willow vaulted out of her seat and bounced against the mesh guard overlooking the ice.

Oliver's heart seized with panic, but of course the steel barrier didn't collapse.

"Yes, definitely in need of food." Gillian stood and reached for Willow's elusive hand. "Plus this way you'll be able to focus," she told Oliver as she hurried after her daughter toward the exit. "Shall we bring you something?"

He'd been hungry, but now his stomach was in knots. "No thanks." He watched Willow nearly collide with a spectator at the top of the stairs.

Oliver took a deep breath to calm his pulse, but he couldn't block the mental image of Willow plummeting from the stand onto the cold, hard ice. Sometimes he wondered whether other people played out these disasters in their minds the way he did.

Out on Sheet E, his team were up by a point with the hammer in the seventh end over Team MacDougall. Despite their kilts winning them loads of new fans, MacDougall had had a disappointing bonspiel, coming into this game with a 1-2 record. By Oliver's calculations, a loss to Boyd would end MacDougall's chances to make tomorrow's Glasgow Open playoffs—and their already slim chance at winning the Scottish Challenger Tour.

Oliver knew he should be pleased with Boyd's performance in the round robin thus far. They'd won all three games by at least four points, and statistically they stood head and shoulders above the rest of the field. But in this game he'd noticed their confidence starting to waver for reasons he couldn't grasp. During the fourth-end break, he'd asked how they were feeling, and they'd replied with tight-lipped affirmations of *Fine* and *Good*, avoiding one another's eyes.

He sensed the pressure was getting to them. Each win brought them one step closer to the dream they'd worked so hard to reach. Oliver had to find a way to loosen them up, to remind them to have fun out there. In his experience, major competitions were won by teams with the mental toughness to *dial back* their intensity in big moments rather than ratchet it up.

Like Team Riley seemed to be doing. Their three victories had all been nail-biters won on Luca's final stone of the game. But from what Oliver had seen, they never got rattled. He wondered whether Luca's teammates were following his meditation regimen as well.

I would've killed to play for a skip like that, Oliver thought. *Someone who kept me out of my own head.*

Or maybe he just wanted to be near Luca again, to spend more hours gazing into those dancing dark eyes as the two of them talked about anything, everything, late into the night, ideally after a long session of—

Oh shit. Oliver noticed Jack looking up at him with his hands in a *T* formation, signaling a timeout. How long had he been trying to get his coach's attention?

Oliver lurched out of his seat, banging his knee against the armrest, and hurried downstairs to the rink. As he approached their sheet, his curlers were discussing the next shot.

"If we miss," Alistair was saying, "we give up one."

"But then we're still tied going into the last end with hammer. What do you think, Coach?" Jack traced the proposed path with the edge of his brush head. "I hit that guard of ours and run it back for a takeout? That'd give us three points, maybe four."

Oliver examined the house, where two of Boyd's yellow stones and three of MacDougall's reds were cluttering up the back. A lone yellow stone sat at the top of the house, but it was second shot to one of MacDougall's, the one Jack wanted to take out.

Boyd's opponents were clearly trying to force them to draw for a single point, thus giving up the hammer going into the crucial final end. It was the far easier shot, but Oliver knew it wasn't Jack's style. He tended to throw too hard for the sort of finesse draws that Luca was known for, and his keen competitive edge rarely let him back down from a challenge, even when it would be wiser to do so.

"That's a super long angle-raise takeout you're proposing," Oliver told Jack. "Ice could be tricky this late in the game." After several ends of play, a sheet often developed idiosyncrasies.

"Ali just made a hit on that side. Ice is still good there."

Jack seemed to be asking for permission rather than advice. Oliver searched the house for a safer option that would still appeal to his skip's ego. There was another takeout available, but a miss on that one risked knocking out one of Boyd's own stones and giving MacDougall an even bigger steal.

For the first time, Oliver wished a curling coach could behave more like a hockey coach so he could just tell Jack what to do. But he'd always loved the autonomy this sport offered its players. The first time his own hockey coach had yelled an order at him, Oliver had thrown down his stick and wobbled off the ice in protest over such "bossy bullshit."

Then again, Jack was thirty years old, not six. He could handle a bit of pushback.

"If it were me," Oliver said, "I'd go for the draw and take the point."

Jack blinked up at him, blue eyes wide with dismay. Then he cleared his throat. "Okay, I…guess I'll try that, then."

Crap, I've dinged his confidence.

"But I'm not you," Oliver hurried to add. "If you're fine with the risks, then go for the takeout. It's definitely doable."

Jack tugged the red cuffs of his white jacket, showing a new uncertainty. "I think I can make it."

Oliver had to build consensus behind Jack's decision. He turned to the front end. "What do you guys think? Can you sweep it past their long guard up there for the runback?"

When they nodded eagerly, game as ever, Oliver asked Alistair, "And you can call it?"

The vice looked between his coach and his skip, then gave a thumbs up. "Let's have a go."

"Great," Jack said, though his jaw shifted as he scanned the house. "Thanks, Coach."

Oliver hurried back through the warm room and up the stairs, reaching it just in time to see Jack's delivery.

As soon as the stone was released, Oliver knew it was doomed. "Way wide," he whispered.

The shooter skimmed the side of the yellow Boyd guard, which drifted harmlessly along the edge of the house, affecting absolutely nothing. Jack let out a loud curse, audible over the murmurings of the crowd.

Oliver applauded anyway. "Good try, Jack!"

The skip's eyes flashed up, then he raised his broom in acknowledgment, though he looked like he wanted to bash it against his own head. The teams were now tied 6-6, but because Boyd hadn't scored, they retained the hammer and therefore the advantage going into the final end.

Oliver looked over at Sheet A, where Team Gillespie had just taken two points in the seventh to lead Team Riley 8-7. Statistically speaking, Gillespie had a sixty percent chance of winning.

Yet Luca seemed unconcerned, an attitude shared by his teammates. They'd stuck to their game plan and kept up their banter, staying true to their "Team Smiley" reputation throughout every end.

Oliver watched Luca closely, wondering how the skip maintained such a steady equilibrium. Did he truly have no doubts in himself or his teammates? Did he simply not care about victory?

Or was his serenity a carefully crafted facade obscuring a

whirlwind of angst? What was he afraid of, other than clowns and balloons?

Oliver needed to know, and not so he could use those fears to Team Boyd's advantage. Until he understood the shadows lurking within Luca's heart—assuming the man wasn't completely shadowless—Oliver could never reveal his own.

Especially not the shadow no one else had ever seen.

———

LUCA HUMMED to himself as he wiped the bottom of the red-topped curling stone. The tune was a jingle from an old Irn-Bru advert Garen had found on YouTube. Its silliness somehow calmed him—and more importantly, helped block out the questions bombarding his mind: What if he missed? What if they lost? And less important but still insistent: Was Oliver watching?

None of the answers mattered. All that mattered was this final throw of the game. He kept his eyes fixed on the yellow pad of Garen's broom, using it as a guide to angle his entire body. *Be the line.*

Luca was still humming as he propelled himself out of the hack, dropping forward into the slide, letting gravity add momentum to his delivery. He kept humming until the instant of release.

When the rock was halfway down the sheet, he joined Garen in shouting, "Yes! Hard! Haaaarrrd!"

Ross and David furiously brushed the ice in front of the red stone to keep its path as straight as possible until it got past the guard. Luca eyed the line, visualizing the end of the rock's journey in the four-foot ring, where two of Team Gillespie's yellow stones sat side by side. For Riley to win, Luca's shooter had to roll off one yellow stone's inside edge, then strike its companion with enough force to send both flying from the house—without removing the Riley stone at the back of the twelve-foot as collateral damage.

Luca held his breath as the stone reached the second hog line. It passed the guard with an inch to spare.

"Off!" Garen shouted. David and Ross lifted their brooms.

The stone entered the house, knocked out both of Gillespie's, then spun to settle on the button.

Boom.

As Luca stood to shake hands with Team Gillespie, he noticed his knees were trembling. That was odd.

Ross and David looped their arms around Luca's shoulders and squeezed hard.

"Is it me," David said, "or are we in first place now?"

"There's still one game left. But we've started as well as we could do." Luca put his free hand in his pocket to hide its shaking. "Thanks, guys. That was a total team shot."

Ross nodded, still panting. As usual after a hard, fast sweep, his face was nearly as red as David's hair.

"Were you worried?" Garen asked as they stepped off the ice onto the catwalk. His voice echoed inside the rink, now empty but for their two teams.

"Not worried." Luca picked up his gripper and slipped it back onto his sliding foot. "Just alert to the possibilities." As he headed for the warm-room door, he saw Oliver turn away from the glass.

So he *had* been watching. Luca was glad he'd not known of his secret spectator before that last throw, or it might have affected his shot.

He stopped, only now realizing what David had said about being in first place. He looked at the Sheet E scoreboard to see that Team MacDougall had come from behind in the final two ends to beat Team Boyd.

Ooft, Jack must be fuming. Luca hoped his brother-in-law wasn't taking out his frustration on their coach. How would Oliver handle this surprise setback?

Luca shook his head hard to dispel these musings. He would spend the next hour resting his brain—and feeding his stomach, which was already growling from the smell of catered buffet wafting from the warm-room kitchen.

A tension was growing inside him, only slightly alleviated by this latest win. If Luca didn't rein in his nerves, that pressure would build to a boiling point at the worst possible time —tonight, when Team Riley would finally meet their match.

OLIVER MADE his way through the bustling warm room toward the lounge area in the back corner. He needed to collect his thoughts for the post-game meeting, which would start as soon as Team Boyd finished broomstacking with their jubilant conquerors.

Honoring his and Luca's agreement to ignore each other, he barely looked up from his tablet when Team Riley and Team Gillespie entered the warm room. (He did, of course, join the customary applause that greeted them—and every other team after a game—in keeping with the spirit of curling.) All eight curlers seemed cheery, as everyone always did when Luca was around.

Oliver's phone vibrated in his pocket. He took it out to see a text from the skip of his Nova Scotia champion women's team, Nina Patterson.

Watching Glasgow Open webcast with the whole gang here. Just saw our own Oliver on the ice at the timeout!!!

Attached to the message was a pic of the four curlers holding up their Labatt Blue bottles in salute.

He smiled as he thumbed in a reply.

It wasn't my best work, as you can see from the result.

She answered quickly.

You got this, b'y.

Nina's Cape Breton term of address gave Oliver a pang of nostalgia for last season, when he'd made the daily two-hour drive north to work with Team Patterson. It had been almost a year since anyone had called him *b'y*.

His new team appeared then, sinking one by one into the worn brown-leather cushions of the chesterfield across from him, their faces still shell-shocked.

"Thought you could one of these, Coach." Jack handed Oliver a bottle of lager, then slumped beside him on the love seat. "Sorry we let that game get away."

"Thanks for the beer," Oliver told him. "And no, *I'm* sorry. I shouldn't have undermined you in the seventh end."

"But you were right," Jack said. "The draw was the wiser shot. I knew it even as I was going for the takeout."

"And your uncertainty showed in your delivery. That's on me. I made you question your choice."

"Isn't that why you're here?" Alistair asked. "To steer us right when we're wrong?"

"During practice, maybe. But during a competition, I should step back. At most I should offer alternatives, not tell you what I'd do if I were you. You're tightly wound enough as it is."

Ian and Bruce shared a significant look, then let out simultaneous sighs.

"I cannae think straight," Ian said.

"I cannae think at all." Bruce pressed his palms to his brows. "My eyes hurt from trying to see everything at once."

"I've never wanted a drink so bad in my life," Alistair said. "This isn't even a wee bit fun."

"Fun?" Jack sat up straight. "It's not meant to be *fun*, Ali. This is serious. This is our future."

"If our future is as stressful as our present," Bruce said, "then I'm not having it."

"So what, we just give up because it's hard?" Jack pointed his can of energy drink at his front end. "Do you want to win or not?"

"Of course we want to win," Ian said. "We just want to keep our sanity while we do it." He turned to Oliver. "You've competed at much higher levels than this. How did you keep the head? What's the secret?"

"There's no secret, there's just..." Oliver searched for the right word. "Acceptance. You gotta acknowledge that this is a huge moment for you and that you feel stressed—which is totally normal, by the way. But once you've done that, shift your mind back to the thing in front of you. Focus on making that shot, not what happens if you don't make it, and definitely not what happens if you win that end or that game. Stay in the present."

"Easier said than done." Jack fiddled with the pull tab on his can of energy drink, making a repetitive *thonk*-ing noise.

Oliver sat forward. "Look, you guys did a shit-ton of work to get where you were before I came aboard. Then in the last month, you've put in a *mega*-shit-ton of work. It shows in your play. So just trust that."

Jack *thonk*ed his pull tab one last time. "You're right." He looked at his teammates. "Sorry I got so crabbit. I'm not raging at you, I'm just frustrated with myself because I want to win so bad." He pounded a fist against his knee. "I wish I could be like Luca and not care."

"Obviously he cares," Alistair said, "or he wouldn't be here. He's just got a different way of showing it."

Jack snorted. "Yeah, a way everyone loves."

"Pish," Bruce said. "Our fans love when you're pure beel-in'. People fancy a fighter."

Beelin', crabbit...somehow Oliver wasn't surprised there were so many Scots words for *angry*.

"They're right," he told Jack. "Every skip has a different style, and there's nothing wrong with yours unless it starts to affect play. Just keep talking to your teammates—and listening to them—when things get tough. You'll get each other through this."

They all nodded but looked a bit dubious.

"So what do our numbers look like?" Jack asked him, clearly looking to change the subject.

"Spectacular." Oliver picked up his tablet, but instead of showing them the figures, he closed the spreadsheet and opened his video app. "Overall this weekend, each of you is shooting over eighty percent on both hits and draws, which is phenomenal." He stopped himself from adding *for non-Canadians.* "As for the MacDougall result, shit happens. You know that. What matters is not how you got knocked down, but how you get up again. When you walk out onto that blue carpet at Nationals, nobody will be talking about the team who missed one runback angle-raise takeout at the Glasgow Open. They'll be talking about the team who does this."

He set his tablet on its stand in the center of the coffee table between them, then hit play on the video he'd made last week for just such an occasion.

"Team Boyd's Greatest Hits" was a montage of their most stunning takeouts and raises from the last two seasons, set to Franz Ferdinand's "Take Me Out."

"Oh my God, that's my favorite song." Jack moved over to the chesterfield, squeezing in between Ian and Bruce.

"I know. Gillian told me." Oliver sat back and watched his curlers come to life. Their eyes lit up, their silence turned to laughter and cheers, their bodies went from slumps to fist pumps.

As they started watching the video a second time, offering each other high fives and *gaun yersel*s after each shot, Oliver went to the bar and ordered a round of lagers from Craig, the club president and current volunteer bartender.

"I know beer's not the world's best recovery drink," Oliver said, "but they could use a little loosening up."

"Oh aye." Craig opened the four bottles and set them in front of Oliver as he spoke. "This last month, those lads have come in nearly every day to practice for hours. I think they're trying to impress you."

"Well, they're succeeding."

Craig lowered his voice. "Jack told me your job depends on Boyd winning the Tour and going to Nationals. Everyone in this club would be pure devastated to see you leave."

"Really?" Oliver looked around at the packed warm room. "Most of them don't even know me."

"They've seen the magic you've worked on Team Boyd. That pride carries over to every club that takes to the ice at Shawlands—the women's, the juniors, the seniors, even the purely social curlers. I've not felt that sort of spirit here in..." Craig looked at the wall-mounted gallery of past Shawlands greats. "Ages."

A bit dazed, Oliver returned to his team, who were watching the video for what must have been the fourth time.

"If you play like that," he told them as he handed out the beers, "then no one in this building can touch you." He pointed to Team Riley lounging at their table with their opponents, watching a televised soccer match as though this was just another bonspiel. "Not even them."

12

Heavy out of Hand

HEAVY OUT OF HAND: *When a curler knows upon release that they've thrown the rock too hard and there's nothing the sweepers can do but gnash their teeth, then lie and say, "It's all right."*

LUCA HATED how much he wanted to win this game.

The outcome of Riley vs Boyd didn't really matter, he reminded himself as they stepped off the ice for the fourth-end break, down by three points with the hammer. Thanks to the results of the other teams in their round-robin pool—none could finish better than 2-3—Riley and Boyd would take the top two spots in the standings no matter who won tonight's game.

That meant both teams would advance to tomorrow's playoff round, with the first-place team playing the other pool's second-place team in the semifinal, and vice versa. Due to the caprices of a random draw, the other pool consisted of generally weaker teams, so Luca didn't much care which one he played in the semifinal.

"Remember the game plan," he told his teammates as they

munched their mid-game snacks. "This is a chance to experiment, to work out what sort of shots and situations will rattle Team Boyd, in case we meet them in the final tomorrow night." *Like the entire world seems to expect.* "Any thoughts along those lines?"

Garen stopped peeling his banana and squinted at him. "Did you shave?"

"What? No." Luca rubbed the spot where his beard met the now-smooth part of his neck, then pulled his hand away, realizing it was a sure tell. "As I was saying—"

"You do look more tidy," David said.

Luca sighed. "I just trimmed a wee bit and cleaned up around the edges." He'd done it an hour ago, furtively, at the sink in the men's toilets.

"But we all agreed not to shave," Garen said.

"I didn't shave," Luca said. "I trimmed."

"Can I shave too?" Ross asked.

"No!" Garen turned back to Luca. "Trimming counts, mate. The good-luck magic is in every hair, like with Samson. Why did you need to trim?"

"Vanity, of course."

Garen gave him the side-eye. "Big plans tonight?"

"No plans." Luca stroked his jaw again, hoping he'd left his beard symmetrical. "Just possibilities."

"Fantastic." Garen flapped his banana skin. "We're now doomed, thanks to your 'possibilities.'"

Luca knew Garen could be right, but not for superstitious reasons. Luca's desperation to win this game was all about impressing Oliver. It was a totally understandable and utterly human reaction, but in sport, too much desire was dangerous. If Luca made his calls with the same instinct as a peacock spreading its tail feathers, he didn't deserve to be skip.

"Doubles," Ross said.

Luca blinked at the non sequitur. "Sorry?"

"We bait Boyd into trying double takeouts." Ross sipped from his squeeze bottle of protein drink. "They like the glamor shots. Maybe they'll miss under pressure."

"But if they don't miss," David said, "our stones are gone and we lose by a million."

"And then we'll know not to do that tomorrow." Luca looked at Team Boyd conferring with Oliver, their faces as intense as ever. "Good idea," he told Ross. "Let's have fun with it."

As luck would have it—"beard luck," according to Garen—Boyd did not miss. At all. Riley set up harder and harder configurations, only to watch Alistair and Jack smash out their rocks with extreme prejudice. Whatever Oliver had said after today's loss to MacDougall, it had clearly injected Team Boyd with confidence.

His tranquility dwindling with every shot, Luca managed to blank the next two ends and keep the hammer, which took Riley into the seventh and penultimate end still trailing by three points. To make matters worse, they'd spent so long discussing how to make life difficult for Boyd, their thinking-time clock was running down. If it reached zero, they'd automatically lose.

"All right, lads," Luca said as he gathered with his teammates near the hack. "It may seem like things are going pear-shaped, but we've got to stick to the game plan. If we change style now to avoid losing, we'll have learned nothing."

"Surely we're confusing them with all this chaos," Garen said. "If nothing else, it'll keep them awake tonight wondering if we've lost the plot."

"I like that. 'Chaos' on three." Luca held out his fist for a four-way bump. "One, two, three."

"Chaos!" they all shouted, crashing their fists together, them raising them into the air.

As Luca glided to the other end of the ice, his cheeks ached from forcing a grin. Chaos wasn't his style. But if it kept Team Boyd and their coach guessing, it couldn't hurt in the long term. And in the meantime, Team Riley would have a bit of fun. It wasn't all about winning, right?

For the first four stones, each team played as though the other didn't exist. David threw a pair of perfect red corner guards while Ian put two yellow stones in the house. Ross got around Bruce's slightly off-center center guard to take out both shot rocks, his shooter rolling to the front of the eight-foot behind the center guard, completely protected.

See how you *like it*, Luca thought toward his rival skip.

It was a perfect start for Team Riley—until Bruce performed a slick runback takeout, bumping Boyd's yellow center guard straight back to remove Riley's shot rock and sit straddling the line between the eight- and twelve-foot rings.

Luca gritted his teeth. Again Boyd seemed invincible. But there was no time to waste on regrets.

"Draw to the outside here behind our corner guard?" Luca asked Garen, tracing an arc through the house where he wanted the stone to travel. "It'll be hard for them to take out."

"Aye, especially since the sheet's getting pure frosty out on the wings." Garen hurried toward the hack to deliver the message to Ross and David.

As Luca set his broom for Ross to aim at, he again resisted the urge to look up into the crowd at Oliver. It was distracting enough to hear Willow singing, "C'mon, Daddy! 'Mon, Uncle Luca! Everybody win win win!" to the tune of a pop song he couldn't quite place.

Behind him, Jack murmured to Alistair, "Ice is getting a run left of center."

Was it? Luca stared at the pebbled surface ahead of him, trying to remember if Ross's last rock had hit any sort of anomaly on that side. It was hard to compare, as that had been a totally different shot curling in the opposite direction.

If Jack was right and Luca didn't move his broom to reset the line, Ross's stone would catch that dip in the ice and sail through the house without curling. If Luca did move the broom but Jack was wrong, Ross's stone could crash on their corner guard. But at least it would still be in play.

He went to move his broom, then stopped. Maybe Jack was just playing mind games with him, spouting disinformation knowing that Luca was listening. Surely Oliver wouldn't suggest such underhanded spy tactics.

Luca looked at the Team Riley clock. He'd not conferred with Garen about the ice, and there was no time to do it now. So he stayed put.

Ross came out of the hack bang on line, and his release was calm and sure.

"I don't think he heard me," Jack told Alistair.

With a sinking feeling, Luca crouched down to examine the line. "Clean only!"

"Weight's good!" David called out as Garen gently brushed the ice in front of the stone to clear any debris.

"Gotta curl!" Luca said. *Please curl. Please curl. Please please please curl.*

But it wasn't curling. Jack was right, and he'd not been playing mind games at all.

"No," Luca said. "Never."

As the stone entered the rings a hair too fast, Luca stepped aside so Jack could sweep it once it crossed the tee line, ensuring it did in fact leave the back of the house and out of play.

"Bad luck," Jack said with what sounded like sincere regret. "Been a long day for this ice."

Luca nodded, but inside he was seething. His usual mindfulness methods weren't working—recognizing his frustration just frustrated him more than ever. He wasn't used to caring so much, especially not about a meaningless game like this. How had one missed shot turned him inside out?

There was no time for reflection, as Alistair immediately drew another stone into the four-foot, about two feet behind his first one. Time for Riley to start smashing.

Unfortunately, Garen's runback takeout jammed, leaving Boyd still sitting two—which became three with Alistair's next draw to the back of the eight-foot. But then Garen promoted one of their corner guards into the back of the four-foot, a brilliant shot that brought the crowd to its feet, ringing cowbells and waving those creepy Team Riley heads.

As impressive as it was, Luca knew that at this stage of the game, a single point wasn't enough. Riley had to stay aggressive.

But Boyd didn't play along. Instead of trying to take out Garen's shot rock like Luca predicted, Jack put up a guard to block the center of the house.

Oh, now *the wild man learns a bit of discipline.*

Luca examined his options with Garen at his side and their front end listening a few feet away.

"I could try and draw in from the far left there," Luca said, "but that's the same path Ross's stone rode straight through the house."

"What about the right side?" Garen asked.

Luca looked where his vice was gesturing. He'd have to get it past three stones—their own guard and the two yellow Boyd ones at the top of the house—but he could do it with a delicate in-turn draw, *if* that part of the ice had enough curl. "When was the last time someone drew into the house from that side?"

"Alistair's second stone in the sixth end," David said. "It curled just fine."

Luca gave him a grateful smile, in awe of his lead's ability to keep up with ice conditions by mentally cataloguing every shot. "Thanks, mate. Okay, let's do this."

Less than a minute later, Luca came out of the hack, using all his strength to keep his quads engaged, holding himself steady and controlled. The moment he released the stone, that feeling of utter rightness sailed straight up his throwing arm. Sometimes this game really was magic.

He got to his feet and followed the stone, yapping along with Garen at David and Ross as they swept to keep it straight until it passed every obstacle. Then they lifted their brooms, letting the stone spin toward the button.

The rock settled onto the white circle like it had been drawn there with a magnet. Luca raised his arms and let out his loudest whoop of the season.

"Come on!" he shouted, pumping his fist and sharing high-fives with Ross and David. He didn't care there were still two stones left in the end. The relief of not being humiliated in front of Oliver was sending his adrenaline off the charts.

As he joined Garen behind the hack, Luca released a whooshing breath. "Not bad, aye?"

Garen gave a tight nod. "Look at what they're contemplating."

Luca turned to see Jack tapping his broom head against his own guard. He swept the brush back toward Riley's stones, then mimed sending them both out of the house.

"He's trying a double takeout?" Luca looked at the other side of the rings. "It'd be easier to throw the same draw I just did, to try and lie second shot."

"Ross was right." Garen crossed his arms. "Jack likes the glamor throws."

Luca could only watch, his head wanting to explode, as the Boyd skip executed his fancy runback double takeout, ridding the house of Riley's stones with a series of resounding bangs. Jack jabbed his fist into the air and yelled to the adoring crowd.

Luca turned to his vice. "We should shake now."

Garen gaped at him. "Are you off your head? Just throw another draw with your last stone. It's even easier now there's no guard on the left side."

"Then we go to the last end down two without the hammer." *That's if I make it.* "Look, it's been a long day. Everyone's shattered and this game means nothing."

"You keep saying that, but I don't believe it. And I don't think you believe it either." Garen leaned closer. "You're feart you'll miss this last shot, aren't you?"

Luca's hands formed a death grip on his broom handle. He *was* afraid. He *did* want to leave the crowd—specifically Oliver—with the memory of his spectacular draw.

But if he conceded now, Luca would leave them with the memory of a quitter. Besides, there was always the chance Boyd's infamous overconfidence would lead to a mistake Riley could capitalize on. It had happened before.

"You're right." Luca tapped his brush head where he wanted Garen to put his own. "Let's play it out."

Luca made the draw, rescuing one bittersweet point. But the eighth end went quickly, as Team Boyd shut down every Riley scoring chance with a newfound patience and precision. Jack executed one final takeout on his last stone to win the game 8-3, Riley's biggest loss of the season.

As he led his team off the ice, Luca couldn't think of a single joke to cheer them up, swamped as he was with shame.

"Sorry I almost gave up," he whispered to Garen. "Thanks for not letting me disgrace us like that."

"Och, that's what vices are for, talking skips off ledges. I don't get enough practice, thanks to your chill self." Garen poked him in the ribs with the end of his broom. "But don't ever do that again. It pure freaked me out."

Luca opened his mouth to make that promise, but no words would come.

THE BOYD-RILEY SHOWDOWN had confounded all of Oliver's predictions and formulas. Whether the two skips were trying to out-macho each other or simply entertain the crowd, from the stands it had felt more like a bullfight than a curling game.

While the teams held another awkward broomstacking, Oliver sat alone in the rink's cramped office, analyzing the results of the other matchups. They confirmed his happy hypothesis: Thanks to the relatively poor performance of Team MacDougall, Riley and Boyd were now the only teams who could earn enough points this weekend to win this season's Scottish Challenger Tour. Since they were currently tied on the Tour leaderboard, whichever team finished better tomorrow would win it all.

He reviewed the three possible outcomes:

1) If, as widely predicted, Boyd and Riley both won their semifinal games in the morning, they would meet in tomorrow night's final, with the winner taking the Glasgow Open tournament—and the Challenger Tour, with its accompanying five-figure check and trip to Nationals.

2) In the unlikely event Boyd lost their semifinal but Riley won theirs—or vice versa—whichever team progressed to the

finals would automatically win the Challenger Tour, even if they then lost that final.

3) In the *extremely* unlikely event both Boyd and Riley lost at the semifinal stage, they would play each other in tomorrow afternoon's third-place game, the winner of which would take the Challenger Tour.

Oliver decided it would be counterproductive to share these permutations with his team. If they knew they might need to win only once tomorrow, it could take the edge off their performance—and their style was nothing if not edgy.

Returning to the warm room, he was surprised to find it nearly empty. Luca was sitting alone on the chesterfield, eyes closed, listening to something on his earphones.

When Oliver sat beside him, he opened his eyes. "There you are," Luca said. "Finally."

"Where'd everyone go?"

"Pizza. Or maybe a curry. I don't know which they finally decided on." He gave Oliver a serene smile. "I wasn't hungry, and by that I mean, I didn't want to be with anyone but you."

Oliver could barely keep from kissing him then and there. But a few club members were still lingering at the bar, and though anyone with eyes probably suspected he and Luca were a thing, Oliver wanted to delay the flood of gossip as long as possible.

He pointed at Luca's feet. "If you're not too tired, and if your offer stands, I'd like to give your shoes a try."

Luca gasped. "Yes! Yes, of course." He unlaced his curling shoes and pulled them off. "By now they shouldn't be too sweaty. I'll go and tell Craig we'll be using the ice." He got up and hurried down the hall toward the dressing room.

Oliver slipped on Luca's right shoe, which was a tad tight in the toes, but not painfully so. He tied it snugly, then picked up the left shoe—the significant one, the one with the Teflon sole. He slid his foot inside, feeling like Cinderella. This one fit even better, as if meant to be.

"Okay, we're good." Luca came out of the dressing-room corridor wearing his runners. "Craig said to turn the lights off when we leave and not to exhaust myself ahead of tomorrow's semi, because the club is gagging for a Riley-Boyd final." Luca looked at Oliver's feet. "They fit?"

"Like a dream."

"What sort of dream?" Luca sidled closer, swaying his shoulders. "The good sort or the bad sort?"

"The best sort." Oliver glanced at the bar, where the remaining trio of women were still engaged in their lively debate over Scottish independence. "Sorry about tonight's game."

"Hah, no bother." Luca picked up his brush and examined the head. "We were going to the semifinals win or lose, and we'd rather play the other pool's first-place team, Crawford, than the second-place team, which you now have to play."

"Team Harrison? What's so difficult about them?"

"You'll see." Luca zipped his jacket. "Ready?"

As he followed through the door to the rink, Oliver wondered what Luca had just alluded to. Based on all available data, Harrison should have been an ideal matchup for Boyd.

Deciding for now that Luca was just messing with him, Oliver turned his mind to the moment's pressing matter: how it would feel to throw a curling stone for the first time in years.

He chose a broom from the racks on the wall, then joined Luca at Sheet C.

"Want to take a couple of practice slides before you throw?" Luca asked.

"I probably should." Oliver stepped onto the ice. "But I won't."

"Ooh, look at Doyle, diving into the deep end." Luca slipped a pair of grippers over the soles of his runners. "Shall I call the line for you?"

"Nope. No brushing either."

"Then I'll just stand back here and enjoy the view." He moved behind Oliver. "Gie it laldy!"

"Sorry?"

"Do your best. One hundred and ten percent."

"Oh. In Canada, some say 'give'r'."

"Then give'r!" Luca shouted, sounding like an Irish pirate.

The stones were lined up behind the hack to make room for tomorrow morning's ice scraping, thus putting them in easy reach. Oliver crouched down and reached for the handle of the first red stone. At the last instant, his hand stopped.

Come on, it won't bite.

As his fingers slipped beneath the handle, a lump formed in his throat. It was like taking the hand of a long-lost love.

He pulled. The stone resisted for a moment, having sat on the ice for nearly an hour, but then it slid toward him. Oliver shifted over to set the stone in front of the hack.

Now, his pre-shot routine. He tilted the rock to clean its underside and feel the running surface for its relative sharpness or dullness—unsurprisingly, it was in prime shape, which meant it should curl beautifully. Then he stood and imagined his old skip—no, imagined Luca—standing in the far house, tapping the button before placing his brush head on the tee line to aim at.

Oliver stepped into the hack and aligned his hips and shoulders with the imaginary brush. Then he crouched down to grip the stone in his right hand, tucking his broom under his left arm.

He'd expected this to feel foreign after so much time, yet it was the most natural thing in the world, as natural as breathing or laughing or—

"Erm..." Luca cleared his throat. "I know you're having a moment and all, but I should point out that in this country, we find it easier to slide without a gripper."

Oliver looked down. "Shit."

"But who am I to question the technique of a two-time Brier champion?"

Trying not to laugh, Oliver stood and pulled the rubber gripper off his sliding foot. Then he redid his pre-shot routine, more quickly this time. He inched back the stone and his sliding foot, then pressed forward with the stone, letting its momentum draw his body down and forward into the slide. At just the right millisecond, he pushed out of the hack with his back leg.

And then he was floating, perfectly balanced, like he'd never left the ice for a day, much less years. It was magic.

Until the stone left his hand. *Crap.*

It was light. Way, way light. At this speed, it wouldn't even make it past the far hog line and into play.

"Sweep!" he shouted. "Hard! Hurry hard!"

Luca didn't respond. Oliver turned to see him holding his stomach, laughing so much he made no noise at all.

Oliver jumped up to pursue the stone, slipping slightly and nearly falling on his arse. By the time he caught up with the rock, it was not only coming to a stop but also rolling off the side of the sheet in what was possibly the worst throw of his life (including his first day of curling at age seven).

That's when he started laughing, and couldn't stop. He bent over, knees weak, letting out all the day's tension in one long cackle.

"Was it worth the wait?" Luca called down the sheet.

"For sure," Oliver replied when he'd caught his breath.

"You know, this sport is a lot tougher than it looks. I thought it was all about drinking."

Luca nudged Oliver's second rock in front of the hack. "That throw might've been salvaged with the help of a competent sweeper."

"Yeah, but all I had was you."

"Oi!"

"I didn't want to defile your skip's hands with all that hard work," Oliver said as he glided toward the hack, trying not to wobble.

Luca looked at his palms. "True. They are normally reserved for finer bits of magic." He slung his brush over his shoulder. "And yet I shall make the sacrifice."

As Oliver reached for the second stone, Luca situated himself at the side of the sheet a few feet ahead of him.

"Dead beastie alert." Luca reached down and picked up what looked like a cellar spider. "They get frozen to the ceiling, then fall onto the ice when it warms up in here. Garen calls them 'roadkill.'"

Oliver was struck with the sudden, shuddering memory he could never truly steel himself against. As always, it took his breath away for a moment, but in this case it also reminded him what he'd done wrong just now: On his first throw, he'd forgotten perhaps the most crucial part of his pre-shot routine.

This time, before cleaning the rock, he touched the tattoo that lay an inch above his wrist. It was only for an instant, and through his sleeve he couldn't feel the two letters etched upon his skin. But this one tiny act put everything into place, just as it had done for six years.

"To the button," Oliver said.

This time his delivery felt sound all the way through the release.

"Weight's good," Luca said, accompanying the stone down the sheet, his brush poised above the ice.

Oliver slid past him into the house to check the line. "Yep! Sweep!"

Luca went to work, keeping an open stance with his chest facing the house so he could gauge the trajectory, perhaps not trusting Oliver's judgment.

"Hard!" Oliver shouted. "Haaaaaaard!"

Luca switched to a closed stance to get more power. Now the stone was well and truly on its way home.

"Whoa!" Oliver said, and Luca lifted his brush. The rock entered the house on course, but needed a bit more curl. "Yep! Hard!"

Luca swept again, and this time Oliver joined him. Together they paved the way for the stone to roll those last six inches onto the button, where it came to rest in the very center.

"Ya dancer!" Luca gave Oliver a hearty high-five. When their hands met in the air, they both held on, bringing their bodies together over the triumphant stone.

Their kiss felt as natural to Oliver as throwing that rock, holding this brush, and standing on this ice.

When they parted, Luca whispered, "Good throw."

"Good sweep." He noticed Luca was panting. "Did it wear you out?"

Luca laughed. "Nah." He pulled off his glove and used it to fan his reddened face. "I'm just breathless from hearing you say, 'Hard!'"

"WHEN I WAS A KID," Oliver said as they sat side by side at the empty warm-room bar, "I pretended the twelve-foot ring was radioactive, the eight-foot was full of acid, and the four-foot could, at any point, spontaneously combust."

"That would give curling a much bigger TV audience." Luca popped open the next in the series of lagers he'd retrieved from the fridge behind the bar. "What about the button? What was that made of?"

"Asbestos, of course. To protect it from the fiery four-foot."

"Oh aye, fair dos." Luca twirled about on his favorite stool —the wobbly one—remembering how he and Oliver had sat in this same exact place eight nights ago, barely knowing each other. "What do you miss most about curling in Canada?"

Oliver took a long sip while he considered. "Hanging out with my teammates, for sure."

Fer shur, Luca mimicked silently, enjoying the way the phrase made his lips work. "Specifically?"

"Sometimes during broomstackings we'd challenge our opponents to a game of Hole in the Hole. That's where we pitch Timbits into each other's mouths from across the room." He picked up his bottle and set it down a few inches to the left without drinking from it. "After each turn, the players take a step back and do it again. Whoever misses first has to buy the next round. Not to brag, but I was provincial champion three years straight."

Luca stopped twirling. "Wait—who is Tim and what were you doing with his bits?"

Oliver laughed. "Timbits are doughnut holes from Tim Hortons."

"Ahhh." Luca took a large swig, though his head was already reeling from the first two beers after a long day's curling. "I've always loved the concept of the doughnut hole. I mean, by definition a hole is a void, a lack. At the center of a doughnut is not merely nothingness—which would be sad enough—but lost potential. So a doughnut hole is like—it's like retrieving that potential and making something wonderful of it. Like a form of salvage art. Does that make sense?"

"In theory," Oliver said, "except doughnut holes aren't made from the lost doughnut middle anymore."

"Noooo! Shut your blasphemous mouth."

"Trust me, I used to work at a Timmies. The holes are made by machine using their own designated dough."

"So the very term 'doughnut hole' is a beautiful lie." Luca sighed, resting his chin in his hand. "Its irony almost makes it more poignant."

Oliver nodded slowly. "Gotta admit, I did not expect a Scotsman to have such deep thoughts on doughnuts."

"Wheesht." Luca wanted to put his finger over Oliver's lips to hush him but worried he'd poke him in the eye. "I can't help obsessing over words. It's a side effect of my day job."

"Your day job, right. So how does one come to edit medical textbooks?"

"Ah. Well." Luca took another sip of beer to fend off the sudden sobriety threatening his head. His career wasn't a pretty story, but Oliver had been frank with him about his own mistakes, so it was only fair to tell it like it was.

Mostly, anyway.

"It's a very specific vocational path," Luca said, "First one goes to university to become a doctor. Then one learns all the ways the human body can utterly fail at living. Then one gets very depressed—metaphorically, not clinically—and quits uni, but having already studied Greek and Latin and being not terribly poor with words, one answers affirmatively an email from a sympathetic lecturer who knows of a job at a medical publisher."

"That must have been a tough decision—quitting, I mean."

Luca tried to shrug instead of squirm. "What about you?"

"I was too focused on curling to think about university.

After I got banned, I took some business classes at the local college, but I didn't complete a degree or anything. So do you like your job?" he asked, thwarting Luca's attempt to change the subject.

"I don't hate it." This was the kindest thing Luca could say about his employment. "I know I'm lucky. I've got mates with master's degrees who can't find jobs. And of course I never would've kept curling competitively if I'd stayed in medical school. But my work, it's not what I'd always imagined doing. Saving lives and that."

"Is that why you teach meditation?"

Luca hesitated. "Yes, I wanted to help people in a way that didn't involve blood and disease and death. Besides, our bodies aren't really under our control. We can exercise and eat right yet still die young."

Oliver stiffened. "What's your point?"

"That our minds are more manageable."

"Hm." Oliver moved his bottle again, creating another condensation ring atop the bar. "You think we can control our own brains?"

Luca sensed skepticism. "Maybe not *control*, but definitely influence. With practice, we can learn to see our thoughts and feelings as just that—thoughts and feelings. We can stop confusing them with reality."

Oliver scoffed. "Must be nice having that kind of control— sorry, *influence*." He shifted his bottle a third time. "Not everyone does. For some of us, it's like herding tornados."

"But that just means you need it more than most. And like I said last night, sometimes the harder it is, the more powerful your mind can become." Luca relaxed again now that the subject had turned from his past vocation to his present one. "It's like exercise. For people who find it easy to focus, medita- tion is like a leisurely stroll. For those who have trouble, meditation can be more like high-intensity interval training. But who gets more fit in the end, the stroller or the HIIT man?"

"Is that really how it works?" Oliver asked with what sounded like hope.

"Aye. But it's the same as exercise—you've got to show up every day and do the work. Did you do the work this morning with that meditation app I showed you?"

"I did, believe it or not." Oliver looked pleased with himself, an expression all the cuter for its rarity. "I love how it unlocks higher levels after you finish the basic sessions. And how it gives you rewards for streaks." He shifted his beer bottle again as he spoke, twisting it after he laid it down. "It sounds silly, but that sort of thing really helps ADHDers. Few things in life are immediately gratifying enough to motivate us to do them, so we need reward systems other people don't."

"Hm." Luca was fascinated by the way Oliver's brain worked. He had a million questions, but most were probably too intrusive, so he opted for the oblique approach. "What are those few immediately gratifying things for you?"

"Sketching. Thinking about curling." He brushed his toe against Luca's shin. "Hanging out with you."

Luca felt a rush of electricity pass between them. Suddenly the warm room was more than living up to its name.

He hooked his foot under the rung of Oliver's barstool and pulled himself closer. "So I don't need to offer you a biscuit for each hour we spend together?"

"Not unless 'biscuit' is slang for this."

Oliver kissed him, deeper and more urgently than he'd done on the ice. Luca's insides flipped over and writhed with need, begging him to get this man alone and naked, pronto. He threaded his fingers through Oliver's soft waves of hair, provoking a moan that stoked the heat inside him.

Oliver's lips moved from Luca's mouth, tracing a path

toward his ear. Luca shivered, profoundly relieved he'd trimmed his beard, as the bare skin along his jawline felt more sensitive than ever for having been covered this last week.

He tilted his chin, and with slitted eyes he spied the pattern Oliver had created atop the bar with his beer bottle's condensation:

Five rings in the shape of the Olympic symbol.

Luca felt like his pericardium was peeling back from his heart, exposing it all at once to the pain of his and Oliver's lost dreams.

The front door swung open, and a voice came from the foyer.

"No, I know just where I left it," a woman called to someone outside. "It's behind the—"

Luca turned to see his sister frozen at the threshold, hand over her mouth.

"Erm…" He couldn't really say, *It's not what it looks like*, as it was exactly what it looked like.

Gillian dropped her hand. "What. The. Fuck."

Luca stood, bumping into Oliver, who was also getting to his feet. "Don't tell Jack. Not yet."

His sister groaned. "This is so wrong, lads. It's so…"

"Unprofessional," Oliver filled in. "I know. I'm sorry."

"You are?" Luca asked him.

Oliver shook his head. "Not 'sorry' as in, I wish we weren't, but 'sorry' as in, I know the circumstances are less than—"

"I'm not having it." Gillian stalked past them behind the bar, where she reached underneath and pulled out the phone she'd apparently left behind. "You don't need anyone's approval, but still, I do *not* approve."

"But you won't tell Jack?" Luca asked.

"Of course not. I want you both alive, at least until the end of this tournament." She flapped her hand. "As if things weren't complicated enough. Do you know what it's like, dividing my loyalty? Having you and Jack nipping my head about who's my favorite, like it's some sort of side competition off the ice?"

"But that's got nothing to do with—"

"If you'd just stayed with Team Boyd, all of this, even you two"—she gestured between Oliver and Luca—"would be fine." She shoved her phone into her pocket and headed for the door. "I'll see you tomorrow."

Luca followed, aware that if he kept Gillian more than a minute or two, Jack might come in looking for her.

He caught her near the door to the foyer. "Please don't be angry," he said, softly enough so Oliver couldn't hear.

"Have you lost your mind?" she hissed.

"Yes! I can't help it, Gill. I'm out of my nut over this guy. Do you know how rare it is for me to connect with someone?"

She blinked and looked away, her jaw set. "I know. Any other time, I'd be happy for you."

He gave her jacket sleeve two tiny tugs. "Or you could just be happy for me now."

Gillian sighed. "Whatever. Enjoy yourselves." She wrinkled her nose at their surroundings. "Just not here."

"Oh, like you and Jack never winched in the warm room."

She jabbed him in the chest. "Finish your drinks and clear off. If anyone else sees you two, this whole club will go up in a giant gossip bomb."

"That sounds pretty. Do you think the flames will be purple? I like purple."

"Goodnight, Luca," she said as she spun away. A moment later the front door opened, letting in a puff of cold, damp wind and a brief blare of traffic noise.

Luca turned back to Oliver. "That's my sister. She's nice."

"She loves you."

He shrugged. "That stuff about dividing her loyalty, she was just talking pish. Jack's her favorite, and I don't care."

"He's not." Oliver came closer. "I've seen the receipts."

"Sorry?" Perhaps *seen the receipts* was a Canadianism.

"After I ordered the giant heads of Team Boyd for their fans to bring to the bonspiel, Gillian ordered a set for Team Riley."

For a moment, Luca was too stunned for words. "No one told us."

"She said you might accuse her of trying to freak you out."

"They are pretty disturbing. Still, it was pure sweet of her." His mind zoomed back to what they'd been doing when Gillian had interrupted. He looked up at the wall clock. "It's getting late."

Oliver's face fell. "Yeah, you need your sleep." He emptied his bottle of beer with a swig. "We could share a cab, I guess."

"That seems logical." With his heart pounding in his throat, Luca moved forward and took Oliver's hand. "Since we're both going to your place."

13

Warm Room

WARM ROOM: *A curling rink's social area adjacent to the ice sheets. Often contains a bar, kitchen, and comfy furniture. "Warm" in more than one sense, this room is, for many curlers, a second home where one can always find a friendly face and a kind heart.*

OLIVER TRIED to steady his hand long enough to slip the keycard into his hotel-room lock. It had taken all his self-control—which had never been a deep well to begin with—not to jump Luca's bones during the interminable taxi ride from Shawlands.

But he'd managed, and not only out of courtesy to the driver, or concern for Luca's physical exhaustion after a long day of curling. Oliver was still mindful of Luca's words from last night.

"I don't want you to expect too much."

Was Luca being overly modest? It didn't seem like him. There was something more there, maybe the same something that was keeping Luca uncharacteristically silent right now.

So as soon as they'd shed their coats, and while Oliver still had the courage, he took Luca's hand.

"Listen," he said as they sat on the edge of the bed together, "I think you should take the lead here tonight. I'm totally cool with whatever you want to do. Even if what you want to do is nothing at all."

"Ah." Luca pulled back a little, scratching the side of his neck. "That was...direct."

And already Oliver had screwed up. "Sorry, I didn't mean to—"

"No, it's fine. It's good. See, I was expecting more awkward fumbling and confusing subtext before we got round to being honest." He squeezed Oliver's hand but didn't meet his eyes. "Probably a British thing."

"Right." This gave Oliver an idea. "I could make us some tea?"

Luca smirked. "One sugar, no milk."

Oliver filled the kettle and switched it on, then stood beside the fireplace. "It's pretty fast, being small and all."

"What is?"

"The kettle. It boils pretty fast."

"Ah." Luca leaned back on his hands and started swinging his legs, scuffing his feet against the hardwood floor. He seemed more amused than nervous now.

Finally he patted the bed beside him. "Sit."

Oliver obeyed, placing himself exactly where Luca had indicated.

Luca pulled in a deep breath and let it out. "So here's the thing about me and sex. See, my level of desire tends to, erm, vary." He held his hand flat, then moved it up and down like a scale. "Though so far not with you. With you it's been here since moment one." Luca reached up as far as his arm would go. "But there might be times when it's lower or, like, nonexistent, and it's got nothing to do with you or how I feel about you. It's just how I am. Just as you're...how you are."

For a moment, Oliver couldn't speak. No wonder this man accepted him for who he was. Luca knew what it was like to be different.

Then Oliver remembered Luca telling him last night how other guys had had a problem with this aspect of him. Idiots.

"That's fine," Oliver said. "No, it's more than fine, it's wonderful. It's good to be different. I mean, I know it's not always easy, but if other people don't get it, that's their problem."

"Okay." Luca produced a tiny, hopeful smile. "Cool."

Oliver wasn't sure what to say next, but he sensed Luca wanted to tell him more. Maybe he was just waiting for the right questions. "I know you're into big words and exact language and all that, so...do you have a term for, um, yourself? Not that you need to pick a label," he hurried to add.

"I don't know yet, honestly." Luca frowned. "People toss about words like 'asexual spectrum' and 'gray ace' and 'demisexual,' and I'm not sure any of them fit me precisely, but maybe I'm...somewhere in there?" He gave Oliver a cautious sideways look.

"Well, whatever you decide to call it, I'm on board."

Luca's shoulders relaxed, but he rubbed his palms against his thighs a few times before speaking again. "So, in case you were wondering, that's why I've not been very active of late. It's been ages since I met someone who turns me on enough to want to-to do something about it." His gaze fixed on Oliver's mouth. "I want to do something about you."

Every inch of Oliver's body flared with heat. *That is the sexiest thing anyone's ever said to me.* "Yeah," he managed to utter. "Me too. I want...yes. To do..." He leaned forward. "Something."

Their kiss held none of last night's casual caution. The moment their mouths met, Luca pressed forward, his slim body urging against Oliver like he could never get close enough. Oliver pulled him in tight, then tighter still when Luca moved to straddle his lap.

As Oliver lay back on the bed, drawing Luca down to stretch atop him, the kettle dinged. "Water's ready. You want some—"

"I don't need tea just now." Luca went to kiss him, then stopped. "I mean, unless you do."

"No, I really hate tea."

Luca laughed, and Oliver joined him. For a moment he relished the vibration of breath between their bodies, imagining what else besides a good chuckle could bring about that sensation, and how much stronger it would be with their clothes off.

This musing made him realize their discussion was unfinished.

"Hey," Oliver said before Luca could kiss him again. "You know that thing where you sometimes don't want to do stuff?"

"Aye, despite your vague description there, I know what you're referring to." Luca tensed. "Is it a problem?"

"Not at all. Just be sure to tell me when those times happen." He slipped his fingers into Luca's hair, smoothing his thumb over the beard at his jawline. "I'd hate for you to do something you don't want to, just to please me."

Luca's eyes softened. "Thanks. That means a lot." He leaned his head into Oliver's touch. "I promise I'll be clear with you. But to be equally clear with you now…" He shifted his hips a bit, rendering his next words unnecessary. "This is not one of those times."

Then Luca gave him a kiss that Oliver felt all the way to the base of his spine. The sensation shot out in every direction, stealing his last coherent thought.

He kept his word, letting Luca take the lead as to what they did and which clothes came off when. Luca's kiss and touch were all hunger and no hesitation.

Until he pulled down Oliver's boxer briefs.

"Oh." Luca sat back on his heels. "Oh."

Oliver lifted his head from the pillow, slightly dizzy from the rush of blood out of his brain. "Is that a good 'oh' or a bad 'oh'?"

"A surprised 'oh,'" Luca said. "I knew there was a seven percent chance, but still…"

"Chance of what?"

"That yours would be, you know, different to mine."

"You mean circumcised?"

"Yes. That." Luca kept staring. "Huh."

After a moment, Oliver said, "I promise it won't bite."

Luca tittered. "Right." He reached out and wrapped a tentative hand around it.

Oliver gasped at this first delirium-inducing touch. "Jesus…"

"Is that okay?"

"Yes. It's good." Oliver could feel every pulse point in his body throbbing at once. "Real good." The sight of Luca's face made him (almost) wish for his sketchbook to capture that look of utter fascination. "You okay?"

"Oh aye. It's softer than I expected."

"Sorry?"

"Soft like 'smooth,' I mean." Luca offered a light caress, smiling at Oliver's response. "I like it."

"The feeling is mutual." While Oliver could still think, he asked, "So what's seven percent?"

"Hm? Oh. Nova Scotia men circumcised."

"Ah." That seemed about right, based on Oliver's own experiences throughout the province. "I was born on PEI."

"Oh no." Luca pulled his hand back into his lap. "Did your mum have liver cancer?"

Oliver stared at him, certain he was hearing things. "What? No, why?"

"Usually that's what a percutaneous ethanol injection is used to treat. Or was it her thyroid? Did they not know she was pregnant?"

Oliver laughed so hard, he had to shield his mouth to avoid waking the neighbors. "PEI is Prince Edward Island. The province where I was born."

"Oh my God." Luca covered his face and sank down onto the other pillow. "Please forget I said all that."

"I will never forget. Unless…" He turned toward Luca, then took his hand and drew it back where he needed it most. "Okay, I've forgotten."

Luca continued, his strokes gaining confidence. "Forgotten what?"

Everything but this, Oliver thought, gazing into those wide, dark eyes. *Everything but you.*

LUCA HAD STOPPED DREADING the moment when his body and mind lost interest. That wasn't going to happen tonight; and even if it did, they would deal with it together. Knowing Oliver wouldn't see him as deficient—or worse, feel hurt or rejected himself—made Luca feel freer than he'd ever felt in his life.

Following the circumcision talk, they didn't say much apart from *"Can I…?"* and *"How's this, then?"* With few exceptions, these phrases were followed by variations on the theme of *YespleaseohGodyes*.

Only once did Luca nearly break the spell, when he saw the letters *ND* inked in black just above Oliver's right wrist, a tattoo previously hidden by his sleeve and even now shadowed by the brown hair of his lower arm. After the PEI misunderstanding, Luca wasn't about to guess aloud what ND might stand for (North Dakota? Nuclear Disarmament? Ooh, maybe Neurodiversity!).

He'd ask later about the letters, or maybe Oliver would offer the information. It didn't matter right now. Nothing mattered but the taste and feel of skin and breath, and the rhythmic rush of heat through every inch of their entwined bodies.

Luca had never felt so much the center of the universe as he did right now under Oliver's gorgeous green eyes. They studied his face with a steady focus, noting his reaction to every touch, their edges crinkling when he moaned or sighed at a particularly adept maneuver.

Oliver's experience in bed was evident, but not in a way Luca had often found intimidating with other men. It felt like everything Oliver did, he'd invented just for this night. Just for Luca.

And the way he asked permission for each act, in the most explicit terms possible, turned Luca on to no end. He didn't know whether Oliver was simply more enlightened than other lovers or if this was an extension of Canadian politeness, but whatever the reason, it was hot as fuck.

With Luca's consent—insistence, really—Oliver slid down, slowly, his mouth reminding Luca of all the inches of skin he possessed but routinely ignored.

He buried his hands in Oliver's hair and held on tight all the way, the soft brown strands his only anchor to the earth.

Near the end, Luca's fingers clenched so hard he worried he'd leave Oliver with a pair of conspicuous bald patches. But then he stopped worrying, stopped thinking, his mind and mouth abandoning words, then syllables, then consonants, finally uttering one long, lone vowel that seemed to rise through the ceiling and beyond the sky.

As his vision cleared enough to focus on Oliver's face appearing beside him again, Luca had but one thought: *I want to make him feel like that—tonight, and every night. Well, maybe not every night. But definitely tonight.*

So he did, with a little guidance from Oliver on the finer points. Luca briefly envied Team Boyd in having such a patient, good-humored coach. He could only imagine what strides Team Riley could make with Oliver's help.

But this envy soon passed as Luca returned his thoughts to this time and this place and this man—to the best here-and-now he'd ever had.

14

Burned

BURNED: *A rock accidentally touched while in motion, usually with a foot or broom. When one burns a stone, one is expected to confess immediately. To quote the World Curling Federation handbook: "No curler ever deliberately breaks a rule of the game or any of its traditions. But, if a curler should do so inadvertently and be aware of it, he or she is the first to divulge the breach." To quote an old Scottish proverb: "Open confession is good for the soul."*

WATCHING the firelight flicker on the ceiling, Oliver wondered whether his pulse would ever return to normal.

Beside him, Luca stretched and sighed, pulling the covers up over his bare chest. Then he began to laugh.

When he didn't stop, Oliver asked, "What's so funny?"

"A minute ago, when you were on the verge of orgasm, I pure wondered if you were going to shout, 'Oh jeez!' when you came."

"Remind me to hit you with this pillow once I can move again."

"For sure," Luca said in a bad Canadian accent. "I should

be away home now." He snuggled closer against Oliver's shoulder. "There. That's me home now."

"Good." Oliver angled his head to kiss Luca's temple. "So did I?"

"Did you what?"

"Shout, 'oh jeez!'?"

"Almost." Luca snaked an arm around Oliver's chest. "Gives me something to work for tomorrow night."

This mention of the future poked a hole in Oliver's haze of ecstatic contentment. Tomorrow night, everything could be different.

But that was tomorrow, and this was now. Oliver had never wished so hard he'd been born with decent eyesight. Then he could just fall asleep in this perfect moment without taking out his damn contact lenses.

Luca murmured against his shoulder, words that sounded like gibberish.

"Sorry, what?"

Without opening his eyes, Luca turned his head and spoke more clearly. *"Munit haec et altera vincit."*

"Wow, you're the first guy who ever spoke Latin to me in bed. I gotta say, it's pretty hot."

"It's the motto of your own Nova Scotia." Luca pulled the covers up another inch. "It means, 'One defends and the other conquers.'"

"Who's the one and the other?" Oliver asked.

"Scotland and Nova Scotia."

Oliver didn't get it. "Why would we conquer you? You're the ones who came here—I mean, who went there. Not that I'm complaining, since my grandparents are Scottish."

"Don't be so literal." Luca's arm tightened around his chest. "You've conquered me, Oliver Doyle."

"I doubt that."

"The very fact I'm in your bed proves it." Luca's eyes closed again, and his voice turned dreamy. "I'm not usually so attracted to someone I don't know well. Though we do know each other well for two people who just met. But I wanted you from the moment I saw you. Anyway, that's just not...me."

Oliver's mouth went dry with fear. "What do you think it means?"

Luca didn't answer. Oliver could feel his breath, steady and slow, against his skin.

He didn't need an explanation. It was clear from those words—and every wordless act in this room—that their connection was something extraordinary, and that Luca sensed it too. If Oliver had to leave in a few days, he could handle his own heartbreak, but he couldn't handle Luca's pain on top of it.

He lifted Luca's arm. "Before you get too cozy, I need to take out my contacts and set the alarm."

"Good idea," Luca mumbled. "Seven o'clock, please."

With a great effort, Oliver pulled away. As he put his boxer briefs and T-shirt back on, then stepped into the bathroom, he tried to cling to the fantasy to which he'd escaped these last few hours in Luca's company. But by the time he'd cleaned his contact lenses, those feelings had dissipated like fog under a hot sun, replaced with a gnawing dread.

Oliver stared himself down in the mirror as he brushed his teeth. *He needs to know.* It wasn't fair to keep Luca in the dark, not when they'd grown so close, so fast.

When he finished, Oliver went out into his room and picked up his phone from the nightstand. "You said seven o'clock, right?"

"What's wrong?"

Oliver froze. "Sorry?"

"You pulled away after I blethered on about my feelings for

you. Then just now when you were brushing your teeth, you let out one of those 'My God what have I done?' sighs."

"I did?"

"I could hear it through the door. It sounded dire."

Oliver stared down at his phone, trying to remember why he'd picked it up. "Seven o'clock, right?"

"Yes, seven o'clock!" Luca sat up. "Are you already having regrets?"

"No. Jeez, no. Just—hold on a second." Oliver set the alarm time, made sure it was toggled on, then put down the phone. "I need to tell you something."

"Oh God."

"It's not what you're thinking."

"How do you know what I'm thinking?"

"I meant, it's not about you and me and all this." Oliver switched on the bedside lamp, then slipped under the covers to sit close beside him. "I really like you."

Luca squinted into the lamp's soft glow. "But…"

"No *but. And.* I really like you, *and* that's why I want to be honest." He managed to meet Luca's eyes before taking the plunge. "If we don't win tomorrow, I'm out of a job."

Luca blinked at him. "That's definitely not what I was thinking." He sat back against the wooden headboard. "Jack will sack you if they don't win? What a prick!"

"It's not like that. Our contract was only for this tournament and the weeks leading up to it. The team needs the prize money from the Challenger Tour to keep paying me. This was always the agreement."

"I don't understand." Luca peered up at the dark television above the mantle, as if it might offer an explanation.

"I'm so sorry. I thought you knew, and by the time I realized you didn't know—"

"I can fix this!" Luca grabbed Oliver's hand. "If we win, we'll hire you directly. You can be Team Riley's coach."

"It's not that simple. My visitor's visa depends on this contract. I had to prove I could support myself while I'm here. My lawyer said Team Boyd can't transfer the contract to you or anyone else."

"Then I'll give them my share of the purse to keep you on."

"Your share is less than four thousand pounds. It's not enough."

"Then I'll convince the lads to give up their—"

"No. Luca, please." Oliver's face burned with shame. "Going begging to your teammates—Jesus, I couldn't live with myself. I came here to take Team Boyd to Nationals, and if I fail at that…honestly, I wouldn't want to show my face in Scotland again."

"Great." Luca smacked his palms against the covers. "So what, you just slink back to Canada?"

"I've had other coaching offers, from teams in the States and in Eastern Europe. Even Australia."

"Australia? That's-that's like a hundred hours from here."

"But I'd probably try to go to China, since that's where—"

"*China?!*"

"—a lot of the growth in curling is right now." Oliver knew his babbling would only make it worse, but he couldn't stop. "The Olympics'll be in Beijing in 2022, so the government is funding winter sports big time."

"Why are you telling me this?" Luca's voice was rising into another register.

"About China?"

"About you, ya knob!" Luca picked up his pillow and smacked Oliver in the chest with it.

"Would you rather I kept it a secret?"

"Yes!" He hit Oliver with the pillow again. "I'll be curling tomorrow knowing I either lose the trophy or I lose you. How could you do that to me?"

Oliver groaned. "See, this is what I wanted to avoid."

"Then why didn't you?"

"Because I needed to be honest." He felt his voice crack, the words scraping his throat. "Only I wasn't at first. I let you get close to me knowing I might have to leave in a few days. The best thing would've been to tell you right away, and now I realize the second-best thing would've been not to tell you at all. I fucked up, Luca, I fucked up again. I'm so sorry." He gripped his head, tugging at his hair. "I suck at lying, but I suck at honesty, too."

"Och, you're—I can't do this." Luca lurched out of bed and started to gather his clothes from the floor near the clown crate.

"I understand if you want to leave." Oliver felt a rising panic as he watched Luca yank on his briefs, then shove his arms into the sleeves of his blue undershirt. "But I really wish you'd stay."

Something in his voice must have betrayed the rawness inside, because Luca stopped and turned to him. "What is it?"

"What is what?"

"You sound like there's more." Luca pulled down the front of his shirt to cover his belly. "Is there something else I should know?" He pointed to Oliver's right wrist. "Like maybe what 'ND' is and why it's so important you need to touch that tattoo before you throw every stone?"

Instinctively Oliver put his hand over the initials, which seemed to flare with a sudden ache. He could tell Luca the official version, the one he'd told Heather last night, the one he'd told everyone everywhere, the one that had appeared in all the papers on that April day nearly a decade ago. It would satisfy

Luca's curiosity and gain Oliver some much-needed sympathy.

But it wouldn't explain why Oliver always cut and run when things got tough, why moving to China would be easier than facing Team Boyd if he let them down. It wouldn't explain what must be, to Luca, a bewilderingly deep well of shame.

"I've never told anyone," Oliver said. "But I'll tell you."

LUCA TOSSED ASIDE HIS TROUSERS, then climbed back under the covers, where he was met by a wave of warmth from Oliver's body. "Go on," he said softly.

Oliver took a deep breath and ran a hand through his hair, which was still mussed where Luca had clutched it. "I don't know where to start."

"Maybe at the beginning?"

"Yeah." Oliver pulled his knees up under the covers and rested his forearms upon them. "I was nine when Noah was born. I hated him at first. After all, I'd been the only child for a long time and was used to getting all the attention. Now there was this screaming baby waking me up at night, and my parents couldn't come to all my games anymore."

ND stood for Noah Doyle, then. But Luca was fairly certain that last night, Oliver had said he had no siblings.

"But once Noah got to be a toddler and actually had a personality," Oliver said, "I really loved him. He was quiet and sensitive—and like me, he was into art, only he was way more talented. We'd draw and paint and stuff together. But unlike me, he was small, and he couldn't play sports to save his life." He gave a crooked smile. "Except for Hole in the Hole—he was a champion at that. Noah was the one who named it, by the way."

"Genius."

"Yeah." Oliver's smile faded. "Anyway, he got bullied a lot."

Luca clicked his tongue. "Lads can be wee shits."

"It got so much worse after I came out. Everyone *I* knew accepted me, at least to my face. But to Noah's bullies, the fact I was gay was confirmation that he was too. They'd follow him around and ask if queerness ran in the family, and whether I was teaching him to—" He gave a quick shudder, then tugged the covers up higher over his faded red T-shirt. "The bus was the worst, because he'd be trapped for half an hour with these monsters."

"And drivers are too busy keeping the bus on the road to play referee."

Oliver wiped his nose, though he wasn't sniffling. "Anyway, Noah could tell ahead of time when a bus ride would be bad. He said he could almost smell it on those bullies—the way wolves smell fear, except it was the opposite. Like if rabbits could smell hunger, he said. So on those days, he'd call me from the pay phone at school and ask me to pick him up." He paused for another deep breath.

"Did you do it?"

"Yeah, if I wasn't working or training. I'd go rescue him. That was his word, 'rescue.' Kinda ironic, if you think about it."

Luca didn't know what he meant but assumed it would soon become clear.

"There was this one day." Oliver rubbed his throat, tugging the skin over his windpipe between his thumb and fingertips. "I'd had a heavy training session that morning and I'd been out drinking with my teammates the night before. I needed a nap, so I turned off my phone and set my alarm clock to wake me up before Noah got out of school, in case he called." Oliver glanced at Luca. "This was back before you could set your phone to Do Not Disturb with exceptions for important people. Back then, the choices were On and Off."

"And you missed his call."

Oliver nodded, swallowing hard. "So he, um...eventually he gave up on me and started walking home."

"Oh no. Your mum must have been raging." As soon as the words left Luca's mouth, they felt incongruent. Hadn't Oliver said he'd never told anyone about this? Maybe he'd been referring to a part of the story he'd not yet reached.

"Noah wouldn't tell our parents he was too scared to ride the bus home," Oliver said. "They didn't even know he was being bullied. He'd sworn me to secrecy because he knew Mom would make it worse by calling the school or the other kids' parents. And Dad..." He scoffed. "Dad would've just told him to man up."

"So did Noah grass you up?"

Oliver blinked at him. "What?"

"Did he tell your parents?"

Oliver's face contorted, then his breath jerked in, startling Luca. "I know what—" He nearly hiccuped. "I know what 'grass you up' means. And no, he couldn't tell them. Noah couldn't tell them anything...ever again."

Luca's heart and stomach seemed to swap places. "Oh my God." It all made perfect, petrifying sense now. "What happened?"

"It wasn't the truck driver's fault, they said." Oliver's eyes lost focus as he spoke, staring ahead into the glimmering fire. "On a blind curve like that, Noah should've been on the other side of the road. But he was doing what he'd been taught, which was to walk against traffic. He had his iPod in, so I guess he couldn't hear the…" He swayed a little, as though the memories were buffeting him like a gust of wind. "God, he loved that fucking iPod. He'd wanted one forever, but this was the first year people like us could afford them. He'd put those earphones in and just…bliss out. He'd just leave this world."

A sob leapt from his chest. Luca took his hand, wishing he could do something, anything more.

"The weirdest thing?" Oliver drew his wrist over his mouth. "That iPod was totally undamaged. The coroner's office gave it back to us later. I tried to listen to it. I knew it was totally masochistic, but I wanted to see which song he was hearing when—" His breathing turned short and shallow. "Of course the battery was dead. Which meant any of the songs could have been his last. So I hate them all, but I listened to that playlist over and over, wondering. I still play it every year on the day it happened, and on his birthday." Oliver's voice broke. "He would've been twenty years old next month."

"Christ…" Luca wanted to pull him close but sensed he'd be pushed away. "I'm so sorry. You poor thing."

"Me?" Oliver practically spat. "*I'm* not the poor thing. I'm not the one who died because his stupid brother forgot to hit an alarm switch."

"That's not why he died." Luca tried to steady his voice. "He died because he did something unsafe."

"Because I wasn't there for him. I promised I'd *keep* him safe, and I failed."

"You were exhausted."

"Everyone else can be exhausted without killing their—" He yanked his hand out of Luca's and shoved his palms against his eyes. "I woke up later—a lot later—when our land-line rung. I heard my mom answer it. She started screaming And I knew. I knew before she even told me, before I turned on my cell phone and heard his voicemail."

Oh God. Luca's eyes grew hot with tears. He could never have survived the horror of that moment, which Oliver must have relived a thousand times since. "And you've never told anyone?"

"No one ever knew." Oliver lowered his hands and took a moment to collect himself. "I'd always pick him up at this little park around the corner—out of sight of the school, you know? He was scared a teacher would see us and tell our mom." His lips twitched. "Sometimes we'd pretend we were spies."

Luca risked a soft touch on Oliver's shoulder. "It sounds like you were a brilliant brother."

"I tried to be." He coughed away the rasp in his voice. "I did the best I could, but it wasn't good enough. That's when I finally faced the fact there was something seriously wrong with me."

"There's nothing wrong with you."

"There is. There was. There is." Oliver snorted. "You know, some people with ADHD actually call it a blessing? A superpower, even? They're so fucking delusional." He swiped his thumbs over his glistening eyes. "Or maybe they're just lucky. Maybe no one they love ever got hurt because of them."

"Look at me." Luca took Oliver's chin and turned it toward him. "Anyone could forget to switch on an alarm."

"I know that." The furrows in Oliver's brow softened as he looked at Luca. "But it wasn't just that day. My whole life up to that point was a series of forgotten things. One time, the year before Noah died, I forgot my dad was having surgery. I was in Thunder Bay for a bonspiel. It was a minor procedure, so he said I didn't need to be with him, but I didn't even call the night before to wish him good luck, because I totally fucking forgot. My mom had to phone me that morning from the hospital to remind me."

Luca didn't know what to say. He couldn't imagine something like that slipping his mind.

"It was like people who weren't in front of me didn't even exist. I would still be like that if I hadn't gotten help. It took someone with a Ph.D. to teach me how to remind myself I'm not the only person in the world. And it doesn't always work. I mean, here I am telling you about my dead brother and somehow making it all about me. Nice superpower, eh?"

Luca chose to ignore this bit of self-flagellation. "When you say you got help, you mean like therapy and all?"

"Therapy, medication, a million tools and strategies to help me remember things." He gestured to the pair of jotters on the bedside table, then the neon-yellow sticky notes arrayed around the room. "My psychologist and psychiatrist, they changed my life. They *saved* my life."

Luca felt a swell of awe within him. It must have shown on his face, because Oliver asked, "Why are you looking at me like that?"

"Because you're amazing. Listen." He took hold of Oliver's shoulders. "Those doctors didn't save you. *You* saved you. You could've disintegrated, and no one would've blamed you after what happened to Noah. But you saw something was wrong and you made it right. That's the best way to honor his memory."

"I shouldn't *have* to honor his memory." Oliver's voice rose. "He shouldn't *be* a memory. He should be a man. He should be *here*."

"Aye, he should be." Luca pressed his forehead to Oliver's, trying to calm him. "But he's not. And you are. You deserve to live without punishing yourself."

"What do you mean, punishing myself?"

"You could've gone back to the ice after your suspension. You could've told your story and formed a new team." Luca pulled back to look at him. "Now I understand why you didn't even try."

"Because of Noah?"

Luca nodded, expecting pushback against his armchair psychology.

"Losing a curling career is nothing compared to losing a brother." Oliver massaged the tattoo above his wrist. "But getting banned, yeah, it was like a reminder that I was the worst person in the world, that even the best medical treatment couldn't keep me from being a total failure."

"'Total failure'? My God, Oliver, you've stood atop the podium at a world championship."

"That was a long time ago, in juniors. Before Noah died."

"And then years after he died, you won the Brier." Luca poked him. "Go on, try and minimize that feat. You weren't skip, after all, and you'd a home advantage because it was held in Halifax. It doesn't count, does it?"

Oliver looked away without protesting.

"What about the next Brier, two years later?" Luca asked. "How many medals do you need to stop telling yourself you're a piece of shit?"

Oliver covered his face, and the rasp of his breath broke Luca's heart.

"I'm sorry," Luca whispered. "I shouldn't—"

"You're right, I'm not a *total* failure. But it doesn't matter now. I made my choices, and I can't go back. You saw me out there on the ice tonight. I've lost whatever talent I once had."

"Are you daft?" Luca immediately regretted using that word, but pressed on. "After years without throwing a single stone, you put one on the button on your second try. What I saw on the ice tonight was a curling genius who just needs a wee bit of practice and a great bit of courage."

Oliver frowned, no doubt resenting being called a coward, but not denying it.

"You thought quitting was a punishment to yourself," Luca said, "but what about the rest of us? What did the sport lose when you stopped playing?"

"It lost a good curler. But maybe it gained a decent coach." Oliver shook his head. "I won't fake regrets I don't have. If I'd never quit playing, I wouldn't be here with you."

"You're here *now*, and I'm glad. But to hear you talk of moving on to China when you've not even been sacked yet—it makes me want to shake you so hard you forget your own name."

"You don't understand."

"No, I don't. I'm not you. I only understand what *I* want." He bumped his shoulder against Oliver's. "Which is to be with you, by the way."

"You barely know me."

"Well, now you're really talking pish. I know you miles better than 'barely.' You've just told me your deepest, darkest secret."

Oliver's eyes softened. "And yet you're still here."

"More than ever." Luca reached out and pulled him close. A moment later, Oliver wrapped his long, strong arms around him, as tightly as a drowning man with a piece of driftwood. Luca wished he could go back in time and comfort the nine-teen-year-old Oliver as the loss of Noah nearly pulled him under.

When their embrace finally eased, Luca risked a wee bit of levity. "So just to confirm...that *was* your deepest, darkest secret, right?"

Oliver tilted his head toward the crate in the corner. "You mean other than the carefully preserved corpse of the last guy who told me he hated clowns?"

Luca's fist tightened on Oliver's shirt. "On second thought, you *are* the worst person in the world."

Oliver almost laughed, but then his face grew pained again. "What are we going to do about tomorrow?"

A fair question. How would Luca be able to curl knowing that winning could tear them apart, perhaps even sending Oliver into a fresh spiral of grief?

"Tomorrow will see to itself. It can't help it." Luca slid down to rest his head on the pillow. "All I know—all I need to know—is that tonight I'm sleeping in your arms." He shut his eyes, then opened them again. "But if you could be so kind as to lock that crate…"

15

Flash

FLASH: *When a stone passes through the house, completely missing its target. Probably named for the feeling of one's life flashing before one's eyes as it occurs.*

OLIVER HAD NEVER FELT SO raw, or so alive.

Last night's emotional tsunami had left behind an almost eerie stillness within him, the likes of which he'd never experienced. The effects lingered now as he sat in the stand watching Team Boyd approach the end of their semifinal game. Neither the biting cold of the rink's air nor the raucous cheers of hungover fans enjoying a Sunday morning hair of the dog could breach the warm, quiet place inside of him.

Luca knew it all now, every stupid, senseless act of Oliver's life—the major ones, anyway—and he still wanted to be with him. Maybe in time Luca's acceptance would prove contagious, and Oliver could make peace with what had happened to Noah. It was either that or continue to let his past devour his present and future.

"Kevin, love, maybe shift to your left a wee bit so you can

get a better angle on Sheet D?" Heather said into her comm. "Cheers." She switched it off and looked at Oliver. "I don't think he realized this was the final shot of the game."

"Hopefully." Oliver rubbed his breastbone to ease the ache brought on by his thoughts of Noah. "There's no likely scenario for a tie to send it into extra ends. Either Jack makes this draw to win, or he misses it to lose."

Team Boyd were up by one with the hammer. They'd tried to blank this final end, but as Luca had hinted last night, Team Harrison had been tough to put away. With one red stone on each side of the twelve-foot, Harrison had made a double takeout impossible. Even a single takeout risked leaving the shooter either lying second or rolling out, resulting in a tie.

Jack shouldn't miss. He'd been practicing his draws for weeks, and this wasn't a finesse shot—there were no guards in the way, and he only had to get it to the eight-foot ring.

That didn't mean he *wouldn't* miss. The mind did funny things under pressure.

While he waited for Jack to get into the hack, Oliver peered over at Sheet B to see Luca's opposing skip, Dougie Crawford, throwing his last rock of the eighth and probably final end. The score there was tied, but Team Riley had the hammer. Crawford had done everything they could to steal a point, but now their best hope was to draw to the four-foot behind their center guard and force Luca to make a hit to score.

Crawford drew back, then delivered. As he watched the release, Oliver knew the throw was too heavy. Not only would it go too far, but it wouldn't curl enough to hide behind the center guard.

Sure enough, Crawford's stone drifted to the back of the eight-foot ring, completely exposed. Luca now had a choice of two straightforward shots for his final throw: a draw to the four-foot or a hit-and-stay. Most curlers would have found the hit easier, but Luca always seemed to prefer a draw. Oliver couldn't help smiling at the image of Luca as a tightrope walker saying, "No thanks" to a net beneath him.

Tonight's much-anticipated Riley/Boyd final was nearly a reality.

"Here we go." Heather clutched the edge of her notebook as Jack got into place.

Oliver tried not to hold his breath, then remembered nothing bad would happen if he did. He wasn't the one settling into the hack to make the shot that would take him one step closer to his dream. It just felt like he was.

Jack's delivery and release were smooth as melted butter. The weight looked perfect. The line looked perfect. Ian and Bruce probably wouldn't even need to sweep.

Oh Jack, I'm so fucking proud of you right now. The Boyd skip could have chosen to finish with the riskier, more viscerally satisfying hit, but after all these weeks, Oliver's message had finally gotten through.

He stood up, ready to cheer. The yellow stone kept gliding down the ice, its handle merrily rotating—

Wait. Oliver rubbed his eyes, hoping he was seeing things, that the handle hadn't started turning the other way.

"Oh my God," said a Team Boyd fan behind Heather. "Was that a pick?"

Oliver opened his eyes to see Jack drop his broom and cover his face, unable to watch as the stone veered drunkenly off course, bounced against a corner guard, then came to rest on the edge of the empty adjacent sheet.

"Kevin, are you getting this? No, I've no idea what just happened. Hold on." Heather stood and touched Oliver's arm. "Coach?"

He couldn't reply. He could only watch his new life fade before his eyes. This job, this city, this man he was falling for…

"It was a pick," said the fan behind them, a middle-aged woman with a pink tartan blanket covering her lap. "That's when the rock hits a piece of debris on the ice."

"I don't see any debris," Heather said.

Oliver covered his mouth to hold in a groan of anguish. How could this happen? He'd seen Bruce and Ian clean the throwing path with their brooms before Jack's shot. Whatever the rock picked on must have dropped onto the sheet in the last half minute.

"Could be a hair or maybe some lint," the fan said. "Happens all the time, but och, on a final throw? That's some cruel fucking fate, so it is."

"So now what?" Heather's voice pitched up as Team Boyd started shaking their opponents' hands. "It's over? He can't redo it?"

"Nah, it's got to count." Pink-tartan lady sighed. "That's curling for you."

"You're joking!" Heather's ponytail lashed the air as she looked back and forth between Oliver and the ice. "They lose everything because of a piece of lint? What kind of sick sport is this?"

Heather continued to rant, wondering why anybody would play this game if something so small and random could alter one's destiny.

Oliver envied her innocence. His whole life had been a series of small mistakes and stupidities, which, when combined with accidental acts by an indifferent universe, created life-shattering disasters.

Down on the ice, Bruce bent over to peer at the spot where the stone had gone off course. He reached down and picked up something Oliver couldn't see.

"What was it?" Jack called to his second.

Bruce held up the invisible object. "Dead spider!"

THE CROWD'S sudden silence broke through Luca's titanium concentration as he headed toward the hack to throw his final stone. He'd been glancing at Team Boyd's scoreboard and knew they were leading with the hammer in the final end. But those sounds from the fans were the opposite of the roar he'd expected.

He stopped beside David and Ross, who were staring over at Sheet D.

"Holy balls," David said.

Luca turned to see handshakes being exchanged. The game was over. All eight players looked shell-shocked as the crowd offered a polite round of soft applause. "What happened?"

"Boyd lost," Ross said. "I heard someone say 'pick.'"

"Lads!" Garen was gliding down the ice toward them, his hair floating off his shoulders in the breeze he created. "Not to pressure anyone, but we've got ninety seconds on our clock. Also, if we make this draw, we win the Challenger Tour." He held up a hand. "But again, no pressure."

Luca continued toward the hack, his head spinning. He'd expected the Moment of Truth (always capitalized in his head) to come during tonight's final, not this morning's semifinal. He wasn't ready.

But he had to be. He had to treat this like any other shot in any other bonspiel. How many times had he made a draw to win an event? He carried perfect weight in his back pocket, as Oliver would say.

He stopped short.

Oliver.

If Luca made this shot, his team would be guaranteed to finish ahead of Boyd in the Glasgow Open, thereby winning this season's Scottish Challenger Tour before they'd even played in tonight's final.

Then Team Riley would go to Nationals. And Oliver would go away.

If Luca missed and lost the game...honestly, he wasn't sure whether Boyd or Riley would win the Challenger Tour. The teams had had identical records coming into the final event this weekend. To break the tie, the Tour officials would use a complicated collection of shot statistics, which meant Boyd would probably prevail.

But what about the third-place game this afternoon? If Riley and Boyd played each other then, surely that result would decide the Tour.

Luca shook his head as he approached the hack. None of those contingencies mattered if he made this shot. With Crawford sitting two stones, one at the back of the eight-foot ring and the other on the far left of the twelve-foot, Luca just needed to make a clean draw to the four-foot. On any normal day, he could do it in his sleep.

"Go light," Ross told him as he and David got into position. "We'll get it there."

Luca looked at his front end. Had he forgotten to mention the pro-side error for this shot, that it was better for him to throw light and let his sweepers extend the journey rather than throw heavy and send it through the house? Good thing his team had his back.

"You're not too tired just now?" he asked them with an attempt at a smile.

"Nah, we live to sweep, man." David gave Ross a fist bump. "We live to sweep."

Luca crouched down and cleaned the rock, desperate for the head-clearing power of his pre-shot ritual. A quick peek at their clock showed thirty seconds remaining—plenty of time to start his throw, but not enough time to contemplate all the possibilities, permutations, and consequences. Perhaps that was for the best.

Just make the shot, Luca told himself as he stepped into the hack and positioned himself to face Garen's broom. *No need to think*. With a single long, deep breath, his mind went quiet and calm. As always.

But as he slipped his fingers beneath the stone's red handle, Luca's eyes betrayed him. He looked up into the crowd—only for an instant, but long enough to see Oliver sitting forward, elbows on his knees, palms pressed to his nose and mouth, watching the man who held his fate in his hands.

Luca looked down at those hands, noticing how cold they'd grown. Returning his gaze to Garen's broom, he lifted his hips, drew back, then launched into his delivery.

The moment he was out of the hack, he knew the weight was far too much for a draw. He dropped the knee of his trailing leg to slow himself down, but did it too hard, skewing his body and the angle of his throw.

As he released, Luca tried to push the rock back in the correct direction—a totally amateur move. "Heavy out of hand," he called out, not that David and Ross couldn't tell by the sheer speed at which the stone was traveling.

At the other end of the sheet, Garen started to spread his arms in confusion. Then his shoulders dropped. "No, never," he called to the sweepers, who were already holding their brooms waist high, knowing there was nothing they could do, short of developing spontaneous superpowers that would let them slow the rock with their minds.

Then Garen lifted his arms. "We can hit this one out!" He set his broom in front of the nearest yellow stone. "Sweep, lads! Hard! Haaaaaaard!"

David and Ross ran to get in front of the stone, then brushed like fiends, shuffling sideways to match its pace.

Luca saw Garen's new call. Yes, they could take out Crawford's stone at the back of the eight-foot. If the shooter struck it on the nose and didn't move an inch, it would sit close enough to score.

Luca held his breath as Garen's voice crescendoed and cracked. Was it possible he'd screwed up the shot yet still won? Was the Challenger Tour trophy and a trip to Nationals still within reach?

Was Oliver about to be sacked?

Luca's stone knocked into Crawford's, but on the edge. Both rocks spun out of the back of the house, leaving behind the single yellow in the twelve-foot. Crawford had won by one point.

Garen held out a congratulatory hand to his stunned counterpart. The crowd above fell dead quiet once again.

In the silence, Luca heard something inside him scream.

He stood, knees aching, and approached Dougie Crawford. "Good luck tonight," he told his fellow skip, who could only manage an awed "Cheers" as the moment hit him. Over on Sheet B, Team Harrison were milling about looking similarly shocked. The two underdogs would meet in the tournament final tonight, with Boyd and Riley mere spectators.

After the handshakes, Luca joined his teammates behind the house. "Lads, I'm so sorry. I don't know what went wrong."

"Adrenaline," David said with a shrug.

"Happens to everyone in the big moments," Ross added.

Not to me, Luca thought as Garen gave him a wordless hug. Usually before a high-pressure shot, he would assess his breathing and pulse so he could adjust his delivery to compensate for the adrenaline. Had he done that check before this shot?

Luca couldn't remember. All he could remember thinking about was Oliver receding down the overseas-flights corridor at Glasgow International Airport.

This had been no ordinary miss. This had come from that deep, dark place within him where fear alone resided.

LUCA SPENT the broomstacking in a daze. Team Crawford insisted on buying doubles, seeming almost apologetic about beating them. Then the victors wished Team Riley good luck before convening their own strategy session ahead of that evening's final.

"Again, I am so sorry," Luca told his team the moment they were alone at their table.

"We could've salvaged that shot," Garen said as he scooted over into the chair beside Luca, "if only I'd seen that hit sooner and had them sweeping straight off. My bad."

"*I* should've seen the hit," Luca said. "It should've been Plan B. Maybe even Plan A."

"Nah." David dropped his burly frame into the chair across from him, then grabbed the bowl of crisps the volunteers had set out. "You're more likely to miss a hit than a draw."

Beside him, Ross nodded. "And if a hit had rolled even a wee bit outside, they would've had shot rock anyway. The draw was definitely the right call."

"Maybe." Luca didn't like to second-guess himself. It was best to leave a poor shot in the past where it belonged.

But every time he blinked, he saw his red stone spinning out of the house again. Team Riley's dream had been within their grasp, and Luca had literally thrown it away.

"Forget it." David waved his hand at the air between them. "Gotta focus on the third-place game against Boyd now. Winner gets the Challenger Tour title and goes to Nationals, right?"

Luca nodded. "According to Craig." The club president had just stopped by their table and Boyd's, trying to ease his teams' disappointment with this fact. "Crawford and Harrison were in sixth and seventh place on the Tour leaderboard coming into this bonspiel. Neither of them can win the whole Tour by winning tonight's final, so it's still down to us and Boyd."

Garen snorted. "Weird how the third-place game will mean more than the final." He reached across the table and took a handful of crisps from the bowl. "Big picture-wise, at least," he added as he crunched.

"Yes." Luca swallowed hard. "Which is why I think you should be skip."

They all stared at him.

"Mmph-hmph?" Garen said, his mouth full.

"I can still throw fourth if you want," Luca told him, "but you should decide our strategy and call the line."

"Whatever the fuck for?" David asked.

"After that last throw, I don't trust myself to make the right choices."

"How not?" Ross said. "Aye, you bottled that throw, but it could happen to anyone. It's not like you did it on purpose."

When Luca didn't respond, his teammates sucked in a collective breath.

"What are you saying?" David lowered his voice to a whisper. "You lost the game on purpose? Were you betting on Team Boyd?"

"No! And I didn't lose on purpose, at least not consciously." Luca rubbed behind his ear, wondering whether even that was true. "But maybe subconsciously."

"Because Jack's your family?" Ross asked. "That's taking the brotherly love thing a bit too—"

"It's not Jack, it's Oliver." Garen kept his eyes on Luca. "Isn't it?"

"Ahhh." David sat back and stroked his beard. "*L'Affaire Canadienne.* It all makes sense now."

Luca looked at his lead. "You knew too?"

"Knew what?" Ross asked.

"Luca, you and Oliver are an open secret." David spread his hands to encompass the warm room. "Everybody knows." He patted Ross's shoulder. "Apart from this one, apparently."

"I've no aversion to beating Oliver *or* Jack," Luca said, "but that coaching contract is contingent on them winning the Scottish Challenger Tour and going to Nationals. So if we beat Team Boyd today, then Oliver's gone." He set his fists on the table, feeling more resolute with every word. "I can't be trusted with that power."

"Right." Garen pushed back his chair and stood up. "Front-end conference, lads." He beckoned David and Ross to follow him to the bar.

Luca contemplated the bowl of crisps in front of him, then shoved it away, feeling sick and hungry at the same time. How had his inner and outer life gone so topsy-turvy in one short week? The answer was clear.

"Hey," came a soft voice.

The answer was also standing right beside him.

"Hey." Luca gestured to Oliver to take the seat across the table. "Sorry about your semifinal. Brutal time for a pick."

"Yeah, really bad luck there." He sank into the chair with a sigh. "What happened with your draw?"

"What happened was me not being able to get you sacked."

"God...." Oliver pressed his palms to his temple, then dragged them down his cheeks, leaving them flushed in streaks. "This is exactly what I was afraid of."

"I thought I could put it out of my head, or at least not worry about it until the final. But then Jack lost and suddenly there was no time to think. I didn't mean to miss, I swear. I guess something in me just couldn't do it."

"I'm so sorry I told you."

Luca shook his head. "It's good you were honest. If I'd found out from someone else, I would've been raging you'd not told me, and that would've affected my performance. Or worse, if I'd found out after we'd won that I'd unknowingly snuffed out your job..." Och, the thought was unbearable. "The fact is, you and I can't control your circumstances. All I can do is try and have the smallest influence possible. That's why I've asked Garen to skip."

"And Garen says no."

Luca turned to see his vice, with David and Ross flanking him.

"I won't do it." Garen sat on the table and put his feet on the chair beside Luca's. "I *could* do it, and I'd probably be brilliant. But you're the one who got us here, and you're the one who'll take us to the bitter end."

"But how can you trust me after what I just did?"

"Mate." Ross leaned in on Luca's other side. "You trusted *us* when you put us in your team last year. We were a sorry bunch of pretenders, but you wanted us anyway. So it's our turn to have faith in you."

"Lads, I can't—"

"You will." David put a firm hand on Luca's shoulder. "Or we'll forfeit."

Luca looked across the table at Oliver, who stood quickly and said, "I'll leave you guys alone." He met Luca's eyes. "See you later, either way?"

Luca opened his mouth to say yes, but the word stuck in his throat. After what had just happened, it was obvious where his loyalty belonged. There was only one way to give his teammates the single-minded skip they deserved.

"No," he told Oliver. "I can't see you anymore." Luca's jaw trembled as every cell in his body rebelled against the sentence he'd just uttered. "I'm sorry."

Oliver stared at him, his eyes growing wider with each rapid blink. Then he turned and walked away.

"What just happened?" Garen slapped the table top. "Did you just break up with him?"

"I think so," Luca said in a small voice.

"I don't get it!" Garen made claws with his hands as though ready to strangle Luca. "You finally find a nice guy— and I know how hard that is, because I'm *not* a nice guy and neither are my boyfriends—and you just shove him away because of one bad shot?"

"It's all I could think to do." Luca felt close to hyperventilating. "I've got to clear my head."

"I don't know, man," David said. "It feels like a 'shoot the hostage, take them out of the equation' maneuver, but whatever works, I guess."

It's not working, Luca thought as he watched Oliver stride into the foyer and out the front door. All at once he felt a gaping void open up inside him, telling him he'd just made the most massive mistake of his life.

THE COLD AIR was a welcome antidote to the heat in Oliver's eyes. He paced in front of the rink entrance, resisting the urge to run to the next street and hail a taxi to the airport.

Instead he dialed his voicemail.

"You have one saved message. To—"

-Beep!-

"First saved message, received—"

-Beep!-

The front door opened with a jingle of sleigh bell, revealing Jack Boyd.

Oliver turned away from his skip, the phone still at his ear. "I just need a minute."

"Okay," Jack said, but he didn't go back inside. He simply put his hands in his jacket pockets and started rocking on his heels.

"Agent O, this is Agent N," said Noah's long-lost voice. "Jeez, that sounds so—"

Oliver hung up. "What do you want, Jack?"

"Just wondering what you were chatting to Team Riley about."

"Nothing much," Oliver said, though he wanted to scream *None of your fucking business!* "Just commiserating on our losses."

"Hmm." Jack rocked twice more before speaking again. "I'm not brain-dead, Coach. It's obvious you and Luca are...something."

"Shit." Oliver slumped onto the bench beside the front door. "Does everyone on the team know?"

"They've not mentioned it to me, but they've probably figured it out."

"I must really suck at hiding my feelings."

"Well, you're not British, so you've no formal training."

"Eh?"

"Our primary schools teach a mandatory course in repression. The 'Stuff it Down and Carry On' initiative, it's called. Quite successful, by all accounts."

Oliver realized Jack was joking. "It's over now, anyway, me and Luca. At least I think it is. It should be. It was stupid to get involved with him knowing my gig here was temporary."

"These things happen." Jack stepped on a dead leaf, then shifted it back and forth against the pavement, making a scratching noise. "Passions run high in the pressure-cooker world of bonspiels," he said with no trace of irony. "That's how Gillian and I met, back in juniors."

Oliver had heard the story four times, twice from each of them. Gillian and Jack had been the classic curling couple, hooking up at successive events and eventually making it a permanent thing.

Jack sat beside Oliver on the bench. "You know I'd give anything to let you keep coaching us, no matter what happens today. Gill feels that way too. She said you could stay with us to save money on board and lodging. I should warn you, though, there'd be babysitting duties involved."

"That's not the problem. I adore Willow. But without a salary, I can't make ends meet."

"I get it," Jack said. "You could make a fortune coaching in Asia."

"Not a fortune, but at least a living, doing what I love and what I'm best at." *Or what I thought I was best at.*

The front door opened again. Willow ran out ahead of Gillian, arms held high.

"Mister Ollie!" She planted herself on the bench between him and her father, then peered up at Oliver's face. "Are you sad cos Daddy lost?"

There was no point in lying to the kid. "A little. Are you sad?"

"Noooooo!" She punched the air with both fists, arms spread like a cheerleader. "Mummy says he can still win even though he lost." Willow stopped, then put a finger to her lower lip. "I don't know how."

"It is confusing," Oliver said. "You know how a curling team can lose an end but still go on to win the game?" When Willow nodded, he said, "It's a little like that, only bigger."

Willow looked to her dad for confirmation, then asked, "Can Uncle Luca win too?"

"No, lass, we can't both win today." Jack tucked his daughter's hair behind her ear. "But we can all do our best, play fair, and have fun. That's what matters most, right?"

Willow wrinkled her nose, then looked over her shoulder at Gillian. "Mummy, Daddy's talking pish!"

Oliver laughed, though he knew he shouldn't. "On that note." He stood and beckoned Jack to join him. "Let's go strategize."

16

Out of Stones

OUT OF STONES: *A hopeless situation in which the trailing team's number of stones left to throw is less than the deficit between the two teams. With a comeback now arithmetically impossible, the game ends in handshakes of concession. It's the decent thing to do.*

"I THINK we're in serious trouble."

Luca looked at his vice in disbelief. "What are you talking about?" Team Riley were playing the game of their lives. They'd just stolen a point for the second end in a row to lead Boyd 3-2 at the fourth-end break. The crowd was totally on their side, partly due to their play and partly due to the presence of a certain aristocrat leading their chants. Seeing his newly fragile meditation student Lord Andrew out and about in public had placed a warming balm on Luca's broken heart.

Garen fidgeted with the hem of his blue-and-black shirt and frowned at the sheet behind them. "I'm pure worried about the ice."

"What's wrong with it?" Luca's pulse sped up as he looked

at David and Ross. Had he missed an anomaly that could thwart his flawless draws?

"I've just got this bad feeling," Garen said. "Like it's going to melt the moment we step onto it."

"Why?" Luca wanted to shake the answer out of his flatmate.

"Because we're on firrrrrre!" Garen howled at the ceiling, then licked his finger and made a sizzling noise as he swiped it over all of them.

Luca laughed so hard with relief, he felt a twinge within his ribcage. "I will kill you later in your sleep."

"Not if we kill him now while he's awake." David shook his broom at Garen. "Ya wee bam."

"I thought we could do with a bit of loosening up." Garen rolled his shoulders, then regarded his banana with unease. "My stomach's been in knots since the first rock. Thought I was gonnae boak all over Jack's shoes during the pre-game handshakes."

"Me too," Ross said. "I literally can't wait for this to be over."

The fact that Luca couldn't bother lecturing Ross on the literal meaning of the word *literally* worried him. Apart from Garen's fire joke, their team had been dead serious throughout this entire game. And they were winning. Maybe the "Team Smiley" approach had undermined their potential all along. Maybe they should raise their intensity every day.

Or maybe this game was an exception, when no rules of the universe applied.

Luca decided to save the philosophy for later and focus on the four ends ahead of them. No matter what, he would *not* look behind him at Team Boyd conferring with the man who had pried open Luca's heart and taken up residence there, despite his decision this morning to banish him.

Breaking up with Oliver had clearly been the right thing to do, given how focused Luca had been on this game and his teammates. To think he'd risked everything for the sake of...

For the sake of what? he wondered as his vision blurred with uninvited tears. For the sake of the first man he could imagine falling in love with since he was a teenager?

Luca felt the vibration of Oliver's footsteps as he passed them to return to the stand. He kept his face toward the ice to avoid the sight of Oliver walking away.

Then he felt a nudge against his arm. Luca looked down to see Ross offering him a tissue.

"Cheers, mate." He took the tissue and dabbed at his nose. There was nothing odd about a case of the sniffles in cold air. But it never happened to Luca indoors, as he'd told Oliver on the boat to Ailsa Craig.

The memory rocked him now, just like the merciless waves they'd navigated that day.

A *boop!* sounded on the timing clock behind them, signaling the end of the break. Luca stuffed the damp tissue into his pocket, blinking rapidly to let the cold air dry his eyes.

With a deep breath, he banished all thoughts of Oliver, of everything but the game in front of him.

This. Here. Now. There'd be plenty of time later to cry, to curl up in a ball in the center of his bed and mourn the loss of his lover.

It was time to fight.

OLIVER HAD STOPPED TRYING to calm down.

He'd spent the fifth end counting his breaths, the sixth end imagining himself on a beach in the Caribbean, and the seventh end pretending his water bottle contained whisky or at least chamomile tea.

Now, heading into the eighth end, he was beginning to accept and even embrace the fact he was losing his shit.

On the inside, at least. On the outside, he was stoic as ever, scoring shots and calculating strategies on his tablet. He should have been reassured by the fact Team Boyd were up by two points with one end to play. But Riley had the hammer, so nothing was certain—nothing except the heartbreak Oliver felt at the sight of the man who'd just dumped him.

Not that he hadn't deserved the dumping. He'd known all along that his stay in Scotland could be short, and still he'd encouraged Luca's feelings for him, even after learning how rare and precious those feelings were. Then, to assuage his own guilt, Oliver had tossed a giant truth grenade between them. How could he be shocked when it exploded in his face?

At every step Oliver had made the wrong choice, as blind as ever to the consequences. But maybe if he had more time here in Glasgow, he could still fix things. Maybe Luca could forgive him.

On the ice below, Ian had put up a red center guard and drawn behind it. Riley's lead, David, had done the same with a corner guard, but his stone in the house had curled a bit too far, leaving part of it exposed. Bruce took it out with a swift throw along the left wing. Ross responded with a half-successful attempt at a runback double takeout.

"That was a bit crap, right?" asked Colin, one of the friends of Ben, the lad who'd rescued Oliver from Heather Friday night. The three mates were sitting behind Oliver to his left. "Cos he left one of the red stones in the rings?"

"Well, Ross cleared a path to the center," Ben said, "which you always want when you have the hammer."

"So it wasn't crap, then?" Colin asked.

"It was and it wasn't, for different reasons."

Colin sighed. "I'll never understand this game."

His frustration reminded Oliver of Colin's football team-mate Heather, who was now down on the ice with her cameraman, catching all the action. Oliver missed her company, but with only one game in play, she no longer needed a bird's-eye view to tell Kevin which sheet to focus on.

Bruce attempted to draw his second stone behind a Riley corner guard, but it came up short, leaving Ross with a redemptive double takeout, which he made to the delight of the crowd—especially his girlfriend, Claire, who'd brought what sounded like the world's biggest cowbell.

Oliver grew queasy as he surveyed the house. A yellow Riley stone sat up front, straddling the line between the eight- and twelve-foot rings. Jack would want to get rid of it right away to reduce the chance of Riley scoring two. But there was no takeout shot that wouldn't leave their shooting stone exposed—or worse, rolling out of play. Alistair would be better off ignoring it and drawing behind the corner guards on the other side. It was the same shot Bruce had just missed a minute ago, so they'd know exactly how to adjust.

Tell him to draw, he thought in Jack's direction, wishing telepathy was a real thing. *Or call a timeout so I can tell him to draw.*

Jack called for the takeout, of course. Oliver looked down the front row at Gillian, who was shaking her head with the same dismay he was feeling.

Alistair's shot hit the wrong side of Riley's stone, sending both out of the house. The vice slapped his broom against his palm in frustration.

"Why is he raging?" Colin asked. "Didn't he want to hit the yellow one out?"

"He did, but—well, you'll see," Ben said. "It's complicated."

Luca called for Garen to draw to the top of the house behind the corner guards—the shot Oliver thought Alistair should have attempted.

Garen's line was good, but the weight was far too heavy.

"Whoa, whoa, whoa," Luca called out to his sweepers, and then to the yellow stone itself as it sped toward him. It finally slowed just across the tee line, coming to rest in the back of the twelve-foot ring, despite Jack's attempt to sweep it out.

"Sorry!" Garen said.

"It's actually fine," Luca called back. "Look what they're doing now."

Jack was crouching behind the cluster of two corner guards, lining up a double peel to remove them. Luca was right—Garen's shot was better protected where it was, far out of Alistair's firing line.

"I want to come around!" Alistair shouted to Jack from the other end of the sheet. "Sit behind those corner guards."

Uh-oh. It was as if Ali had received Oliver's telepathic message but with a tragic satellite delay. Drawing behind the guards was no longer the best option—and could prove to be the *worst* option.

Jack moved back and examined the line. "Why?"

"If we get rid of those guards," Alistair said, "they can split the house for two to tie."

Oliver's jaw tightened so hard it nearly cramped. Giving up two points was an acceptable outcome. It meant playing an extra end, but one in which Boyd would have the hammer and an advantage for the win.

His mind fast-forwarded through the shots that lay ahead, like the end game in a chess match. A small mistake on Alistair's attempted draw could let Garen set Luca up to score three points with his final rock and win the game.

Call a timeout. Call a timeout. For the love of sweet baby Jesus on a pogo stick, call a timeout.

"Works for me!" Jack tapped the side of the four-foot ring to show where the stone should finish.

Oliver fought back a grimace. Coaches weren't allowed to communicate with players except during a timeout and the fourth-end break. That rule covered any reaction in the stand that a team could interpret as a signal.

Vindicated—or so he thought—Alistair settled into the hack. His delivery was clean, but just like Garen, the weight was off, and his red stone stopped in the back of the four-foot ring, completely exposed.

Both thirds had overthrown their draws, perhaps a sign that adrenaline and nerves were taking over. But Garen's second shot took out Alistair's stone and rolled only an inch, essentially taking its place in the back of the four-foot.

"That was good, right?" Colin asked as the Team Riley fans cheered and rattled their cowbells.

"Certainly looked impressive," said Colin's boyfriend. Oliver couldn't remember the young man's name, but he was apparently a lord—a Scottish lord, even though he sounded totally English. This country was so confusing.

"It was a brilliant throw," Ben said. "Now there's a remote chance Riley can score three to win."

Gnawing what was left of his fingernails, Oliver watched Jack finally choose a shot he agreed with: a double takeout to remove both of Riley's yellow stones from the house. It wasn't horribly difficult, and even if the throw went narrow, it would still take out one stone, vastly shrinking Luca's chances of scoring three.

No, wait—Jack should opt for the single takeout, just to be

safe. Again Oliver found himself wishing his skip would call a timeout to ask his advice.

As Jack drew back, his jaw was set with a fiery confidence. He let the rock sail. It was perfectly on line, with no need for sweeping.

"Yes!" Jack shouted, with Alistair joining in. "Haaaaaaard!"

"What the hell?" Oliver whispered, but then he saw it. By having their brushers sweep, Jack and Ali were trying to make sure the shooter hit both Riley rocks, rather than hit one rock for sure. They wanted to err on the side of...whatever the opposite of caution was.

The shooter flew through the house between the stones, touching neither.

"Well, that was definitely crap," Colin said.

For a moment Jack just stood in the center of the sheet, bending over like he was about to hurl. The crowd was silent now, an appropriate response for such an egregious and unnecessary miss.

Garen and Luca were already busy in the house, trying to figure out how to capitalize on Jack's mistake. They discussed several options, clearly surprised and maybe a little rattled at having this opportunity dumped into their lap. Eventually they decided on a draw to the very top of the house to guard their shot rock. If they made it, they'd be sitting three.

Luca stood behind the hack for a full five seconds, pulling back his shoulders and taking a deep breath. He seemed serene as ever as he lined up, no doubt thinking about how the last few shots had been overthrown, and how going too far into the house would set Jack up for a double or even triple takeout.

This situation called for a delicate touch, which was Luca's specialty. Oliver tried not to think about how that touch had felt last night on his—

"Weight's light!" Luca called out the moment it left his hand. "Real light."

"Yes! Hard!" Garen shouted. "All the way, lads! All the way!"

David and Ross bore down on the ice like they were trying to crush it out of existence. Oliver's own arms ached as he watched them brush with all their might, urged on by Luca and Garen. No doubt they were at the end of their strength.

Oliver held his breath as the yellow rock seemed to take forever to stop. But stop it did, just outside the rings.

"Och," Colin said. "Missed it by a bawhair."

"Sorry!" David called to Luca as the skip approached.

"My fault. You guys did all you could do." Luca looked at his stone and mouthed a profanity that was easy to lip-read.

Oliver got to his feet, anticipating Jack's timeout call. It came in an instant.

When he entered the rink, Oliver tried to hurry without looking like a hospital worker answering a code blue. His team was amped up as it was and needed a calm, reassuring presence.

"Hey," he said to Jack as he reached the sheet. "How's it going?"

To his relief, the skip gave a little laugh at Oliver's fake-casual tone. "Not bad. You?"

"A little hungry, but otherwise okay. So what are we thinking here?" Oliver was acutely aware of the fact they'd be discussing Luca with him standing ten feet away behind the hack. Even if he couldn't hear what they said beneath the crowd's murmurs, it would be picked up on the webcast audio —not to mention Heather's video—for later listening.

"Maybe a runback double takeout?" Jack traced an arc from the yellow stone Luca had just left outside the rings, to Riley's shot rock on the four-foot, then finally to Riley's other stone in the back of the house. "If I get rid of all three, it's pretty much over."

Oliver admired how Jack's confidence had been unshaken by his miss, and he knew how much the skip would love to win on his own spectacular shot rather than on Luca's failed one. "But if you miss by a little, he's got an easy two points for a tie. If you miss by a lot, he's got an easy three for the win."

"And with the way their stones are lined up," Alistair said, "it'd be dead tricky to get the angle we want."

Oliver nodded. "So we gotta ask ourselves, what's the hardest shot for Riley to make? Then try to leave him with no choice but to make it."

Jack thumbed his chin for a moment, then looked at Oliver. "We're running out of time. Just tell me what to do."

Hoping he was worthy of Jack's faith, Oliver pointed to the center of the house. "Ideally you draw to the button or the top of the four-foot. Then he's got nowhere to draw to and has to hit. His shooter will probably go out, and maybe even take one of his own shot rocks with it. He gets just one point and you win."

Jack crouched down to check out the line. "I know I can come around those guards, but will it curl enough to make the four-foot? Ice is pretty keen down the middle now. That's why I was thinking takeout."

Oliver knew Jack was less comfortable with draws, and this morning's fluke pick hadn't helped. "That's okay, because if you're a little heavy, you're still second shot and he's only lying one. Worst case, he draws for two and you go into the extra end with hammer."

Jack snorted. "Worst case, he'll hit ours out for three and win."

Oliver pictured the shot Jack had just described. It wasn't Luca's style. "He'd need to give it an in-turn rotation, which he doesn't favor for a hit. According to the numbers," he added, in case anyone thought he'd picked up this tidbit from his time with Luca off the ice.

"You're right." Jack stood quickly. "He'll go for the safe draw, like always. I don't even need the numbers to know that."

"Here, then?" Ali asked as he laid his brush head on the tee line for his skip to aim at.

Oliver started to tell him to move it in a bit more, but Jack said, "Yeah, I like it."

Oliver debated contradicting him, but it wasn't the coach's job to call the ice. Besides, Jack and Ali had been playing on this sheet for nearly two hours, so they knew its perks and pitfalls better than he did. And ultimately, if Jack thought he needed that much ice to make the shot, then that's what he should get. Better to be on the safe side.

"Thanks, Coach." Jack gave him a fist bump as he glided by.

It was time to return to the stand, but Oliver's feet felt stuck to the ice. He didn't want to leave. He wanted to be the one settling into the hack and readying the stone to make a saving shot.

But that wasn't his life now. It hadn't been for ages.

"Good luck," he told Alistair as he left the ice.

By the time Oliver reached his seat, Jack was already releasing the stone. As predicted, the line was a tad too wide, but the rock settled into the back of the four-foot ring near Riley's to lie second shot.

Behind Oliver, Colin's aristocrat boyfriend said, "I quite fancy when they yell, 'Hard!' at each other."

Ben laughed. "See, Andrew? I told you this sport is filthy hot."

Oliver let out a long breath, feeling the space between his

ribs expand a tiny fraction. Boyd's victory wasn't assured yet, but they'd made Riley's choice for last rock very obvious. The Luca he knew wouldn't hesitate to take the safe route.

But after this morning's breakup, Oliver wondered if he knew Luca at all.

LUCA STEPPED FORWARD. "I can draw for two," he told Garen, then tapped the top of the stone Jack had just thrown into the four-foot. "And use this to catch it."

David and Ross nodded and began to head down the sheet.

"Luca, wait." Garen bent over to look at the gap between the center guard and the corner guards. "A draw would get us the tie." He pulled his lower lip between his thumb and forefinger. "But then we go into the extra end without the hammer."

"We'll deal with that when it comes, like we always do," Luca said. "Besides, I don't see how we can get more than two here." *Thanks to me bottling that last draw.*

"Unless..." Garen went over to Boyd's lone red stone. "Instead of drawing, you hit this wee bastard out of the house. If your shooter stays, we're lying three for the win."

"Are you joking?" Luca looked at the gap between the guards. "If I throw it heavy enough for a takeout, then it won't curl enough to avoid those rocks up there." *And we lose spectacularly.* "Even if it gets through, it'll spin out after the hit, and we'll still be left with only two." Given the choice between an easy two points and a hard two points, the decision was clear.

"Maybe. Maybe not." Garen stood up and signaled a timeout to the timekeeper. Immediately David and Ross started making their way back to them.

When their front end arrived, Garen crouched down and

extended his broom in front of him like a golfer sizing up a putt. "It could work. Look." He moved aside and let Luca take his place.

Luca sighted the shot. Garen was right. With a lighter hit weight and an in-turn rotation—and with David and Ross sweeping all the way past the guards—it was theoretically possible to score three.

Garen could probably make it. Jack and Alistair could definitely make it. But Luca? Maybe once in ten attempts—a fact Jack was counting on. Team Boyd had gambled on Luca opting for a safe and comfortable draw, living to fight another day in an extra end. The old Luca wouldn't even consider this shot.

But a new Luca had been born this weekend. The shame of last night's near-surrender and the horror of this morning's loss had shattered his shackles of false security. On Friday he'd told Heather, *"We're not afraid to lose,"* but in these last twenty-four hours, that boast had been a lie. Luca had to make it true again.

If he tried this takeout and missed, at least they would have gone down fighting. It would be a glorious defeat to end a scrappy performance they could always be proud of.

And Oliver would stay in Glasgow.

"What are we thinking, lads?" David asked.

Luca stood and tapped his broom on the inside of Jack's red stone. "Takeout?"

David laughed, then looked at Luca's face. "Oh, for real." He cleared his throat. "Ooookay."

"Can you get it there?" Luca asked his sweepers. "With this ice?"

Ross peered back and forth along the sheet, his eyes tracing the proposed path. Then he nodded once. "We can get it there."

"Okay, then." Luca turned to Garen. "We're doing this."

His vice grinned. "We're pure doing this. Blaze of glory and all."

"Woo!" Luca headed for the hack, ready to give it laldy—or *give'r*, as Oliver would say.

A voice behind him shouted, "Wait!"

Jack.

Luca slowed but didn't stop as he glided along the ice, lightly brushing his stone's intended path to clear any debris (even though David had already done it for him). "Skips don't talk to each other before a shot," he said as Jack caught up. "You naughty boy, you."

"You're going for the takeout?"

"Yup."

"You can't make it. I know how you curl, Luca, better than anyone else does."

"Good, I've surprised you. Always like to keep things exciting."

"Is this about Oliver?"

Luca stopped. Heather and Kevin were standing about twenty feet away on the adjacent sheet, microphones pointed at the skips.

He turned to Jack and whispered, "He told you? Or was it Gillian?"

"I guessed." Jack lowered his voice. "Look, I've got no problem with—"

"You think I'd lose a game on purpose because I don't want to upset some random guy I'm hooking up with?"

"You don't hook up with random guys," Jack said. "Obviously he means something to you, but your feelings shouldn't interfere with—"

"My feelings?" Luca nearly clocked him with his broom. "It's not *feelings*, Jack, it's *reality*, the reality *you* created with that contract. The reality that says if I win, he'll leave." His voice broke. "It doesn't matter now, because Oliver and I are over. Win or lose, we're over."

Luca moved away before the officials could interfere and before his lungs seized up entirely.

He didn't believe his own words for a second. Of course it mattered. After all Oliver had been through, losing his brother and then his career, he deserved a new start. He deserved a place to heal. Even if Luca couldn't give him that as a boyfriend, he couldn't be the one to take it away.

All at once he felt a weight lift from him, replaced by a deep sense of peace. The moment Jack had spoken Oliver's name, Luca knew what he had to do, the sacrifice he had to make. There would be other seasons to win the Scottish Challenger Tour and go to Nationals. And if there weren't, if this was Team Riley's one chance...well, there were more important things in life than curling.

Luca sped through his pre-shot routine, exhilarated by the flood of freedom in his arteries. It was so liberating not to care about making a shot. Every muscle felt loose, and his breath flowed in and out with no stutter.

He made a show of aligning his body with Garen's broom head, so that no one in the crowd—especially Oliver—would know he was missing on purpose. All that mattered was that he looked like he was trying to win.

The rumble of the crowd that had swelled during his argument with Jack now receded, replaced by an awed hush as quiet as new snowfall. Luca lifted his hips and drew back, a bit farther than usual to get enough weight behind the throw. He was going to hit one of those guards with spectacular force. It would sound like a gunshot.

3...2...1...Liftoff!

His velocity out of the hack took his own breath away. With

his eyes glued to a spot to the right of Garen's broom, he sped forward, then released the stone.

Garen's shouts of "Hard! Hurry! Haaaaarrrrd!" rose over the roar of the stone and the scratching of broom heads against the ice. Luca pulled his trailing foot up to keep himself in a crouch as he readied his face to look disappointed.

Oh no.

Luca stood quickly, nearly losing his balance. He opened his mouth to tell David and Ross to stop sweeping, but it was too late. His stone was already passing those guards, on its way to hit—

Crack!

Boyd's red stone slid toward the back of the house, with Garen frantically brushing the ice to keep it moving. From where he stood frozen, Luca couldn't tell how far it would go.

Then Garen tossed his broom into the air. "Yaaaaaas!"

They'd scored three. They'd beaten Boyd.

What have I done? Luca sank back into a crouch and wrapped his arms around his head. *Whathaveldonewhathaveldonewhathaveldone?*

Somehow, despite his mind's fiercest intentions, Luca's body had made that shot. Had it known deep down that despite all the hurt it would cause, he really wanted to win?

His guts seemed to crush together in a stampede toward his mouth. He'd lost Oliver once and for all. The man who'd suffered so much, who hated himself for so many imagined failures, would soon be gone from his life. No more apple eyes, no more *R*s turning Luca inside out. No more Oliver.

A firm hand touched his shoulder. "Good game," Jack said.

Luca just shook his head.

"Come on, mate." Jack wrapped his fingers beneath Luca's arm. "Get yourself up."

Luca stood on shaky legs, only to fall into his brother-in-law's embrace. "I'm sorry, Jack. I'm so sorry. I tried to-to…" His words drowned in tears.

"Shhh. I know." Jack rubbed his back. "You're going to Nationals, wee man."

Luca opened his eyes to see David, Ross, and Garen gathered into a group hug at the other end of the sheet, bouncing up and down like lunatics. It made him feel better, but only a wee bit.

Jack let go of him and patted his cheek. "And now I'll have time to play mixed doubles with Gillian, so I'm the real winner here."

Luca gave a weak laugh, then wiped his face with his sleeve before moving off to shake hands with the rest of Team Boyd.

"Belter of a takeout there," Alistair said, almost knocking him over with a hearty back thump.

"Thanks," was all Luca could get out before his teammates mobbed him.

"We did it!" Garen screamed in his ear. "Even though you shaved, we still did it!"

Luca tried to reply, but his face was buried between the giant chests of David and Ross, their howls of joy meeting his ears in stereo. So he just closed his eyes and hung on to his mates, knowing that if *this* and *them* were all he ever had, he'd still be the luckiest lad in Glasgow.

17

Thinking Time

THINKING TIME: *Total amount of time each team has to plan and execute its shots within a game. A concept that should be—but unfortunately rarely is—applied to real life.*

OLIVER'S STANDING ovation had nothing to do with sportsmanship. He couldn't be sorry Luca had won like that, no matter the consequences. That final throw had been a thing of beauty.

Luca's reaction afterward, though, threatened to gouge open Oliver's chest and dig out his heart with a spoon. He'd seen men and women weep after victories—he'd done it himself after winning Junior Worlds and his first Brier—but they'd been crying tears of joy. Luca had looked devastated.

Even now, as the two teams made their way off the ice and toward the warm room, Luca's smile for the crowd was strained around the edges. He seemed ready to wallop Garen, who was jumping up and down, holding up three fingers and chanting, "Third place! Third place! Third place!"

Oliver sank back into his seat, his mind scrambling to pivot toward this new reality, grasping for any consolation to stave off the anguish.

Maybe the loss was for the best. Now Oliver could leave this city that already felt too much like home and never set eyes on Luca Riley again. Then both teams could recover from the chaos he'd injected into their lives.

And maybe another new challenge would be good for him. Maybe next time he'd fail to fail.

"Is this seat free?"

Oliver looked up to see Ben, whose two friends were already heading downstairs to the warm room. "Sure, I guess."

Ben sat beside him, the corner of his *Riley Rocks!* sign swinging dangerously close to Oliver's face. "Sorry about the result. I know how hard you must have worked."

"It's disappointing, but there's still a lot of season left for Team Boyd."

"That's the spirit." Ben buttoned up his coat. "Ooft, it gets pure Baltic in here once the crowd clears out, doesn't it? Anyway, enough chit-chat. What's going on with Luca?"

Oliver started. "What do you mean?"

"I've rarely seen him risk a sure tie for the sake of a win, especially not with a shot like that. And I've *never* seen him so emotional, win or lose."

"It's a big deal, going to Nationals."

"That's the thing," Ben said. "Usually the bigger the situation, the calmer Luca gets. He keeps the head when everyone else is flailing."

No wonder Oliver had been so drawn to him. He'd needed someone like that in his life. But by pulling him close, he'd destroyed the very serenity that made Luca special to everyone.

"I should get downstairs." Oliver put his tablet in his bag and stood up. "My team is probably—"

"I kinda like the change," Ben said, then nodded as if he'd just convinced himself. "Maybe our Luca needs to come down off that Zen mountaintop once in a wee while and be a mere mortal." He took off his glasses, held them up, and frowned at the lenses. "Just saying."

When Oliver entered the warm room, he spied his team and Luca's sitting at the far table. To avoid inserting himself into this of all broomstackings, he approached the presidents of the women's and men's competitive clubs near the coffee machine. They seemed to be having an intense conversation, but Oliver interrupted them anyway.

"Hey," he said, "I just wanted to thank you guys."

Anya looked up at him, startled. "For what?"

"Putting on a great tournament, for one thing. But mostly for making me feel at home." He lowered his voice. "I guess you're aware I'll be moving on soon."

Craig and Anya shared a significant look. "Shall we discuss this now?" he asked her.

"Why not?" she said. "I'll go and fetch Jack and Luca. We can all meet up in the office for some privacy."

Oliver followed Craig on feet that felt numb. He could sense it: He was in trouble for his affair with Luca. Maybe someone else had guessed the Riley skip had tried to throw the game to save Oliver's job.

The club office was a glorified supply closet perhaps twenty square feet in area. Oliver had never been claustrophobic, but the moment he took a seat on a low plastic step stool, he felt the walls begin to close in.

Why had he come to Glasgow? Why had he thought he could ever make a new start when the problem was never a place or time or any person but his own damn self?

Anya returned with a bewildered-looking Jack and Luca. Craig motioned for the two of them to take a seat together on a box of copy paper. Luca didn't look at Oliver, at least not during the fleeting moment Oliver could bear to look at *him*.

"First," Craig said, "massive congrats to Team Riley on winning the Scottish Challenger Tour and qualifying for the national championship. We'll schedule a celebration party, pronto."

"Cheers, Craig," Luca said hoarsely, then cleared his throat.

"And Jack, please know that everyone here is dead proud of Team Boyd and its accomplishments so far this season."

Jack's lips twitched, but he said nothing.

"Of course," Craig continued, "we'd love for both teams to go to—"

"Oh, for God's sake," Anya said, "stop torturing the poor lads and tell them our idea."

"Right." Craig stood up straight and tugged down the front of his snowflake sweater. "Like most curling clubs, ours are completely volunteer organizations. We've got no paid employees, and we operate on a shoestring budget."

Oliver shifted on the stepstool. Was the club about to ask for donations from its two prominent teams, maybe for a share of any sponsorship money they might bring in? The timing seemed odd.

"But we want to change that," Anya told Oliver. "If our boards will allocate the funds, we'd like to hire you."

Oliver stared up at her, not sure he'd heard correctly. "Hire me?"

"As an instructor," she said, "once you've got yourself certified here in Scotland. Until then, you'll just be a coach."

"A-a coach? A coach for—wait, I don't understand."

"That's why we asked Jack and Luca to join us." Craig turned to them. "Our condition for hiring Oliver is that he coach Team Boyd *and* Team Riley, as well as our top two women's teams."

Luca sat up straight. "Coach both of us? Is that allowed?"

"It's done at the highest level in nearly every country," Anya said. "Curling associations hire coaches and assign them to more than one team, sometimes even rivals."

"She's right." As Oliver spoke, it felt like someone else was reciting his words—and so calmly, too, considering a tornado was raging inside his head. "Those coaches don't work for the teams themselves. They work for the association—or in this case, the clubs."

"So Oliver's mission," Craig said, "would be to advance the game of curling in Glasgow, which means making our best teams as competitive as possible. Hiring a former world champion like Oliver would put this city back on the map as a hub for serious curling."

"This is—my God, this is amazing!" Luca said, the animation returning to his face. "It sounds ideal."

"What about when Luca and I compete against each other?" Jack asked. "Who does he coach then?"

"Neither," Anya said. "He'd coach Team Riley at Nationals, but any time you two go head to head—including in league games—he'd have to stand down. So Team Boyd would have less of him than you do now."

"Better than not having him at all." Jack looked at Oliver. "If the clubs sponsored you with an endorsement from our national curling association, you could get a work visa. You could stay as long as you're in this job, which could be years."

Oliver clutched the side of the stepstool, certain it was tilting. This offer was everything he could have hoped for, so why did he feel like throwing up?

Jack nudged Luca. "Frankly, I'd hate to share him with any other team. But you and I already know each other's curling inside and out."

"Exactly!" Luca smacked his palms against his thighs. "There's no secrets to be stolen via some sort of spy coach."

"No cloaks, no daggers," Jack said. "But I forever and always get credit for finding him."

"Deal," Luca said as they shook hands.

"And I call bagsies on Tuesday night practice."

"Deal again! I teach that night, anyway."

Craig cleared his throat. "Maybe instead of treating Oliver like a kid you're sharing custody of, we should ask him if he's okay with this arrangement."

The room seemed to shrink further. Oliver swallowed hard. "Um…you said you need to check with your boards, right?"

"Aye," Anya said, "which means it's far from done and dusted. They could balk at spending that much money. But we'll sell it as an investment, just like that video feature Heather's doing. These days, curling clubs either grow or die."

"But we needed to ask you first," Craig said. "I'll not beg my board to pay for a job you don't want."

"Of course he wants it." Luca started to turn to Oliver. "It's everything we—" He froze, as if just now remembering there was no longer any *we*. "I mean, it's everything you could've hoped for."

Oliver tugged at his shirt collar as the heat waves kept rising from his neck to his scalp. "I need to think about it."

"WHAT?" Luca stared at Oliver, doubting his own ears. "What's there to think about?"

"Lots of things," Oliver said. "Like whether I'm the best person for the job." He looked at Jack. "I let you down. I was supposed to take you to Nationals, and I failed."

"I'm not exactly thrilled with the weekend's results," Jack

said, "but it was never your fault, mate. We lost two games today, one because of a pick and one because of a miracle throw by this lad." He slung an arm around Luca's shoulders. "Coach, you've taught us so much, not just since you've been here but in the weeks before. And it's showed in our play."

"Has it?" Oliver turned to Anya. "I want to see the numbers."

Luca exchanged a perplexed look with Jack. Hadn't Oliver been tracking the stats himself all weekend? Maybe this was a ploy to buy time for him to think.

She scoffed. "I'll go and see if the scorekeeper's finished with that last game, but listen to me, lad. Don't go making a life-changing decision based on a few percentage points. You might as well flip a coin." She stalked out of the office.

Oliver sat for several more silent moments, staring at the floor and bouncing his knee up and down. Then he shot to his feet. "I need some air." He swept out the door, leaving the crowded room feeling deserted.

Luca looked at Craig and Jack. "You think I should—"

"Yes!" they said, Jack adding a wee shove.

Luca didn't need to be told twice. He dashed into the warm room, through the foyer, and out the front door into the cold, dark Glasgow evening.

The pavement was empty.

Had Oliver fled in a taxi? Was he already gone forever? Luca grasped his hair, regretting every single thing he'd said and done today. He'd been so off-balance, so unlike himself. Was Oliver to blame, and if so, wouldn't his departure be a blessing?

It felt like anything but. Perhaps Luca had acted less like himself since falling for Oliver, but he'd *felt* more like his real self than ever before. It hurt to admit that his real self didn't have it all together, but rather was a bit of a daftie like everyone else.

A gust of frigid air blasted its way down the street. Luca gave one last scan for Oliver, then retreated inside.

In the warm room, Heather was interviewing David and Ross, who looked well on their way to hammered, based on the emptiness of the whisky bottle they were sharing and the way they were leaning on their girlfriends. Willow was cheering up the rest of Team Boyd with a goofy jig, while Anya sat with the scorekeeper at one of the tables, no doubt discussing the quantitative proof of Oliver's miracles.

A soft hand touched Luca's back. He spun around, his heart leaping with hope.

"It's only me." His sister frowned at him. "I wanted to buy you a drink to celebrate your win, but unfortunately there's no time."

"Sorry?"

"There's somewhere else you need to be." Gillian took his shoulders and turned him to face the window overlooking the ice.

Luca peered through the glass into the rink, where the empty ice lay waiting for tonight's Glasgow Open final. A man stood alone in front of Sheet C.

"Thank God." Luca turned to Gillian and hugged her hard.

"Och, away and let me breathe," she said, but she was hugging him back and laughing anyway.

Luca kissed her forehead as he let her go. "Cheers, lass." Then he moved through the crowded warm room and pushed open the door to the rink. "There you are."

Oliver turned halfway to look at him from the corner of his eye. "I'm not done thinking."

"Again, what is there to think about?" Luca went closer—

but not too close, for fear of spooking him. "Help me under-stand. What is it about this situation that's not ideal to you?"

"I don't need it to be ideal, I just—" Oliver rubbed his temples. "I didn't come here looking for something perma-nent. I didn't come here looking for a commitment."

"Then why *did* you come to Scotland? To conquer it? To show the people back home you could still rule the ice? Were Team Boyd just part of your grand plan to win back the respect of the people who shunned you?"

"You're giving me way too much credit. I don't do grand plans. I don't plan at all." Oliver spread his arms. "I came here because I thought it'd be cool, okay?"

"And was it? Was it 'cool'?"

"Yeah, of course, but—"

"No, it wasn't *cool*, Oliver. It was more than that. You made a difference. You're something special here, and not because of your stupid spreadsheets and video-analysis rubbish. Because of *you*. You're clever and funny and tough and more than a bit mental, and that's all it takes to earn a Glaswegian's respect."

Oliver let out a long, shaky breath. "I lost, Luca." He sounded on the verge of tears. "Even though you tried to throw the game to save my job, I still lost."

Luca staggered back, feeling like his brain had been pried open for inspection. "What are you—I didn't..."

Oliver just laughed. "You're incredible, you know that? The only thing you fail at is failing."

"That's not true," Luca said. "That's not true at all."

"Do you know how hard it is for someone like me to even be near someone as perfect as you?" The way he spat out the word *perfect* made it clear it wasn't a compliment.

"So that's why you're leaving? Are you afraid you're not good enough for this job, or that you're not good enough for me?"

"No! Maybe." Oliver turned away, hunching his shoulders. "I don't know."

"So you'll just run away until you figure it out?" Luca said. "You'll never make peace with what happened to Noah if you keep giving up on yourself."

Oliver spun to face him. "Giving up, eh? This from the guy who quit med school because he had to learn about disease."

"I didn't quit!"

Luca's hand flashed up to cover his mouth, but it was too late. He'd said it out loud for the first time ever.

Oliver stared at him. "What?"

"I mean, I did quit, but..." Luca forced out the sickening truth. "I was failing. I couldn't do it. I wasn't clever enough or hardworking enough. I wasn't good enough."

Oliver's eyes softened. "I'm so sorry. That must have been heartbreaking."

"Yes." Luca wrapped his arms around his own waist. "And not just for me. I failed my family, too, not to mention all the patients I never got to treat."

"But you tried. You did everything you could."

"I didn't try." Luca ground out the words between his teeth. "Not enough. It was hard, impossibly hard, so I quit and told myself and everyone else that med school had given me an existential crisis, because that sounded and felt a lot better than 'I'm too stupid.'"

Oliver took a step closer. "Believe me, I understand feeling stupid."

"I know you do. That's my point."

"What do you mean?"

"Every day I get up and go to a job that reminds me of what I could have been. I stare my failure in the face and get on with the work of making books for medical students who are better than I was. And I do what I can to help people."

Luca pointed to the ice. "That's what you're doing right here. So how dare you walk away from that chance just because it'll be hard?"

Oliver didn't reply. He simply cast his gaze over the ice, then the ceiling, then the spectator stand above their heads.

Luca closed the space between them. "It's time to stop exiling yourself. It's time to stay home."

Oliver's lips echoed the word *home*, soundlessly.

"Aye," Luca whispered. "This can be home. I know it's not the most glamorous place in the world, and you've not had time to see all this city has to offer, but—"

"I've seen enough of Glasgow," Oliver said.

Luca's stomach dropped to his toes.

The door to the warm room opened, and Anya poked her head in. "Oliver, I've got the numbers from the last game."

"Oh." Oliver brushed past Luca and took a step toward her. But then he stopped. "I'll be there in a minute."

"Okay." She looked between them with a faint smile. "Don't hurry yourself."

When the door swung shut, Oliver turned back to Luca. "Where was I?"

Luca braced himself for the knockback of all knockbacks. "You said you'd seen enough of Glasgow."

Oliver winced. "I meant, I've seen enough of Glasgow to know that it's..." He met Luca's eyes. "It's not a place I want to leave."

Oh. "Then maybe don't leave it? Maybe take the job and stay?" *With me.* "If the numbers add up, that is."

"I don't need the fucking numbers, Luca. All I need is—" Oliver shut his eyes and rubbed the back of his neck. "Won't it be weird having me as a coach? With our history?"

"History?" Did he mean they were permanently over?

"Yeah, history." Oliver looked at him sideways. "Was I

dreaming, or were we kind of a thing for a few days before you dumped me?"

"No! I mean, yes, we were, and no, you weren't dreaming." Luca moved forward, sensing they were almost there. "I'm sorry about this morning. I didn't know the right thing to do, so I did the wrong thing. Can you ever forgive me?"

"If you can forgive my idiocy." Oliver crossed his arms over his chest and gave a coy chin tilt. "And if you un-dump me."

YES! Luca straightened his posture and raised his right hand. "I hereby formally forgive your so-called idiocy and officially un-dump you."

"Hmm." Oliver put on a faux skeptical look. "Seems like there should be restitution of some kind."

"Make a request."

"Make an offer."

"How about..." Luca stepped forward and took Oliver's wrists to unfold his arms. "I'll give you all the adoration you deserve. Which is a lot, according to my secret spreadsheet."

"Ooh, secret spreadsheet? Where do you keep that?"

Luca pointed to his own head. "In here." He placed Oliver's warm hand over his heart. "And in here. And other places."

Oliver twitched an eyebrow. "Other places?"

"Oh aye. It's got loads of backup locations so I don't lose it."

"Wise," was Oliver's last word before they kissed. A muffled roar of approval and clang of cowbells came through the warm-room window.

Luca pulled back to give an embarrassed wave to their audience. The sight of the Team Riley fans sent a brand-new reality hurtling through his brain. "Oh my God, we're going to Nationals!"

"I know!" Oliver laughed. "I was there when you won, remember?"

"But it just hit me that I'm happy about it. I'm really, really happy. And scared." Luca put his hands to his cheeks. "Can you imagine, the lads and I playing against Olympic medalists? I'll probably pass out during pre-game handshakes."

"I'm sure the other skips will catch you before your head hits the ice."

"They would do, wouldn't they? They seem very nice fellows." More intimidating facts struck him. "Och, I'll need to learn to play on arena ice. For ten ends. In front of a massive crowd!"

"I can help you with all that. I'll be with you every step, as a coach and as a friend." Oliver took Luca's hand. "And as anything else you want."

I want everything, Luca thought, then repeated the words out loud.

Perhaps, in the right time and place, desire wasn't such a dangerous thing after all.

18

Buried

BURIED: *When a rock sits fully behind another rock and is thus protected from a hit. For now, at least.*

A few weeks later

"Sorry about the snow."

"It's okay," Oliver told Luca as the two of them made their way from the bus stop to the tiny park beside the River Kelvin. "Noah loved snow."

"Did he?" Luca's warm hand slipped inside his, a sign that he wanted to hear more. It amazed Oliver how long his boyfriend was willing to hear him ramble on about his little brother.

"He used to bury himself in it," Oliver said, "then jump out at me when I walked by. I'd always pretend to be surprised. Of course, sometimes I actually *was* surprised. I wasn't as nice about it those times."

"Och, weans can pure do our heads in, can't they?"

Oliver just smiled, marveling how many Scottish phrases there were for *crazy*. It made him feel very much at home.

They reached the bench he'd chosen out of what seemed like dozens they'd scouted around Glasgow. The search for the right park had been an excellent excuse to tour the city, especially the parts rarely visited by tourists.

Until yesterday's board meetings at Shawlands Ice Rink, Oliver wasn't sure he'd still be around to see this park or any other come springtime. But last night he'd received an offer of full employment through the end of next year's curling season, which meant he could apply for a Tier 5 work visa. Between the coaching salary, his graphic-arts business, and "clowning for cash" (as Luca called it), he'd soon earn enough to move out of the Boyds' house into his own apartment.

"Can we just sit for a minute first?"

"Of course." Luca helped him brush the newfallen snow off the bench, the one most like that in the park where he used to meet Noah. As they sat on the cold iron seat, Luca shivered and tucked in his hat's bunny ears to cover his neck. "I must say, winter is miles better with a beard."

"And it looks great." He drew his thumb along Luca's jaw. "Especially now that you've learned to use the trimmer."

"Och, I was such a facial-hair amateur last month. Now I'm ready to take on the best beards in the nation." Luca jogged his knee up and down, as he always did when he spoke even obliquely about the Scottish National Championship starting in two days.

Oliver had bulked up Team Riley's arsenal of strategies and worked with Luca to build his confidence with takeout hits. But for the most part, he hadn't altered the team's overall calm, focused approach. If anything, he encouraged the other three members to step up their meditation regimen (and got Team Boyd—and himself—to start one). Team Riley would need more mental toughness than they could imagine once they stepped under the lights of that Edinburgh arena this weekend, followed as ever by Heather's documentary crew.

"You'll do Glasgow proud," Oliver said softly.

The crease of anxiety between Luca's eyes smoothed out. "I know." He pressed his shoulder to Oliver's. "Have you brought it?"

"Of course. I wouldn't forget this." Oliver pulled the datastick from his pocket and stroked it through its plastic bag. "It's time, right?"

"It is his birthday, so…"

"Okay." Oliver stood and opened the bag. "Here goes."

"Shall I come with you?"

Oliver hesitated. "Not yet." He took the flash drive from the bag, which he handed to Luca. "You'll know when."

Then he walked past the bike path to the side of the riverbank, where he sat on the low stone wall, clutching the datastick so hard he feared he'd crush it.

He set the flash drive on the wall and imagined the digital information inside, zeros and ones combining to form the songs on Noah's final playlist. Oliver had listened to it one last time this morning during his run. Hearing those tunes had only strengthened his instinct that it was time to move on. Since meeting Luca, he was slowly learning to trust his instincts instead of fear them.

Oliver had not, however, listened to Noah's voicemail again before deleting it from his phone, then moving the sound file from his tablet to this flash drive. It was the same sound file he'd transferred from one computer to the next for nearly ten years, always playing the recording into his voicemail account when he got a new phone or carrier—simply to torture himself, as if that would accomplish anything.

This datastick was now the one place in the world where Noah's plea for rescue lived on.

"I promise I'll never forget," Oliver whispered.

He picked up the flash drive, kissed it quickly, then let it slide from his open palm into the River Kelvin.

A gust of biting wind blew then, threatening to freeze the tears to his cheeks. He tugged his tuque down over his ears, then turned to look for Luca.

But Luca was already on his way. A moment later, he sat beside Oliver and wrapped his arms around him.

"I love you," Luca murmured into his neck.

"I love you, too," he managed to say, though between his numb lips and waterlogged throat, it sounded more like, "Aah uhv ooh hoo."

They held onto each other for what felt like ages but was probably only half a minute. Then Oliver took a deep breath. "You know what Noah would want me to have right now?"

"I do know." Luca stood and adjusted his rabbit-ear flaps. "There's a bakery up the road that makes them just the way you like them."

Oliver took a tissue from his pocket and dabbed at his nose. "Crispy on the outside but soft in the middle?"

Luca nodded, his soft, dark eyes full of understanding. "And just the right size for Hole in the Hole."

Thanks for reading!

I hope you enjoyed this first Glasgow Lads on Ice novel, one of only three (?) novels about curling currently in print. Soon I hope to see many more authors writing about the wonderful people who play this addictive sport!

This series crosses over with the original Glasgow Lads football/soccer books (which are a bit steamier) in terms of both timeline and characters, so be sure to check those out as well.

If you fancied this book, please consider introducing the Lads to others—online, offline, or anywhere in between. Thanks.

Want more Lads all to yourself? How about exclusive bonus material like deleted scenes, commentaries, and photos of characters and settings? Then sign up for my mailing list at averycockburn.com/signup and join the fun!

Author's note: ADHD

In the five years since my diagnosis at age [redacted], I've been dying to write a character with adult Attention Deficit Hyperactivity Disorder (ugh, such a perjorative and inaccurate name, but it's all we've got just now). Few novels address the subject —which is odd, considering the disorder affects about ten percent of the population (and probably a much higher percentage of authors). As for the books that do feature those characters…well, I've rarely recognized myself in them.

My dream was to create a character who could take readers past society's stereotypes and misconceptions of ADHD—and maybe help some of us cope with its corrosive, crippling shame. But I was writing a series that takes place in the United Kingdom in 2014-2015, a place and time in which ADHD awareness was even less than that of today's North America.

Enter Oliver Doyle, whose nationality and personal history lent itself perfectly. The time had finally come. (*Cue angels singing.*)

There are as many manifestations of ADHD as there are humans who have it. Oliver's struggles and triumphs closely parallel my own, so while his portrayal as an ADHDer is authentic, it may not precisely match the experience of others with the disorder.

If you recognize yourself or a loved one in Oliver, or if you just want to learn more about ADHD (did I mention ten percent of us have it?), check out these online resources. They just might change your life (for the better, I promise).

- *How to ADHD* YouTube channel: I suggest starting with "How to Know if You Have ADHD," then continue from there on a rollicking roller coaster of self-discovery!
- ADDitude Magazine (additudemag.com)
- CHADD (chadd.org)
- Totally ADD (totallyadd.com)

And of course there are books, marvelous books!

- *Taking Charge of Adult ADHD* by Russell A. Barkley, Ph.D.
- *Driven to Distraction* by Edward M. Hallowell, M.D. and John J. Ratey, M.D.
- *You Mean I'm Not Lazy, Stupid, or Crazy?* by Kate Kelly and Peggy Ramundo

All About Curling

As Oliver says, "Curling is the hardest easy-looking sport in the world." It's also the most complicated simple-looking sport, so here's a brief rundown for easy reference in case you get lost while reading (it's okay, I've been there many, many times):

A curling game is divided into scoring periods known as *ends*. In each end, all four players from each team take turns throwing stones in this order:

- Team A lead
- Team B lead
- Team A second
- Team B second
- Team A third (usually the vice)
- Team B third
- Team A fourth (usually the skip)
- Team B fourth

After all stones are thrown, points are won by the team

with stones lying closer to the center of the *house* (the three concentric rings that look like a bullseye).

Only one team can score in each end.

One point is scored for each stone that lies closer to the center than any of the opponent's stones.

During a throw, the skip (or the vice, when the skip is throwing) stands in the house and places their broom head on the ice to give the thrower a point to aim at.

The remaining two curlers are the designated sweepers. They can affect the stone's trajectory by brushing the ice in front of it as it travels. This action melts the surface to reduce friction and help the stone maintain its current path—if it's going straight, sweeping will help keep it straight, and if it's already curling, sweeping helps it curl more.

The sweepers usually judge the stone's *weight* (how fast it's traveling), while the skip or vice standing in the house judges the *line* (how well the stone is staying on course). They will holler "Hard!" to indicate it's time to sweep, or "No!" when it's not.

There are countless variations on "Hard!" that are all equally suggestive.

When the game is over, we drink! Winners buy first round.

Some great curling books:

- *Break Through Beginner Curling* by Gabrielle Coleman
- *Curl to Win* by Russ Howard
- *Fit to Curl* by John Morris

And curling podcasts:

- 2 Girls and a Game
- The Extra Extra End (USA Curling-focused)
- From the Hack

But the best way to learn about curling is to try it yourself. It's a sport enjoyed by people of all ages and abilities, so why not give it a go? You might be surprised to find there's a club near you.

About the Author

Avery Cockburn (rhymes with Savory Slow Churn—mmmm, ice cream…) lives in the US with one infinitely patient man and two infinitely impatient cats.

Reach out and say "Hiya!" to Avery at:

- www.averycockburn.com
- avery@averycockburn.com
- Twitter: averycockburn
- Facebook: averycockburnauthor